Home

a *Songbird* novel

MELISSA PEARL

ISBN: 1514848899
ISBN-13: 978-1514848890

NOTE FROM THE AUTHOR

I never learned to play the guitar, but I always wished I had. I love singing. There's so much power in music, and being able to project a melody out of your body is a magical experience. Well, it is for me, anyway.

I wasn't a big country music fan before writing this book, but I have fallen in love. Every song on the HOME soundtrack I have listened to so many times and have memorized most of them. I hope you enjoy the playlist as much as I do.

Rachel and Josh have been on my mind and in my heart for probably twenty years now. I heard Joshua Kadison's CD—*Painted Desert Serenade*—when I was in my late teens and his voice and lyrics inspired me. HOME was born from his song "Picture Postcards From L.A.," and it has grown over the years and evolved into so much more than I initially had planned. Rachel's journey was a really tough, heartbreaking one to write, but also so rewarding. People make mistakes. I remember being eighteen and thinking I was invincible. Sometimes the best way to learn is to get burned...then you can rise from the ashes and figure out what really makes you happy and the type of person you want to be.

My hope, as it is with every book I write, is that you will enjoy this journey and that it will make you laugh, cry, and fall in love.

Thanks for reading.

HOME SOUNDTRACK

(Please note: The songs listed below are not always the original versions but the ones I chose to listen to while constructing this book. The songs are listed in the order they appear.)

GIRL IN A COUNTRY SONG

Performed by Maddie & Tae

KEEP YOUR HANDS TO YOURSELF

Performed by John Deer

PICTURE POSTCARDS FROM L.A.

Performed by Joshua Kadison

FALL FROM GRACE

Performed by Amanda Marshall

COME ON OVER

Performed by Jessica Simpson

ANYTHING AND EVERYTHING

Performed by Martina McBride

MELISSA PEARL

THESE DAYS

Performed by Rascal Flatts

YOU SET ME FREE

Performed by Michelle Branch

SUDDENLY I SEE

Performed by KT Tunstall

STUPID BOY

Performed by Keith Urban

SMILE

Performed by Lonestar

KISS YOU ALL OVER

Performed by Joie Starr

TRUST ME (THIS IS LOVE)

Performed by Amanda Marshall

HOME

WALKING IN MEMPHIS

Performed by Marc Cohn

ONE WAY OR ANOTHER

Performed by The Hotstepperz

SHAKE IT IF YA GOT IT

Performed by Kira Isabella

ONE OF THESE DAYS

Performed by Michelle Branch

THESE BOOTS ARE MADE FOR WALKING

Performed by Jessica Simpson

COUNTRY'S WRITTEN ALL OVER ME

Performed by Kira Isabella

LIFE IS A HIGHWAY

Performed by Rascal Flatts

MELISSA PEARL

SEXY LOVE

Performed by Kylie Minogue

I KNEW YOU WERE TROUBLE

Performed by Taylor Swift

LOVE YOU

Performed by Jack Ingram

BEST I EVER HAD

Performed by State of Shock

DO YOU LOVE ME

Performed by The Contours

GOODBYE IN HER EYES

Performed by Zac Brown Band

PERMISSION TO SHINE

Performed by Bachelor Girl

MUSIC

Performed by John Miles

HAPPY GIRL

Performed by Martina McBride

PICTURE TO BURN

Performed by Country Matters

I LOVE YOU

Performed by Martina McBride

COMING HOME

Performed by Diddy - Dirty Money, Skylar Grey

HOME

Performed by Johnny Swim

LONG ROAD HOME

Performed by Sheryl Crow

SAFE

Performed by Miranda Lambert

CHICKEN FRIED

Performed by Zac Brown Band

I HOPE YOU DANCE

Performed by Lee Ann Womack

FEELS LIKE HOME

Performed by Chantal Kreviazuk

I JUST CALL YOU MINE

Performed by Martina McBride

To enhance your reading experience, you can listen along to the playlist for HOME on Spotify.

https://open.spotify.com/user/12146962946/playlist/6 aXFJDi1I5iWfCDqrUxhzV

For Joshua Kadison -

You captured my heart years ago with your song "Picture Postcards From L.A." Rachel came to life in my head, and a story quickly grew from there. Thank you for inspiring this story with your amazing song.

ONE

RACHEL

Clark's Bar buzzed with its usual Saturday night vibrancy. Music blared from the jukebox as people chatted and laughed, throwing back beer like it was water. A dartboard competition that started out as friendly had switched to a serious duel between Trudy and the Baker boy. My money was on the girl, and I couldn't wait to see her kick his arrogant ass to the curb.

I lifted my tray of empty glasses in order to avoid knocking Ol' Dan's head off. That guy sure did thrash around when he laughed. I rolled my eyes as I swiveled my hips and dodged a chair that tipped back before slamming down on its four legs.

"Hey, Rachel." Millie waved to me as I passed by her table. I grinned at her and shook my head. That girl was so gone for Brock Hillard it was actually funny. Apparently she'd loved him since the fifth grade, quietly pining for his oblivious self until he grew a pair and started to realize that girls were good for more than just cooking and cleaning. He grew up in one of those homes where his mama did everything for everyone. Did him no favors, if you ask me. All I can say is that he is one lucky man, because Mille Rae Truman is just like his mama...sweet as pie and wholesome to the core. They'd no doubt be married and popping out babies before her twentieth birthday.

I, personally, could not think of anything worse.

Plonking the tray down on the counter, I slid it toward Josh so he could empty it and reload the thing with a fresh batch of brew.

"How you going, baby?" He gave me that closed-mouth grin of his—the one that made my toes sizzle. He was getting some tonight. Not only did that boy look so damn fine in that fitted T-shirt I made him put on, but he had his hair back in a low ponytail...a short little stubby one that rested against the back of his neck, and it just did things to me, especially when a curl popped loose and he had to tuck it behind his ear.

I smiled at his rugged complexion, peppered with blond whiskers that needed shavin'. "I'm good, honey."

"It sure is busy tonight." He placed two beers on

the tray and swiped his hands over the butt of his faded blue jeans before turning back to pour some more.

"More money for you, though, right?" I winked at him.

His grin grew to a smile, and I spotted a flash of straight, white teeth. "I'm just glad people showed up, even though the band canceled on me."

"Come on, honey, they don't just come here for the band." I pressed my forearms into the counter, lifting my body off the floor and leaning toward him. "They come here because Clark's is the best bar in Payton. Hell, it's the best bar in the county...and that's all because of you." He leaned over to capture my smile against his lips.

He wasn't usually one for PDA, but he couldn't seem to resist me.

His lips were warm and delicious. I savored the taste of them before jumping back down to the floor and grabbing my tray.

"Table eight." Josh pointed to the rowdy drinkers by the window.

"Got it."

"Girl In A Country Song" started playing as I turned for the rabble. It was hard not to sway my hips as I walked across the room. It made me wish I was up on a stage, singing the song myself. That was what I wanted to do with my life. Sing. Play my guitar. Be the girl my mama wanted me to be. But life got in the way, and my grand plans had been put on hold while I saved my pennies.

Stopping at the table, I balanced the tray on one

hand and started distributing beers. They were all drinking the same thing, so I slapped them down in front of anyone. I wanted to get away from the table as fast as I could.

Don't get me wrong. I liked it when the bar was humming. There was this excited buzz in the air that made my blood hot. But what I didn't like was when the idiots barged their way in and made trouble. And I knew from experience that table eight was trouble.

My suspicions were confirmed when my departure was hindered by a fat hand on my ass.

"That's some purty skirt you got there, Rachel."

Here we go.

I lowered the tray to my side and tried to turn out of his grasp, but he stopped me with his other hand on my hip. "It's denim, Roy. You don't need to feel the fabric."

"Come on now, you know my granddaddy was a tailor."

"Your granddaddy was a perverted drunk, just like you. Now get your hands off my ass, sugar." I softened my command with a sweet smile. As much as I wanted to slap him, he was the customer, and I wasn't about to get him all heated up. Roy McGarrett drunk wasn't pretty. Roy McGarrett drunk and pissed off was ten times worse.

His chuckle was breathy and reeked of stale beer. I wrinkled my nose and tried to move away, but he spun me fast and pulled me onto his knee, his arms feeling like tentacles as they wrapped around my waist.

I tapped my hands on his arms, trying to loosen them with a friendly pat. "Roy, don't be doing this tonight. Go home to your wife and sleep it off." I kept my tone light and teasing, still not wanting to upset him.

"I'm allowed to stay out as late as I want on a Saturday and you're my waitress, so if you want yourself a good tip, you better be giving me good service."

His fat, slobbery lips went for my neck. My mass of thick curls protected me a little, but not enough to ward off the fact I was gonna need a blazing hot shower to rid myself of his filth.

"Come on now, let me go." I tried to sound playful, wriggling on his lap to get myself free.

I was tempted to use the tray to bash him over the head, but I'd probably break his nose, and the sheriff would be none too pleased. He and Roy were cousins, whereas I'd only been living in Payton for two years and was still considered a newbie.

He ran his hand down my exposed leg, tickling my skin and making me nervous.

I flicked it off me, my anger starting to spark and fire. Enough was enough already!

"Cut it out." I wriggled some more, fighting his octopus hold on me.

"Oh, that feels good, darlin'. Do it again." He laughed, slapping his chubby hand back onto my naked thigh. His fingers inched toward the frayed denim edging, and I suddenly wished I'd shied away from my ripped-off miniskirt. I knew it was short, but it was decent enough. Besides, it matched my plaid shirt perfectly, and I liked the way it looked with my boots. I just wished Handsy McGarrett didn't like it so much!

I slapped his hand hard this time, warning him to back off before I really made trouble. I'd been nice enough, but my patience was just about done. My main concern was the fact the stupid pig weighed four times what I did, and I wasn't sure how to get free of the beefy arm holding me.

Thankfully, I didn't have to figure that out.

A strong hand I knew all too well landed on the back of Roy's neck, squeezing hard enough to actually make Mr. Grabby squeak.

"You have less than a second to let her go." Josh's voice was deep and thick.

I couldn't help a grin when Roy's arm went slack, and I jumped off his knee. I made sure I was wearing an indignant scowl when I turned to face him, though. Josh hauled him out of his chair, his muscles bulging as he held Roy by the scruff of his neck. I didn't think it was possible, but Chubby Roy actually looked small as my man towered over him.

"I—I'm sorry, Grizz. I didn't mean nothing by it." Roy swallowed, beads of sweat forming on his brow. His forehead wrinkled with a pleading look for mercy.

Josh didn't say anything while he glared at Roy. A low growl rumbled in his throat, reminding me of a Doberman about to attack.

"I'm drunk!" Roy's voice pitched. "I was only

having a little fun."

"Go have fun with your own girl and keep your filthy paws off mine!"

"You say it, Grizzly Bear!" Brock shouted from across the bar, raising his beer for his best friend. Millie let out a whoop beside him.

Roy wanted to frown, I could tell by the set of his mouth, but Josh *Grizzly Bear* Clark was not one to mess with. He'd never lost a fight...ever...and everyone in Payton knew it.

"Take your drunk ass out of my bar, and don't even think about coming back in here until you can treat these ladies right."

"She ain't no lady, Grizz." Roy's fat finger pointed at me. "We all know she's a past whore. I wasn't doing anything she hasn't—"

Roy's words were cut short by Josh's fist. It smacked into his face with a crunch that made me wince. Roy's head snapped back and he let out a pitiful whimper.

"*Don't* talk about her that way," Josh hollered.

My cheeks caught fire, blazing red while my jaw clenched tight and I stared down at the pitted floor. I hated my history. Town gossip had started the day I'd arrived in Payton. They hadn't even given me a chance to defend myself. Rumors were rife about the homeless, sixteen-year-old waif Josh found outside Clark's one morning. Part of the problem was they were right. I'd never had sex for money, but when you're cold and starving and the thought of a warm bed is too good to deny, you do things you're not proud of.

But Josh...he'd never made me feel bad for that. His uncle had given me a roof and a job and for the past two years, I'd been living safe and secure. My only enemy was the constant judgment I faced from stuck-up townsfolk who didn't know what it was to be alone and scared. Hell, half of them had probably never even traveled out of Payton! Them and their sheltered little lives. What did they know anyway?

I crossed my arms, the silence in the bar damn near deafening. I wanted to strangle whoever let the jukebox run dry. The timing was a little too dramatic for my tastes. Every eye in the room was a pistol aimed straight at my head. I loved being the center of attention when I was up on a stage, protected by a microphone and my guitar, but this kind of attention? No thank you, sir!

Roy muttered something under his breath, and Josh pulled his fist back for round two.

"All right! Damn it, Grizz! I'm leaving!" Roy shoved Josh's chest to no avail. It wasn't until Josh let him go that he was able to stumble away.

"Billy, take him home." Josh pointed at one of Roy's table buddies. He jumped-to the second Josh looked at him. "But pay for your drinks first...and you better give her the biggest damn tip you've ever given anybody."

With shaky hands, Billy pulled out a few bills and dropped them onto the table, glaring at his friends to do the same.

Roy leaned against the wall by the window, looking sick and dazed and shooting me a dark glare before turning for the door. I crossed my arms over my chest as he stumbled. Billy caught him near the door and they left together, two swaying trees ready to collapse.

A quick murmur started up the second they'd left and Josh turned to me. His gruff expression was nowhere to be seen as he took the tray from my hand, placing it on the table before gently tipping my chin.

"You all right?" He had his honeyed voice on, the one he only used with me.

I touched his cheek and smiled, my hand small on his chiseled face. "You know what I love most about you? You look like a big grizzly bear, but you're just a soft marshmallow on the inside, ain't ya."

"Only with you, sugar lips." He pulled me into his arms, lifting me off the floor and stealing my breath with a solid kiss. Cheers and whistles filled the quiet space, bringing the hum back into the bar with a rush.

I tipped my head back with a laugh, planting one more juicy kiss on his lips before he let me go. My boots slapped back down on the wood floor and all eyes were still on us.

Realization dawned over Josh's face and his ears turned red. He hated being the center of attention. Now that the judge and jury had left, I didn't mind one bit.

"How about I play y'all a song!" I raised my hand as a second round of cheers rose up around the room.

With a laugh, I skipped over to the stage and grabbed up the electric guitar that I'd been messing around on that afternoon. I preferred my acoustic, but that was upstairs by the bed.

Swinging the strap over my shoulder, I then flicked on the amp and adjusted the mic so I could stand and play.

"I'd like to dedicate this song to Roy McGarrett."

Brock booed real loud, making Josh laugh as he sauntered back around to his safe place behind the bar.

I leaned into the mic and tipped my head. "I don't care how drunk that man gets, he needs to keep his hands to himself!"

A chorus of cheers and whistles erupted as I started strumming "Keep Your Hands To Yourself."

TWO

JOSH

Watching Rachel play always filled me with a sense of awe. She sure knew how to capture a crowd. All eyes were fixed on her. Even Trudy and Lucas stopped playing darts for a minute to watch. Her voice permeated the room, sounding sweet, yet wild, just Rachel's style. Her small fingers danced over the strings as she played the guitar solo, a few drinkers cheering and whooping as she really got into it. Her rowdy, blond curls were like an entity of their own, bouncing around her face and tapping her on the back when she stepped up to the mic and started singing again.

By the end of the song, she had the entire bar singing the main line, hollering and cheering as she flipped a metaphorical bird at Roy. She wasn't the only girl in Payton who'd had to endure that pervert's insufferable hands. His poor wife. I didn't know why the hell she stayed with him.

Rachel finished the song with a final strum, and applause thundered throughout the open space. The smile on her face was like a neon light. That girl sure loved the stage. She was usually too busy working to play and in all honesty, I needed her back on the floor quick smart, but I just couldn't take the moment away from her.

Her eyes darted to mine, dancing with the look of sheer pleasure she got whenever she was performing. It really bothered me sometimes that all I could give her was a waitressing job and the odd stint of singing on quiet nights. She deserved so much more. She was the most talented eighteen-year-old I knew...and she was all mine. Sure, she was saving to leave and all, but I couldn't talk about that, so I just held her at night and cherished every minute I got to be near her.

"Three more beers for table ten, Grizz." Harriet smacked her tray down on the counter.

"Coming right up."

"And you might want to get your girl off the stage before she starts another, 'cause this place needs us both tonight."

"Yeah, I know," I mumbled.

She snorted a laugh and rolled her eyes. "You know, you could always hire someone else and she could sing all the time."

"I can't afford to do that." I placed the first beer down and grabbed a clean glass to pull the second.

Harriet's head tipped to the side, an old smile resting on her lips. "Your uncle was real nervous about giving you this place. It took a lot of convincing to get him to leave and go see the world like he wanted to. He was worried with you being so young and all."

"Come on now, Harry. I turned twenty-two last month." I winked at the fifty-year-old waitress and she flicked her hand to shush me.

"What I'm trying to say, Joshua Clark, is that he didn't need to worry about a thing. You've given him this amazing opportunity by doing a fine job. He's away, free from his troubles, and that's because of you." She tapped the counter then pointed at me. "And if my man stood up for me the way you stood up for Rachel tonight, he'd be getting laid right now."

My ears started burning, and I'm sure Harriet noticed, because she burst out laughing.

"You sweet kid," she murmured, sliding the tray off the counter and heading for table ten.

I rested my palms on the bar and watched her walk away, grateful for her compliment. Uncle Amos had handed over the key to his bar on my twenty-first birthday. I hadn't been expecting it and felt way out of my depth, but he'd stuck around for a year, teaching me everything I needed to know. Truth be told, I actually knew it all already. I'd been raised in the place and had been pulling beers since I was fourteen. Still, when Uncle Amos left for his big adventure, I was like a lost kid for the first few months.

I found my feet soon enough and a year later, I thought of Clark's as mine. Uncle Amos still checked in every week. He owned forty percent of this place, and after investing a lifetime into it, he wasn't about to let it go completely. We used my inheritance to buy in sixty percent, so the bar *was* officially mine. I couldn't help a touch of pride over that.

I owned Clark's Bar.

A smile grew on my lips. Damn, it felt good. It was home for me, and I couldn't imagine being anyplace else. I glanced up as Rachel jumped down from the stage, her petite hips swaying in that sexy little skirt. I didn't like her wearing it on busy nights. Don't get me wrong, I loved the skirt. I just didn't like the way every pervert in the place eyed up her sleek little legs when she was wearing it.

My eyes traveled up her tight frame, from those worn-out boots to the way her plaid shirt was knotted just above her belly button. Put a Stetson on top of that mass of curls and she was an all-American cowgirl. I grinned as she leaned against the counter.

"Table three wants a bowl of curly fries and two beers."

I spun and shouted the order into the kitchen before grabbing two fresh glasses. Rachel blew me a kiss as she took the tray and sauntered over to table three. I couldn't take my eyes off her as she delivered the drinks, my mind traveling back to the skinny little wretch I found huddled in the back doorway, hugging a guitar case.

The rain had been pelting down for days. I was well over it, and my poor dog Duke was going stir-crazy being locked up inside. His barking riled Uncle Amos something fierce.

"Josh, shut that dog up or I'm kicking him outside!" he hollered at me from the kitchen.

I'd clomped after my bloodhound, ready to tell him off, but when I found him with his nose pressed against the bottom of the door, I knew his barking wasn't for nothing.

"What is it, boy?" I scratched the top of his head, the folds of skin soft beneath my fingers. He whined and started scratching at the concrete floor. "Something out there?"

I creaked open the door, my eyes bulging wide at the last thing I expected to see.

A girl with skin like a ghost's was huddled in the narrow doorframe, obviously trying to shelter from the rain. It hadn't helped none. Her clothes were sodden rags, her spiral curls a tatty mess on her head. Her slender fingers clutched a worn-out guitar case like it was the only thing keeping her alive.

"Hey, you okay?" I crouched down to check on her, shaking her shoulder and repeating my question.

She didn't respond. Her eyes were closed and her pasty white skin was freezing to the touch.

"Hey!" I shook her again, scrambling to find a pulse. I was struggling to get my angles right and went to

move her guitar case so I could get better access to her. That's when she flinched, mumbling something in her sleep and wrapping her arms even tighter around the case.

"Thank God," I muttered before turning back into the bar and shouting, "Uncle Amos, you better come quick."

My urgent voice had him running to my side. He peered over my shoulder and his eyes popped wide.

"Well, butter my butt and call me a biscuit, this is unexpected."

I rolled my eyes. "Can you just call Doc, please?"

Uncle Amos nodded, turning for the phone while I gently wrestled the guitar out of her hands. She whimpered some, but was too weak to really fight me. I laid it down with extra care, figuring it meant more to her than I understood, before tucking my arms beneath her. She felt like a fragile bird in my arms.

Duke danced around my feet as I carried her through the bar and up the stairs to my room. His claws scratched on the wood as he followed me. I laid her down on my covers, her head sinking into my plump pillow. Her face still felt like ice as I brushed the back of my fingers down her delicate cheek. She was a small thing — skin and bone really, but there was beauty to her.

Duke muscled past my leg, his wet nose sniffing her out. He looked up at me with his big eyes and whined.

"I know, boy. We're gonna take care of her, don't you worry."

I rubbed his head before reaching for her shirt with slightly shaking hands. I sure hoped she didn't mind me stripping off her clothes, but we needed to get her warm. Lifting her against me, I slid her jacket off then wrestled *the damp cotton shirt over her head. I left her bra on, because that was the decent thing to do, before working off her pants and sliding that freezing body beneath my covers.*

I spent the next hour rubbing her limbs and laying my hand on her forehead while I anxiously waited for Doc. She drifted in and out of consciousness, never opening her eyes but sometimes muttering delirious ramblings I couldn't understand. Time ticked by in slow motion, and I don't know what it was, but with each passing minute, the overpowering need to keep her safe grew stronger.

I sometimes wonder if maybe I'd fallen in love with her that day...or maybe it was the day she smiled for the first time...or the second I heard her carefree laughter, that time when she teased me with that flirty wink of hers. Or it could have been the time I watched her from the doorway while she tuned her precious guitar, bathed in sunlight and looking like an angel when she started singing a soft tune for her mama.

Whenever it was or however it happened, I was gone for Rachel Myers. She was mine and I was hers, and if I could have my way, we'd stay like that for the rest of eternity.

THREE

JOSH

The bar emptied out by two, which was standard for a weekend night. I was looking forward to sleeping past the sunrise. In fact, I was hoping Rachel and I would stay in bed until noon. I wiped down the bar and headed into the kitchen to make sure it was clean. Denny, my main chef, was a real good worker, and he started clean-up at midnight when the kitchen officially closed. I checked the back door, knowing he'd probably already locked it anyway. He had. I chuckled at myself, grateful I had such a good team working for me. When Uncle Amos left for his travels, I was worried I'd lose some staff, but they all stuck around, their loyalty to Clark's unwavering. Crouching down by the back door, I scratched behind Duke's ears. He was dead to the world, his dream-like snuffles making me chuckle. He usually woke near closing, but he looked pretty comfy on his big pillow, and I decided to leave him be.

Pausing on my way back to the kitchen, a smile grew on my lips as I heard the faint strum of a guitar.

As per usual, Rachel had gotten distracted from her chair stacking, the lure of her beloved instrument being too much for her. Her strum was fast tonight, the words popping out of her mouth harsh and emphatic. My brow wrinkled as I stepped toward the door and heard:

What I'd like to do now is throw you to the ground and kick you in the ass
You deserve much more for calling me a whore
But my mama taught me better than that
Walking 'round here with your big boots on thinkin' so great, all that
But the truth be told, you're a low-down toad
But you won't hear me say that, 'cause I'm a little lady
And my mama taught me better than that
You're so lucky, my mama taught better than that

For all that teaching what did I learn?
That sometimes in life you're gonna get burned
So I'll keep my head up high and look you in the eye

'Cause my mama taught me better than that
Whoa yeah, Mama taught better than that

I couldn't help a chuckle. I loved it when she wrote her own songs. Stepping back into the bar, I was about to tell her, when she spotted me. Her eyes rounded and she slapped her hand against the guitar, sealing her lips up tight. Rising from her stool, she placed the instrument down and jumped off the stage.

"Come on, baby, play some more for me."

Her head shook the way it always did when I caught her composing. "I was just messing around."

"You know, people might like what you have to sing."

The curls rustled over her back as she shook her head again. "I can belt out a tune, but I ain't showing them my soul like that."

I walked toward her, gently cupping her face as soon as she was within reach. "You shouldn't be afraid, Rachel. Your soul is beautiful, and the world deserves to see it."

Her soft lips rose into a smile. "You think the world will?"

I hated that question, because I didn't ever want her to leave me. She was my morning star, my constant, and I'd had too many others leave me in the past. I couldn't bear the thought of losing her...but I couldn't say that. I didn't want to see the hope in her eyes fade. I wanted to keep pretending like I was the encouraging boyfriend.

"One day, baby."

It was easy to say it...to live the lie...because I didn't know if she'd ever make it to the big stage like she wanted to. It seemed an impossible dream, and therefore it was easy to support it. I felt a little bad about that sometimes. I didn't want to be a liar, but we lived in a town of less than a thousand people in the middle of America. Payton was barely on the map. She wasn't going to make the big time from this little town. I just couldn't ever see it happening, and a big part of me took comfort in that, while a small part simmered with guilt, knowing that I was helping her keep up the charade.

My quiet words made her smile grow, and she slapped her hands onto my shoulders, jumping up and wrapping her legs around my waist. I held her tight little behind and relished her tongue sliding into my mouth. Her hot breath tickled my insides, making my downstairs spasm with pleasure. I gripped her a little tighter, deepening the kiss so she knew I wanted some.

"Can we go upstairs now?" she puffed into my mouth.

It was an effort not to yell yes, but if I wanted my sleep-in, I needed to clean up the bar first. "We just need to finish sweeping and lock up."

"Okay." Her legs dropped and she slid down my body. Her grin was wicked as she skipped over to the door and flicked all the bolts shut. I went back to the kitchen and snatched out the broom while Rachel stacked the last of the chairs. But before I could get properly sweeping, she grabbed the handle and pulled it out of my hands.

"I'll sweep, you play." She flicked her head toward the piano, and I knew what she was doing.

I always liked to finish my night with a little piano time. There was something soothing about the white keys beneath my fingers and the rich sound that floated into the room. Rachel loved it, too. She thought me playing was sexy, and I just had to oblige her every time.

"What should I play, baby?" I nestled onto the bench and rested my right foot on the pedal.

"Play my song." She shrugged, keeping her eyes on the floor as she started sweeping.

So that's what I did.

FOUR

RACHEL

I didn't know why I asked him to play my song. I guess I loved his voice when he sang it. I gripped the handle of the broom as "Picture Postcards From L.A." filtered into the air. I remembered the first time I heard him playing it and the smile on his face as the words oozed out of his mouth. He was singing just for me...and it was my song.

A small-town waitress wanting to make it to the big time. That was me!

So that's why I loved it, but then I also hated it, because the song talked about how she never actually left. She never made it to LA, because something always made her stay.

I wanted Josh to be my reason...like in the song. It'd be romantic and sweet, and if I was honest, he kind of was a reason, but he wasn't the only thing keeping me in Payton.

It took a fair whack of soul-searching for me to figure it out, and if anyone asked me, I wouldn't admit it, but I think maybe I was scared. So, I kept telling everyone I hadn't saved enough yet. I hadn't really. I mean, I had enough for a bus ticket to LA, but then what? I didn't even know where to begin fulfilling my promise to Mama. I'd be a lost kid in a big city with nothing but the clothes on my back and an old guitar. I didn't know if I was ready for that feeling again...and so I stayed.

Some days it wasn't so bad, but on nights when I'd been called a whore and made to feel like trash, I wanted out. I wanted to prove them all wrong about me. I wasn't the homeless kid I used to be and one day, they'd be reading my name in the headlines and wishing they hadn't been so cruel.

Rachel Myers—country singing sweetheart. Grammy winner. Superstar. That's what I wanted to be.

I slid the broom under table six, capturing a couple of curly fries and a balled-up napkin, a sigh resting in my chest.

The way Roy looked at me, treated me like I was worth nothing more than a good time, it was hard not to believe him. I was probably a fool for wanting anything more than what I had.

Josh and Amos saved my life—taking me in,

helping me get better, and then loving me. No man had ever made me feel the way Josh did. The way he'd stood up for me against Roy, well if that didn't melt my heart, nothing could. That boy would bloody any bar floor for me, and although that sounded kind of gross, it was also so romantic.

Why would I want to leave that?

Because…

Mama's sweet smile flashed through my mind.

Because I had promises to keep.

I wasn't turning into Millie Rae. No, siree. I could fool myself into thinking staying here would be enough, but it never would be.

When I was on stage, that feeling…nothing beat that. I *needed* that life. Imagine being able to sing, for a living! No more sweeping floors or getting beer stains on my favorite shirts. No more Handsy Roy McGarrett and leering, drunken men. I had to make that happen for myself…I just wished I knew an easy way how.

I brushed the dirt into separate piles around the room, trying to focus back on the magic of Josh's voice.

Leaving all that crap behind would be a piece of cake.

But leaving Josh…that would be a little more challenging. I didn't want to hurt him, but he knew. I mean, I talked about it all the time, so it's not like I'd be leaving him high and dry or nothin'.

Guilt skipped through me, and I nibbled on my lip. I was having one of them restless nights. Damn if they didn't keep me awake until sunrise.

Grabbing out the dustpan, I made quick work of clearing the floor. Josh had started up the song again, not singing this time, just gracing the room with the piano accompaniment. His aunt had forced him into lessons when he was a kid. He confessed to pounding those keys in anger every lesson and complaining that he hated it, but he was grateful now...and so was I. If that amazing woman was alive, I'd thank her profusely for what she did. She became Josh's ma when he didn't have nobody. His daddy was a Marine and wasn't around too often, and by the way Josh spoke of Amos and Lindy, I knew they were his parents really. They did all the hard work.

I balanced the broom against the wall in the kitchen, scratching my curls and finally letting out that sigh. I stepped back into the bar and leaned against the doorframe, watching Josh play. He was so beautiful—a breathtaking, all-powerful man. I did love him. I never told him much, not wanting to give him false hope. I showed him in other ways.

A cheeky grin played with my lips, and I slipped out of view, wriggling my panties off with a little snicker. That boy had earned him some and if anything, it'd help settle my restless heart, if only for a night. I ambled back into the main bar and stepped onto the small stage, stopping next to the piano. Ignoring the fact he was playing, I eased my leg over his. He stopped for a second so I could nestle myself against him, my skirt riding high as I straddled his lap. My boots rested against the piano bench, and I grinned at him as he tried to keep playing.

Licking my top lip, I chuckled as his fingers faltered, but it wasn't until I glided my tongue up the side of his neck that the song fell apart. A disjointed chord disturbed the air when I sucked the sweet spot just below his ear.

His large hands cupped my butt, his fingers digging into the denim skirt only just covering it. I rocked against him, feeling him grow hard beneath me. The rough denim against my sensitive skin turned me on, making my insides tingle with urgency. I yanked at his shirt, forcing his arms up so I could whip it over his head. The feel of his rock-hard, smooth skin beneath my hands always made me heady. He was a rippled, hot wonder. I ran my hands down his back, enjoying the power of his body as I rested my lips against his shoulder.

His hands were feather-light as they scooped my hair away from my neck before traveling down my back. Hot, wet lips nuzzled the crook of my neck, a sweet moan slipping from between my lips as he squeezed my breasts.

"I have to have you now, honey. Right here," I whispered.

"Right here?" he puffed back.

"You know it."

And he sure did. His large hands jumped off my shirt and started lifting my skirt out of the way, his fingers lightly scraping my skin.

He paused, his brow knotting when he looked at me. "Please tell me you weren't panty-less all night."

I chuckled, whispering in his ear, "Only for you, Grizz." Sucking his lobe, I pulled away so I could unzip his fly. It was a little awkward, I have to admit, but there was something so damn sexy about making love on a piano bench that we made the awkward work. He held me tight against him as he raised his butt and wriggled out of his jeans. They were soon puddled at his ankles, his naked butt cheeks pressed against the wooden bench.

I stroked him slowly, applying just the right pressure until I got that growling groan of his that told me he was ready. Lifting my hips, I slid onto him—a slow, luxurious slide to heaven. We moaned in unison, my fingers digging into his broad shoulders as he grasped my hips. I started to ride him, slow and easy strokes at first, but it didn't take long for me to build the pace. He felt so damn good inside me, my body was going crazy, my heart beating with a wild thunder.

Yanking out his ponytail, I ran my fingers into his waves, fisting two handfuls as the pressure inside me built to a crescendo. Josh's hot lips sucked and teased the tender skin of my neck, his fingers digging into my butt as he increased the pace for us.

I wanted to cry out his name but couldn't speak. I could barely breathe. All I could feel was the amazing body between my thighs and the thunderstorm rolling through me.

Josh's hold on my hips tightened, and I could sense he was close. I grabbed his face and planted my lips on his, wanting to feel his tongue dancing with mine as he came.

His mouth went slack, a groan firing out of him as he pulled my hips down and drove into me for one final push. I tipped my head back, relishing the way I could bring him to his knees. My body was still on fire, dancing flames lighting my core. A languid smile rose on my lips as his breath puffed against my neck.

"That was good, honey," I whispered, biting my lip as I leaned forward and grinned at him.

"It's not over yet, baby." His voice was husky and deep as he wriggled beneath me, kicking off his boots and jeans before clutching me against him and rising from the stool. I wrapped my legs around him and couldn't help a giggle as his butt-naked self carried me upstairs for round two.

FIVE

JOSH

The bar had a low murmuring hum going on. It was often quieter on a Wednesday, unless an important game was on TV. Baseball season was in full swing, but people seemed more interested in watching my Rachel. She was perched on a stool up on the stage, one leg crossed over the other as she sang and strummed.

The crowd was thin, maybe twenty, which was why I didn't mind her taking the floor and doing her thing.

Her voice had a sexy huskiness to it as she belted out "Fall From Grace" while strumming her acoustic guitar. It was a gift from her mama when she was only eleven years old and the most precious possession she owned. I grinned at her as she caught my eye.

Damn, she was beautiful. The way the light hit her thick blond curls gave her a halo. She'd braided her hair, and the thick locks hung over one shoulder. Tight jeans with rips in the knees hugged her legs, and the tank she was wearing looked so damn sexy, I couldn't wait for closing. Wiping a spill of beer from the counter, I shoved the rag into my back pocket, glanced at table four yet again, and frowned. I wasn't the only one drooling over my woman.

A guy, probably a bit older than me, had sauntered in about an hour ago. He was wearing them skinny jeans that made his legs look like toothpicks and a pair of shoes with points on the end...shiny, pretty boy shoes that didn't belong in a bar like mine. His shirt was pressed, and his hair was slicked back with gel. All them things alone were enough to not like him, but the fact he hadn't stopped checking out Rachel since she took the stage irked me real bad. I didn't like the way his dark eyes roved her body or that greasy little smirk on his pretty boy lips.

"Who're you glarin' at?" Brock glanced over his shoulder.

He'd been sitting up with me since he got off work. He always did that on a Wednesday and I loved it. He'd been my best friend since kindergarten. He'd always been there, and he'd always be the one I'd call in a crisis. Heck, he was the one that sat with me for two days solid after I got the news that my old man had been blown to pieces in Iraq. I still didn't get why that happened. He'd been three weeks away from coming home. I'd lived without him for close to a year. Every time we got to talk, he'd promise me he was coming home. We finally got ourselves a sure date...and he died five days later. I'd been ten years old...and totally devastated.

Brock hadn't said one word after Uncle Amos told him. He just walked over to the couch and slumped down beside me, being exactly what I needed.

I scowled at Brock's question and raised my chin toward table four. "That guy over there," I mumbled. "You know him?"

"Oh, you mean pretty boy?"

I snorted out a laugh. "That's the one."

Brock took a slow pull of his beer before licking his bottom lip. He always did that to me, took his sweet time answering the important questions. I'm sure he knew it riled me something fierce, but he did it anyway.

"Yeah, I'm working on his car right now."

I raised my eyebrows with a nod, silently asking for more.

"He's been in town for his grandma's funeral, although I wonder if it's only to make sure he gets a claim in the estate."

"He's Tilly Peters' grandson?"

"He sure is."

I glared past Brock's shoulder, watching the guy sip at his whiskey with a smug smile on his face. "I've never seen him around here before."

"I don't think he's ever set foot in Payton."

"So, a gold digger then."

Brock shrugged, finishing off his bottle of Corona before tapping it on the bench—his quiet way of asking for another. I snatched a fresh one out of the fridge and opened it for him, plonking it down on the cardboard coaster.

Brock gave me a knowing stare, his lips rising into a grin. "You can't kick him out for that, Grizz."

"I wish he'd do something stupid so I could boot his behind right out that door."

"He's only lookin'."

"He's not just lookin'," I grumbled.

My eyes narrowed as I watched the man. His smirk rose, his dark eyes gleaming as he applauded Rachel.

"Thank y'all. I'll just sing one more and then I'll let the jukebox take over."

"Sing me something sweet, sugar!" Brock hollered from his stool.

I shoved his shoulder, and he nearly toppled off while the rest of the bar laughed. Pretty boy looked our way and I caught his eye, throwing him a steely glare that made him frown.

He turned back to Rachel as she started strumming "Come On Over."

"This one's for my grizzly bear." She simpered, her eyebrows wiggling at me.

I grinned at her and shook my head. That was

not the right song for her to be singing with that leering jackass watching her. She didn't help matters by getting off the stool and dancing around the stage, moving those hypnotic hips and eliciting a few wolf whistles from the crowd.

Brock put his fingers in his mouth and would have whistled too if I hadn't clipped him on the back of the head.

"What?" He laughed at me, rubbing his wayward curls.

I gave him a pleading look that made him turn to face me.

"Grizz, don't be so worried."

"Just fix that car as fast as you can." I frowned.

"He'll be out of here by tomorrow, don't you worry."

I nodded, my jaw clenching tight as Rachel's song came to an end.

"Woohoo!" she cheered, laughing at the crowd as she took off her guitar and gently propped it against the piano. Skipping off the stage, she was heading my way when the last person I wanted talking to her stood from his chair and caught her attention.

SIX

RACHEL

"Excuse me, miss?"

I turned toward the voice, my smile growing as I took in his slick appearance. Hair gel, anyone? I pressed my lips together, hoping my expression wasn't too mocking. I was actually kind of intrigued.

What was a city boy doing in little ol' Payton?

"Hi there." I leaned against the back of the chair parked next to him.

"That was quite a show." He grinned, his white teeth straight and shiny.

I snickered at his funny accent. He wasn't just a

47

city boy. He sounded like he was from the West Coast. "Where you from?"

"California. Los Angeles to be more precise." He reached into his coat pocket and pulled out a business card. "Parker Stewart. I own a talent agency. I represent actors and singers looking to make a career in the entertainment industry."

My heart did a flip-flop as I took the card off him. The black writing was glossy on the cream paper. Struggling for words, I ran my thumb over the lettering. An agent, from LA, in Payton...and he was giving me his business card. What did that mean?

Clearing my throat, I fought for a little composure as I pulled out the chair and sat down.

"So, how do you figure out who to represent?"

"Well, I'm either approached by would-be actors and singers...or sometimes I get really lucky and I stumble across a raw, natural talent just waiting to be discovered." His steady gaze roamed my face, a smile tugging at his lips.

Trying to stay cool about the whole thing was nearly impossible. Was he seriously indicating that he'd like to represent me?

I licked my bottom lip and gazed at his card again. "And, ah, what do you do when you find a raw, natural talent?"

He leaned toward me with a cocky grin. "I mold it and shape it and turn into something magical...and then I make their dreams come true."

My breath caught in my throat and I leaned against the table, my fingers pressing into the wood. "Are you saying…"

"I'm saying I see something in you, and if you're interested, I'd love to work with you."

"She already has a job." Josh's deep voice made me flinch.

I turned with a scowl. "What are you doing?" I gritted out between clenched teeth.

He frowned at me, and I was tempted to kick him right in the shins.

Swiveling back with what I hoped was an elegant smile, I tapped the card against the table. "I am interested. Could you tell me a little more?"

The chair beside me scraped against the wood, and I closed my eyes as Josh sat down beside me. He had his angry face on, and it was irritating as hell.

"Do you mind?" I glared at him.

"Not at all. I'd love to hear what this pretty boy has to say."

Gripping my boyfriend's forearm, I tried to relay my outrage with a quick pinch, but he didn't even jerk. Curse his thick, strong muscles! He was going to ruin everything!

Mr. Stewart seemed unperturbed by Josh's rude behavior and turned his attention to me.

"Well, the way it works is I set you up as one of my clients, and then I find you some work…which hopefully leads to bigger jobs and better prospects, and you start to make a name for yourself."

"A name for myself." My breathy laugh was pathetic, but hello! This was everything I'd been waiting for…and rather than me having to chase it down, it was coming right to my doorstep.

"Okay." I wriggled in my chair with a nod, my excitement making my limbs jiggle. "So, how does it work, do I just sign up with you and wait for a call?"

He fought a grin and leaned across the table. "I know this seems quite hurried, but I have someone in mind that I think would love your style. He owns a club in LA that has live performances each night, and many of the singers who have started out with him have gone on to get movie deals and contracts with record labels. He's looking for something fresh, and I have a feeling that he's going to fall in love with your country charm."

"You think so?" I was blushing like a Valentine's rose, I was sure of that.

"I know so."

Josh jerked beside me. "You ain't singing in no club, Rachel."

A muscle in my neck pinged tight, and it took all my willpower not to snap at my grumpy-ass boyfriend.

Mr. Stewart raised his hand with a reassuring smile. "It's a reputable place. I know 'club' can have bad connotations, but it's just as wholesome as this bar here."

"She's only eighteen," Josh growled.

"I'm nineteen in three months, and stop treating me like a schoolgirl with pigtails in my hair! This conversation has nothing to do with you!"

My words stung Josh real bad. His face pinched tight, his pale gaze growing stormy. Guilt spiked through me, but I bit back my apology. He was being an ass, pooping all over this great opportunity before I even had a chance to explore it. I was not going to let him ruin this for me.

I looked back at Mr. Stewart and mumbled, "Sorry, please continue."

"I'm not trying to pressure you into anything, but you have a beautiful voice and huge potential. I know I could find a place for you in LA."

"Wow, really?"

"LA?"

We both ignored Josh's horrified question.

"It would be a big change for you, and there's no guarantees this first job will pan out, but if you're willing to work hard, I'm confident we can make you a star."

"I am. I can work real hard." My voice was quaking with excitement. I could barely think straight. My brain was buzzing like a beehive.

This is it, Mama. It's happening!

"Can't she just audition here then?" Josh's cold-water tone made my insides deflate. "Rather than going all that way, just to be rejected."

The agent shook his head. "He really needs to see her, and if she does get rejected, being in LA will make it far easier for her to get to auditions." Mr. Stewart was looking at Josh like he was stupid, and I didn't half-blame him. Of course I'd have to be in LA!

"It's just…" Josh shifted in his seat. "LA's a long way and we can't afford to fly, so I'd need to find someone to watch the bar and…" He sighed.

"You'd need to give us some time to figure all this out."

"Well, I'm heading to LA tomorrow. As soon as my car's fixed, I'll be driving to the airport. I'm happy to take…"

"Rachel." I grinned, sticking out my hand and laughing at the fact he was offering me an audition before he even knew my name. "Rachel Myers."

"Miss Myers." His smile was sweet as he clasped my hand and gently shook it.

"I can't be asking you to pay for me to fly to LA."

"Well, let me make some calls tonight. If I can set up a few auditions for you, then it's actually in my best interest to ask you to fly with me. My company will cover the expenses."

"Tomorrow?" Josh's voice sounded small and so unlike him.

I glanced at his ashen face, and my happy buzz took another nosedive.

My grip on his arm softened to a light rub. "Hon, it'd just be for a short while."

"Well, it could take a little longer…" Mr. Stewart gave Josh a kind smile. "I will take care of her, and you don't need to worry about a thing. I've been doing this for years now."

My confidence was boosted by his assuring tone, and I looked to Josh with a pleading grin. He'd never been able to resist my puppy dog eyes, not that I needed his permission, but his support would have been nice. He'd always been the most encouraging, loving boyfriend a girl could want, but as I sat there staring at his grim expression, I knew that was about to change.

*****

Josh had been quiet all night. We couldn't have a proper conversation until everyone had left, and the vibe in the room was pretty somber. Of course everyone sided with Josh, and I instantly became the wench who was leaving him. It only got worse too, when just before closing, I got a call from Mr. Stewart telling me that his guy in LA was real keen to see me. He made me promise not to rush into the decision. I had to think it over and give him my final word in the morning. I already knew what my answer was going to be, and I couldn't even shout it out with a whooping cheer. I got off the call, and the last three stragglers looked at me like I was betraying them all. Thankfully, they left pretty quick after that.

The second the floor was swept, I headed upstairs to check out Parker Stewart's website. Josh stayed downstairs, doing the final lock-up and check of the kitchen.

Leaning toward the screen, I scanned the site. It was pretty fancy and slick...just like Parker Stewart. I was impressed. I didn't recognize many of the stars he represented. They seemed to be working in more small-time soap operas, but they were definitely on the up-and-up. I saw one singer—Maddy Storm—had got herself a record contract and was working on her debut album. She was a pop singer by the looks of things, not really my thing, but Mr. Stewart seemed to represent a range of stars. My excitement reignited as I pored over the website and read his clients' testimonials.

Josh clomped into the room, Duke following in his wake. The bloodhound trotted over to me and rested his chin on my lap, his tail going crazy as I patted his head. Josh glanced over my shoulder and let out a derisive snort. I stiffened, but held my tongue. I wanted to gush about everything I'd read but didn't want Josh pouring cold water all over it. His lack of enthusiasm actually kind of hurt. He'd been telling me I could make it, and then when I finally get the chance, he turns into a cynical grouch.

"You can't be serious about this," Josh grumbled, kicking off his boots. "You're not going, Rachel."

Duke jumped back as I swiveled in my chair and glared at my boyfriend. "You can't tell me what to do."

Josh yanked off his shirt and threw it on the floor, his sharp gaze hitting me right between the eyes. "I don't trust him."

"Oh, come on, you don't trust anybody!"

"He's got a dark smile, and I didn't like the way he was looking at you."

"You don't like the way any guy looks at me." I stood up and threw my hands in the air. "I can't believe you're trying to ruin this!" I slid my boots off, throwing them to the side and nearly hitting Duke. The dog yelped and scampered across to Josh. "Sorry, boy," I muttered at the tenderhearted beast. He whimpered his forgiveness but planted himself at Josh's feet.

Scratching his dog's head, Josh huffed out an impatient snort...a sure sign that his temper was on the rise. I didn't care. If we needed to fight this out then so be it.

Crossing my arms, I met his stony expression with a stubborn one of my own.

With a heavy sigh, Josh ran his hands into his hair and linked them behind his head. "I'm trying to protect you."

"That is not your job."

"What!" His hands dropped, his expression thunderous.

Okay, so that was the wrong thing to have said. I rolled my eyes as his grizzly bear began to show.

"Not my job? Yes it is! I'm your boyfriend!"

Pulling in a breath, I closed my eyes and tried to redeem my mistake with a calm, sweet voice. "Josh, honey, you know singing on a stage is my dream."

"You were singing on a stage tonight." He pointed at the door.

"That's not what I mean and you know it. This is the chance I've been hoping for! I can't spend the rest of my life in Payton—population eight hundred and fourteen."

"We're up to eight ninety-six now."

"Josh!" I planted my hands on my hips and gave him an exasperated glare.

"Okay! I'm just saying!"

"Don't just say!"

"Well, what do you want me to do!"

"Support me! Tell me to fly to LA and make all my dreams come true!"

I gazed at his tortured expression, my eyes traveling down to his heaving chest.

"Your mama doesn't need you to go to LA." His whispered words fueled my anger and maybe my guilt, but most definitely my hurt. Did he not get it?

Keeping my tone steady was a concerted effort. "I made a promise to her. It was the last thing I did before she died, and I ain't going to let her down. I am being offered the chance of a lifetime. It's being served to me on a silver platter, and you're telling me to ignore it?" My voice pitched high, but I was on a roll. "All those times you told me I could make it. They were just lies, weren't they? You could say it to me because you didn't think it was ever going to happen, and now that it actually *is* happening, you're trying to find reason for me not to go. Well, you know what, Joshua Clark? It's happening, and I'm going! I'm gonna do whatever it takes to make this dream come true."

After my flurry of words, the room fell into an awkward silence. My puffy breaths were met with a quiet swallow. Josh looked to the floor like I'd just slapped him in the face. My heart constricted so tight it actually hurt. Josh's lips pursed to the side, his head bobbing like an old rocking chair. He still wouldn't look at me, and it was a painful torture.

Finally he sniffed, snatched the pillow off the bed, bunched it in his hand...and walked for the door, Duke padding after him.

"I'm going to sleep in my old room." He brushed past me while I blinked at my stinging eyes.

It was pointless trying to call him back. Josh liked to stew. That was his way. He'd come around in the morning...hopefully before I left.

Slumping onto the mattress, I fought the overwhelming urge to cry. Part of me didn't want to leave, but I couldn't tell him that. He'd just use it to make me stay and I couldn't.

I could *not* stay.

"You have to go, baby. You have to get out while you can." Mama's voice was weak and breathy.

"I ain't leaving you." Tears were burning my eyes, but I refused to let them fall. I clutched my mother's frail hand like it was the only thing keeping me alive.

"I don't have much time left." A cough rattled her chest, her thin body convulsing.

I waited it out, knowing she had more to say, and desperate to find out what it was.

Wiping her brow with the damp cloth by the bed, I sniffed and pulled her hand to rest against my cheek.

"Once I'm gone, you know Daddy and the boys are going to work you to the bone. You have to get free," she whispered. *"You have to go and live the life that you deserve. Baby, you are so talented. Your voice cannot be hidden away. It needs to be heard. You take that guitar*

and you do whatever it takes to become a star. You fly, my angel. You shine your light and you touch hearts like I know you can."

I couldn't hold back the tears then. They trickled out my eyes and ran down my cheeks, kissing the edge of my mouth with their saltiness.

"You promise me, baby."

"I promise, Mama."

"Whatever it takes."

I nodded.

A weak smile touched her lips. "I'll be watching you, always."

"I love you, Mama."

Those were the last words she ever heard me say. She fell asleep after our chat, and the pneumonia took her that night. I'd stayed for the funeral and she'd been right—the day her body was buried, Daddy and my three older brothers turned me into their housemaid. I no longer had caring for Mama as my excuse, and I was expected to do everything. I hated them for it, but I hated my father more for letting Mama die. Something that started out as a common cold turned into a vicious flu. He couldn't afford no medical bills, and I blamed him for her unnecessary death.

In spite of all that, fear kept me put and I lasted for two more months. But then *that night* happened, and I couldn't take it anymore. With nothing more than my guitar and a small bag of essentials, I split town and never looked back.

I was sixteen years old and homeless, but I was

determined.

My sights were set on the big city. Nashville, originally. I'd planned to busk my way there...do whatever it took to make it, but things didn't go according to plan. I never expected to end up near-dead on Clark's back door, but I guess it was a blessing in disguise. Josh and Amos took me in, helped me get better. I had pneumonia—ironic, right? I don't know why I deserved to live when my saint of a mother was taken before her time, but maybe it was because I had a promise to keep.

Josh had gifted me something I'd never had—a safe haven. He'd made me fall in love, but...

But...

I could never shake my promise to Mama.

I couldn't turn my back on this chance, no matter how much it hurt Josh.

My mama was watching and she'd want me to go.

So...decision made.

SEVEN

JOSH

I couldn't sleep. My old bed was lumpy and uncomfortable. I missed Rachel's head on my shoulder, the way her small body fit against mine, a fragile bird that I wanted to cherish forever.

Why'd she want to leave me?

I tossed over to the side, gazing down at the spot on the floor where I'd slept for months while Rachel slept in the narrow little bed I occupied. She'd been sick with the flu when I'd first found her. Fever had ravaged her skeletal body for near a week before it finally broke. I'd worried the whole time, wondering if she was going to pull through.

Duke had sat by her bed, the perfect guard dog while I worked down in the bar. I'd popped up to check on her whenever I could.

She was a fighter. Her petite frame hid her strength, but I saw it. She was determined to live.

"To live for this chance," I muttered into the darkness, feeling like dirty pond water.

I couldn't deny her this opportunity. I couldn't tell her not to go, but boy did I want to.

I didn't care what she thought. That pretty boy still made me uneasy, but what if I was wrong? What if this was her chance?

The very idea of her walking out my door made my gut clench. I hated the idea with every fiber of my being. It took me back to the last time my father left. He hugged me goodbye, told me he loved me and then went off to war. I wanted to hate him for leaving me again. My ma died when she gave birth to me, and my old man joined the Marines a month later. It was like he couldn't stand to be around me or something. Although, when he was home it was great, but then 9/11 happened and everything changed. He was gone all the time, and I spent my days worrying that I'd never see him again.

I didn't want to go through losing someone else, but if Rachel left...I would.

Sure, she wasn't going off to war, but she was going away. She was leaving me, and I couldn't make her stay.

"Stay," I croaked, feeling more nervous than I ever had.

Uncle Amos had gone out of town for the weekend, and I was in his bed for the night. It was a nice change from the floor.

Rachel stood in my doorway, looking like an angel in one of my old shirts. I could see right through the white fabric, and I knew I had to have her.

I'd resisted for months, quietly falling in love with her and not saying a word. She didn't need some pervert making advances on her. In the still darkness of the night, she'd told me everything. I knew what she'd had to do to survive those homeless winter nights. I ached for her, but it'd made me behave.

I even waited until the day after her eighteenth birthday—the whole time wondering if she'd still be there. As each month passed, talk of the big city grew less frequent and my hope continued to grow.

I kissed her lips for the first time on July fourth, sixteen months after I'd found her, and we'd been playing boyfriend and girlfriend ever since.

The fall leaves were turning red now, and I could no longer resist.

Her eyes sparkled with a cheeky grin as she took in my, no doubt, desperate expression. "You want me, Joshua Clark?"

"I want you." I could barely breathe out the words.

Those supple lips of hers pulled into a giddy smile, her fingers tucking a springy curl behind her ear. "I want you, too." She swallowed, gliding toward me. I drank in her body until she stood at my feet. The top of her head rested just below my chin. I palmed her curls and tipped her head toward mine.

She rose up to meet me, and that night I had my first

real taste of heaven.

I fell in love with that girl...every inch of her...and I promised myself I'd never let her go.

But how did you keep someone who wanted to leave you?

"You can't," I mumbled, squeezing my eyes shut and willing the pain at bay.

*****

The sun rose a few hours earlier than it should have. I stumbled out of bed, kneading my aching temples. I used the bathroom and then peeked into Uncle Amos's old room. Since he'd left, Rachel and I had moved in there and our bed was empty. A suitcase sat on the floor beside it, packed and ready to go.

It felt like a knife was being driven straight through my stomach. Flicking the hair out of my face, I pulled it into a ponytail and clomped down the stairs.

Indistinct conversation was coming from the main bar and I frowned. We didn't open until lunchtime on a Thursday, so who the hell was Rachel talking to?

It was probably Pretty Boy. The anger in my belly stirred just thinking about it. Stopping on the final step, I forced myself to take a slow breath. I couldn't let her leave in anger. As much as I wanted to cuff her to the bar and never let her go, I couldn't do it. What was the point of keeping someone if they didn't want to be there?

Peeking my head out of the stairwell, I took in the sight of Rachel chatting to Duke. His floppy jowls sagged as if he was frowning.

"Now, don't be giving me your sad face. I'll come back to give you kisses soon enough." She grinned, planting a kiss on his head. She was sitting in a chair while he was parked on the floor between her legs. He looked massive beside her.

Snuffling and letting out a little whimper, he bowed his head.

"Please don't be like that. I need you to be happy for me. I need you to look after your daddy. He thinks I'm leaving him because I don't love him anymore, but that could never be true. He owns my heart, that boy, and I'll be calling and sending songs that I've recorded. It's not over." Her bright smile died, her expression crumpling a little before she could catch it.

I closed my eyes, cursing myself for spending our last night in a single bed when I could have been making love to her, kissing every inch of her skin and giving her all the reasons in the world to return.

Her voice dropped to a quiet whisper, which I had to strain to hear. "I love you. Don't you ever forget that."

Duke howled, making Rachel laugh before wrapping him in a tight hug. I gripped the doorframe, resisting the urge to walk into the room and disturb them. If I did, I'd drop to my knees and beg her to stay…and she didn't need that from me.

Heading back up to the bathroom, I turned the shower to scalding and then shoved my head under the hot spray. All I could do was pray I'd have the courage to watch her leave me.

EIGHT

RACHEL

I hadn't seen Josh all morning. Leaving him alone had been real hard yet also a relief. I couldn't handle another battle, so I didn't want to see him, but I'd missed him in my bed and craved his touch, his kisses, his loving gaze. I needed to know we were okay. I didn't want to leave under a dark cloud.

When I went up to grab my suitcase, Josh was locked away in his old room. Who knew what he was doing in there. I didn't have the courage to knock and find out. Instead I muscled that case down the stairs. It landed with a thud on the wooden floor. I left it there and collected up my guitar, resting it gently inside the old black case. I was setting it down just as Mr. Stewart knocked on the main door.

I ran to let him in, forcing a bright smile.

The expression on his face turned my smile genuine. It was actually happening. I kind of wanted to keep pinching myself.

"Good morning, Miss Myers." He slid off his aviator shades, his dark eyes sparkling at me.

"Please, call me Rachel."

"Then you can call me Parker."

"Deal." I nodded.

"Are those your cases?" He pointed over my shoulder and I nodded again.

Brushing past me, he picked them up and then headed for his car.

"Wait, I—"

He stopped and glanced back at me. "Is everything okay?"

"Yeah, I just, um." I swallowed. "I need to say goodbye."

I'd already spoken to Millie on the phone. She'd cried and blubbered her farewell, making me feel like I was dying rather than flying to the coast. Brock had muttered out a swift goodbye. That man was loyal to Josh like a puppy dog. He didn't want me going because it made Josh sad, and he was making me pay for it with short, clipped sentences and an icy tone.

Parker nodded at me from the doorway. "Okay, well, the plane leaves in a couple of hours, so we need to hit the road in five minutes if we're going to make it to the airport in time."

"Right, got it." I nodded, swamped by a nervous agitation that I hadn't expected.

Pressing my lips together, I turned for the stairs and found Josh waiting in the doorway.

My heart squeezed tight at the sight of him—my towering man with his hangdog frown.

"I—" I pointed behind me. "It's time for me to go."

"Yeah." Josh stared at the floor as he slowly moved toward me.

"I'll call you when I get there."

"Okay."

Damn, I was going to miss that deep voice—the soft, husky sound of it.

His pale blue gaze hit me, making me feel everything from guilt to despair. He opened his mouth to speak but couldn't say anything. He'd always struggled to talk about his feelings. I guess I just instinctively knew most of them, and as much as I wanted it, I couldn't expect gushy prose.

I needed to get the goodbye over with.

Stepping forward, I rose to my tiptoes and brushed my lips against his. "I'll see you, Josh." My voice wavered, tears burning my eyes as I spun for the door.

I yanked it open and headed for Parker's car.

"Rachel, wait!"

My boot heel dug into the ground, and I turned to face my man. His large, grizzly bear body strode over to me, his jaw set tight and determined. He stopped right at my feet and pulled a note from his pocket.

"What's this?" I took the one-dollar bill from him.

"I want you to buy me a postcard," he croaked. "Find me one of a sunset or something."

My song—"Picture Postcards From L.A."

Well, ain't that just the sweetest thing.

Tears lined my lashes as I clutched the note in my hand. "I'll sign it with love forever more."

Snatching me around the waist, Josh pulled me into a tight embrace. I clung to him like it was our last. My feet left the ground and I wrapped my legs around him, placing my hand on his face and running my thumb along his jawline.

He didn't have anything else to say, so I kissed him, a hungry, solid promise that I would return. I couldn't promise him that I'd stay, but I also couldn't go the rest of my life without seeing him again. I had no idea when I'd be back, but I knew for sure that I'd never love anyone the way I loved Joshua Clark.

*****

The flight took about four and a half hours. I'd never been on a plane before and I tell ya, I was pretty nervous when we took off, but looking out that tiny window at the world below, that was beyond belief. Mama would have loved it. She would have sat in her tiny, cramped seat going on about how exciting it was.

She would have been right. It was exciting. In fact the further we flew, the more excited I got. The pain of leaving Josh was dulled by Parker's chatter. He was telling me everything we'd be doing. He'd arranged it all the night before. His car was waiting for us at the airport, and he was going to drive me to my hotel.

A hotel!

I'd never stayed in one of them before. I mean, I'd been in the odd, disgusting motel room. The ones with the little kitchens in 'em, but I ain't never stayed anywhere classy. And everything about Parker Stewart was classy.

I stole a glance out the corner of my eye. His thumbs moved like lightning over the touch pad of his phone. I didn't know how he typed so fast. He was such a city boy...and I was a country hick. Tugging on my little skirt, I shifted in my seat, leaning my forehead against the small window to look out again.

The City of Angels was now beneath me, and all I could see were hundreds of houses with bean-shaped pools in their backyards. As the plane began its descent, I swear I was landing on an alien planet.

Could I honestly do this?

Whatever it takes.

Mama's words whispered through my brain, and I forced a smile as the plane touched down.

Parker undid his seatbelt while the plane taxied

for the gate and pulled out his bag from under the seat in front. I waited until the sign flicked off before unbuckling mine and awkwardly rising from my spot.

Parker passed down my handbag and I threw it over my shoulder, lining up with the other passengers and slowly making my way off the plane.

The flying had made me a little nauseous, but I kept my lips sealed. The last thing I wanted to do was puke in front of the man who was about to change my life. We walked to the baggage claim and I waited for my guitar in the special section, squeezing my fingers and praying it'd made the journey unscathed. It came through without a scratch, and I breathed a sigh of relief.

Mama had scraped her pennies to buy me that guitar, and it was my last connection to her. I treasured it and couldn't imagine ever not having it with me. I carried the case back to Parker's side while he lifted off my bag. Resting it onto the trolley, he took the lead and we walked out of the airport.

Throngs of people milled around, and it took a bit of getting used to. The traffic was insane. I'd never seen anything like it, and the frenetic buzz in the air kind of made me feel excited and overwhelmed all in the same minute.

I hustled after Parker who powered ahead at a steady pace, his one long stride equaling two of mine. We reached his car several minutes later. It was buried deep in the parking lot.

With a winning smile, he opened the passenger door for me and I slid inside, feeling a little like a princess. Drivers did not open doors for their passengers where I came from.

The drive was fascinating. Parker put the top down on his car, and I saw all kinds of things on my way to the hotel. It made me feel like I was in a movie. You know the ones where the hillbilly goes to the big city and their eyes pop out as they take in all these strange sights. Well, that was me. I was the hillbilly and Los Angeles was like nothin' I'd ever seen before.

My jaw sat slack most of the way until we reached the ocean, and then my smile grew so wide it actually hurt my face.

"That's the ocean," I breathed.

Parker's head snapped my way. "You've never seen the ocean before?"

I shook my head, lost for words as I gazed at the endless blue. Clutching the top of the windshield, I rose in my seat so I could drink it all in—the white, powdery sand, the foamy lip of each wave. It was like paradise.

Mama, can you see this?

I knew she could, because she was there with me, no doubt just as awe-inspired.

The car slowed to a stop outside a fancy-looking hotel that sat across the road from the beach. The sign said: Hilton Waterfront Beach Resort.

"Here? I'm staying here?"

"Only the best for a potential client." Parker's grin was cocky as he lifted my cases from the trunk.

I took the guitar case and carried it up the stairs behind him, walking into a shiny lobby with plush sofas, huge floral arrangements, and a marble floor that you could see your reflection in.

I must have looked like a kid in Santa's workshop. I couldn't have closed my mouth if I'd wanted to.

My worn-out boots made loud staccato beats on the marble floor. I waited behind Parker as he checked me in, and then he led me to the elevator and took us up to the tenth floor.

The tenth!

I'd never been that high in a building before.

He opened the white door with a keycard and pushed it open, stepping back so I could go through first.

"Lord love a duck." I shook my head, taking in the most gigantic bed I had ever seen. It was covered in a crisp, white quilt and had three of the biggest pillows across it, plus a whole bunch more cushions on top of those. Behind that was glass—just glass—that looked out across the ocean. Everything about the room was elegant and beautiful. I placed my guitar down by the shiny, black coffee table and ran my hand over the pristine couch against the wall.

"Your bathroom is through here."

I followed Parker's finger and walked into a humongous bathroom. It had a tub with jets in it, plus a huge shower with two nozzle heads. The mirror took up most of one wall.

"This place is..." I shook my head again.

Parker chuckled, rubbing his mouth and looking highly amused. "Enjoy it. I'll be back for you tomorrow at ten, and I'll drive you to the audition."

I glanced at my watch. That was about eighteen hours away.

"In the meantime, I suggest you work on an audition piece."

"Something like I did last night?"

"That was good." Parker nodded. "Maybe have a few songs ready to go. Definitely country and maybe something a little poppy, as well."

"Poppy?"

"You know, the fusion of country and pop, like Taylor Swift or Michelle Branch."

My grin was instant. Michelle Branch! I loved her stuff.

"I'm sure whatever you decide will be perfect." His eyes scanned me from my curls to the tips of my boots.

I tugged on my little denim skirt, suddenly three inches shorter with him staring at me that way.

"The skirt and boots are perfect." His lips pursed, his eyes narrowing slightly. "Maybe a more fitted top, something that shows off your body."

I frowned. I couldn't help it. Why would I need to show off my body?

His chuckling grin made his cheekbones protrude. "Not to sound like a shallow person, but we have to sell the whole package. Not only do you have an amazing voice, but you're absolutely stunning and unfortunately in this business, looks

do count. Don't be afraid to show off that gorgeous
body of yours. It definitely won't do any harm."

My cheeks burned with a hot blush. I tucked a
curl behind my ear and nodded. "Okay."

"You have a good night, Rachel."

"I'll see you tomorrow, Parker."

The second the door clicked shut, I let out a loud
squeal and twirled on the spot.

This was happening.

This was actually happening!

I leaped across the room to the couch and
flicked my guitar case open. As soon as my guitar
was nestled on my lap, I gave it a slow strum.
Reaching for the tuning pegs, I adjusted them
before flicking the strings. I retuned it until I was
happy then closed my eyes and strummed again.

"Anything and Everything" came out of me
before I could stop it. That was Mama's song. She
used to sing it, believing just for a moment that
dreams could come true. When she'd gifted me the
guitar, it was the first song she wanted me to learn.
I'd had to teach myself, following along on a little
book she'd bought me, but it had come natural, and
I picked it up pretty fast. I spent every spare second
I could, hiding in the back of the shed and
practicing until the tips of my fingers were
indented with string lines.

"Oh, baby, that's beautiful." Mama clasped her
hands together and looked at me with glistening eyes.
*"You're gonna have your own album one day and
everyone's going to buy it. People are gonna hear one*

second of your voice and fall completely in love."

I hoped she was right.

I so desperately wanted to make her proud.

In spite of the beach calling out the window, I decided to forsake my first feel of sand and stay in my room. I had work to do. I had people to wow in the morning, and I sure as heck wasn't about to let my mother down.

NINE

JOSH

Stepping through the back door, I wiped my boots on the mat and clicked my fingers for Duke to follow. He snuffled and shook his slobbery jowls before walking past me. I ran my fingers through his fur as he trotted by. He was a big boy now, halfway through his life and five times the size of when I got him.

I'd never forget the day Aunt Lindy placed him in my lap. The week earlier, she'd told me about her cancer and I'd been devastated. I'd only just gotten past losing my father, and the idea of losing her too had all been too much. Duke—the perfect distraction—was a godsend. I'd poured all my energy into training him and he'd become the perfect dog.

We sauntered through to the main bar together, Duke heading for the window and stretching out for a nap in the warm sun. I envied him a little. I was up to my second sleepless night in a row. Work the night before had damn near killed me. Everyone wanted to know where Rachel was. Having to explain her absence—having to make it sound like I was excited for her—had been nearly impossible. I'd fudged my way through, ignoring those *I told you so* looks from Ol' Dan and his posse of pessimists. Damn them! I'd never once regretted begging Uncle Amos to let her stay, and I'd never once regretted letting that girl into my bed. I didn't care about her past. That girl was everything I wanted.

Clutching the chair resting upside-down on the table, I pressed my forehead against one of the legs and forced myself to breathe. I didn't usually start prepping the bar until lunchtime, but what the hell else was I supposed to do? Flipping the chair up, I then smacked it down on the floor before moving on to the next. It was usually Rachel's job, but not anymore.

I had to look at hiring someone to replace her, but I couldn't let myself think about that just yet. She still had her audition to go and there were no guarantees she'd get accepted. Yeah, yeah, there'd probably be more auditions just around the corner, but if Parker couldn't find her something quick, I was guessing he wouldn't keep shelling out for accommodations and the like. And with her meager savings, Rachel definitely couldn't afford to stay. Maybe she'd come home sooner than I thought.

"Who are you trying to kid?" I muttered, pulling a chair off the table so fast it nearly flew into the window behind me.

Setting it down, I sucked in a breath. I needed music, something to stop me from wrecking this whole damn place. Thumping over to the jukebox, I started it up.

"These Days" by Rascal Flatts came on. I should have changed it but decided to endure the song, because that was not me. My Rachel *would* be coming back, and not after years of being away either. I wasn't going to wait by the phone for her—I didn't need to. I was going to trust that she'd get this whole *big city, bright stage lights* thing out of her system and return home.

Swallowing back my doubts, I got to work on the next table.

Duke's head lifted off the floor, his low, gruff bark letting me know someone was coming. Checking my watch, I ambled back to the kitchen. Chef Denny never got there early—something must have been wrong.

Just what I needed. Dang it!

"Den, what's the matter?" I stormed into the kitchen only to be stopped by my best friend's lazy smile.

"Howdy, Grizz." Brock held up a six-pack. "I

thought you could use some company."

"You brought beer into my bar?"

"Well, what the hell else was I supposed to bring? You can't be drinking water when your heart's breakin'."

I shot him a dry glare before heading back for the bar. "My heart ain't breakin'," I called over my shoulder.

"You sure about that?" He followed me, placing the beer down and pulling one free.

I stomped over to the tables, grabbed another chair and then slammed it onto the wooden floor. "She's coming back."

"You sure about that?" Same question, entirely different tone.

It hurt, because a part of me—the part I didn't want to acknowledge—believed him.

"It's just an audition," I grumbled.

Brock popped his beer open and took a long guzzle before throwing me a can. I caught it and placed it on the table while I lowered the rest of the chairs.

"When's her audition then?" Brock sauntered over to table ten and got to work.

"I don't know, sometime today."

"She called you yet?"

My lips pressed into a tight line, my fingers gripping the back of the chair.

"I'm sure she's just waiting until after the audition." The lilt in Brock's voice gave away the fact he was lying to make me feel better. That wasn't usually his way.

I met his gaze and saw the truth. His pitying smile made me want to hit him.

"You're gonna have to face it at some point, Grizz. She might never come back."

"This is her *home*."

Brock's head shook. "She ain't never called it that."

"But I wanted her to!" My thundering voice surprised even me. Closing my eyes, I ran a hand through my hair, my shoulders slumping. "I just…" I shook my head, not even knowing how to say it.

When Aunty Lindy died, I shut myself off to any kind of emotion. Losing Dad had cut me pretty deep, but losing the woman who had raised me nearly cut me in half.

Being all open and telling people you loved them…telling them how you really felt, that only led to heartache, because you lost them and you were left with this gaping, raw wound that never really healed. The best thing to do was be numb to everything.

I'd resisted telling Rachel I loved her, like if I let it slip, I'd somehow jinx it. Even so, she'd made me feel again, and that's why I had to believe she'd be coming back, because I wouldn't recover from losing her, too.

I pulled out a chair and slumped into it. Cracking open my can of beer, I pressed it to my lips and drained half of it before slapping it onto the table.

Brock ambled over to my side and took a seat.

"She ain't the only girl in the world, Grizz."

"She's the only girl for me."

Of that, I was sure.

I couldn't guarantee if or when she'd come back, but that girl owned my heart and that wasn't ever changing.

TEN

RACHEL

The audition room was a small space with white walls, two chairs, and a high wooden stool. I followed Parker into the room and gripped the handle of my guitar case. Nerves had been beating on me all night, and the morning had brought no relief. I'd been awake at five and ended up going for a walk along the beach. The sand was cold against my toes, the vast expanse robbing me of breath. My soul soared as the fresh, salty air hit my skin, like a magical morning kiss. I stayed out there for a couple of hours watching surfers and early morning exercisers do their thing. I couldn't wipe the smile from my face the whole time I sat there.

But reality caught up with me soon enough, and I had to brush the sand from my butt and head back to the hotel. I'd been too nervous to eat so I spent the whole time practicing and then making myself pretty. I shaved my legs and put on a little makeup. Millie showed me how to do my hair real nice and tame my reckless curls. I had the smoky eye thing happening and a bright lipstick that made my smile shine. I was wearing my sexy little skirt, and I chose my fitted white tank with the American flag on it. It was low-cut and made my boobs look bigger. I figured it couldn't hurt, right?

"Take a seat." Parker pointed at the stool. "Why don't you get yourself tuned and ready to go while I find Aren."

My curls bobbed as I nodded and headed over to the stool.

Laying down my guitar case, I took out my beloved instrument and sat down to recheck my tuning. I didn't have to adjust anything and was soon tapping my fingers on the wood and waiting.

The door opened and I flinched, unable to stop my embarrassed, breathy laugh.

"Rachel." A tall man with angular features and a long, pointy nose approached me. He was dressed in dark slacks and a white dress shirt that was unbuttoned at the top. He had on a fitted suit jacket that looked pretty stylish and matched his pointy shoes.

I took his outstretched hand and gave it a shake. "Hi."

"I'm Aren Pierce."

"It's nice to meet you." I rested my forearm against my guitar and smiled.

I wasn't quite sure how I wanted to come across. Confident, most certainly, but was that all he wanted? Or was he after a more enthusiastic cheerleader-type girl? I didn't know what to say as he stood there staring at me. His critical, dark gaze traveled the length of my body before coming to rest on my face.

His thin lips eventually drew into a smile. "Parker's right. You are very beautiful."

"Thank you." I grinned, praying my cheeks weren't going bright red.

"Well..." Aren hitched his pants and took a seat on the chair while Parker sat down beside him. "Please, play me a couple of songs, and I'll see if you're what we're looking for."

"Okay." I nodded.

I decided to go with my Michelle Branch song first—"Set Me Free." My boot tapped out a silent beat in the air and I started strumming. A smile hit my lips before the first word left my mouth. I loved the song because it made me think of Mama. I loved the sound of my voice as I sang it. Getting lost within the tune was easy, and I floated through the piece.

The one time I glanced up at the men, I nearly faltered so I decided to keep my gaze down. I knew that was bad performing. It was always better to make eye contact with your audience.

Come on, Rachel, don't blow this!

As I reached the final chorus, I looked straight at Aren, giving him some sunshine. He grinned back at me, his head bobbing in time with the song. I strummed my last chord and sang the final line with a flourish.

A swift silence filled the room after I was done, and my already-tattered nerves went into a frenzy. Thankfully, they didn't leave me hanging for long. Aren and Parker shared a grin, the agent looking pretty smug with his find.

"That was great." Aren's smirk landed on me and he ran a hand through his slicked-back hair. He and Parker were cut from the same cloth—city boys to the core. "Let's hear another one."

Parker winked at me. "That Jessica Simpson one you played the other night was really great."

"Okay." My giddy insides danced with a squeal as I placed my fingers on the strings and strummed out the first rift of "Come On Over." I had to think of Josh as I sang the song; it was impossible not to. I was glad I did. My voice took on a husky quality when I sang it to him, and I could tell by the looks of approval from the two men that they might have found the girl they were looking for.

*****

"He liked you." Parker grinned as he drove me back to the hotel.

"I sure hope so."

"No, he definitely did. I could tell."

I pressed my lips together, trying to contain the squeal wanting to break free. "So, um." I cleared my throat. "What happens now?"

"Well, we'll give him a little time to think, but I'll call him as soon as I've dropped you off and find out exactly where he's sitting. If he wants to take you on, we'll draw up a contract over the weekend, and I'll bring it by on Monday."

"Okay."

"Once you've looked it over and are happy, then I'll move you into your new digs and you can get to work."

"New digs?"

"Yes, Aren provides a little apartment for his singers. The rent comes out of your paycheck, but I can show you all this in the contract."

"So, what's the basic package then?" I held down my curls. They were dancing with the wind and tickling my face as we wove through the sunny streets.

"Well, like I said the night we met, you sign on with him and become a regular act at his club. Throughout that time, he'll train you and help you find your best marketing image—I'll be helping with that, too. Aren has really good connections and gets producers through his place all the time, so working with him, plus having the security of my services, will land you a deal for sure."

"So, Aren doesn't mind losing his entertainment to other producers?"

"Well, he'll get a cut, you see, so it works in his

favor to help his singers and performers get noticed. And in the meantime, he's able to entertain his patrons while training you. His club is amazing and busy every night of the week. This is a great opportunity for you. It will definitely put your name on the map."

"This all just seems so easy." I laughed, still in shock at how it was all coming together.

"Sometimes these things just fall into place. I can't help thinking that it was providence that I walked into Clark's Bar on Wednesday. Who knows, maybe it was providence that had my rental car breaking down, too. Whatever it was, I'm really happy that I discovered you."

I grinned. "I'm happy you discovered me, too."

He chuckled, turning toward the beach and my hotel.

"So, can I check out Aren's club this weekend?"

Parker nodded. "We have to play this carefully. If he thinks we're stalking or hounding him, it might put him off."

"But how do I know I want this job? I kind of feel like I should see what I'll be doing before I sign something."

Parker's grin was wide and toothy. "Trust me, you want this job. You'd be a fool to turn it down, but if it makes you feel better, I could take you out tomorrow night. There's a club near here that's really similar to Club Liberation, so you'll get an idea of what you'll be doing."

"Okay." I nodded, feeling better for asking. I didn't want my sheer excitement overriding my common sense.

"You don't have anything to worry about, Rachel. Struggling singers would kill for a chance like this. I work with Aren a lot, and we've helped many kick off their careers. You give us twelve months, and I can turn you into the superstar you were born to be."

"I like the sound of that." A wide smile stretched across my face and stayed there...until I decided to call Josh.

ELEVEN

JOSH

The bar was meant to open in less than ten minutes, and it was not the time for my phone to be ringing. I'd had one too many beers with Brock and my head was buzzing, which I did not need, especially when I had Denny yelling at me for not ordering in more frozen fries.

"We've got a whole crate of potatoes, make fresh ones!"

"Do you know how long that will take me! I can't be slicing up french fries when I have a million other orders to fill!"

"I'll order some as soon as I'm done with this

call, damn it!"

"They won't get here in time!"

"Then start choppin'!" I hollered over my shoulder before lifting the phone to my ear. "Hello!"

"Hey, honey."

Rachel's voice liquefied my insides.

"Hey." A broad smile lit my lips, and I made a beeline for the stairs. "How's it going?"

I clomped into our room and perched on the bed, my knee bobbing the second I sat down.

"Good. This place is amazing. I can see the ocean from my room!"

"The ocean? Wow, what's that like?"

"So beautiful. Josh, I wish you could see it."

I swallowed, thick emotion clogging my voice. I ran my hand over the unmade bed, missing her with an overwhelming ache. I wanted to ask her how the audition went but couldn't form the words. What if it went great?

"The audition went real great today," she chirped.

Closing my eyes, I held my heavy head and nodded.

"He really liked me, and I think he's going to offer me a contract."

I opened my mouth to speak, but couldn't. A cool breeze from my open window whistled in and curled around my neck. I rubbed at my prickling skin with rough fingers.

"Josh?"

"Yeah," I croaked.

"You not gonna say anything?"

I swallowed, gripping a handful of the crumpled cotton sheet. "What do you want me to say?"

"I don't know, that you're happy for me!" Her sweet tenor disappeared.

My lips pursed to the side, my vocal cords protesting.

"Come on, honey, this is my chance. You can't stay mad at me forever."

"I'm not mad." I cleared my throat. "I'm proud. I knew they'd love you."

"Don't ruin this for me, please."

"I ain't ruining anything. You're over there, doing what you want." I flicked my hand in the air before slapping it down on my knee.

"It'd just be real nice if I knew my man was behind me, supporting me."

"I—I want to. I just…I miss you, baby."

"I miss you, too." She sighed.

"If you—" My jaw worked to the side, fear of her answer making me stumble over my question. "If you sign a contract, how long's it for?"

She paused. Dread seeped through my system. It was an effort to inhale. I dug my elbows into my knees and braced myself.

"Twelve months to start, but more often than not he finds a big producer in that time, so I'd be signing a new contract with them. I really can't say how long I'll be gone."

"Twelve months," I whispered. That felt like a century. I remember crossing off my ol' man's tours of duty. Counting down the days was agony, yet

I'd had to do it.

Twelve months.

I ground my teeth together, holding it all in.

"I might be able to come back and visit. I don't know when, but I'm sure I'd get Thanksgiving off...or maybe Christmas."

Thanksgiving! That was over five months away!

I clamped my teeth together and reminded myself to breathe.

"Well..." Rachel cleared her throat. "I guess I should let you go open up then."

"Uh-huh."

Her sigh was heavy, but short. "Thanks for the riveting conversation. Should I even bother calling you again? I mean, do you even want to know what I'm up to over here?"

"It's just hard, baby. I didn't want you to go, and I can't pretend to be happy about it. I'm proud, but I ain't happy."

"That's fine. Maybe I was asking too much. Have a good night." Her voice was void of cheer when she hung up. I'd managed to slice her enthusiasm in half, and I felt bad for it, but at least I was honest.

Dropping the phone on my bed, I scrubbed my face and sucked in a slow breath.

"Josh! You up there?" Harriet's voice pulled me back to earth.

"Yeah, I'm coming."

"Well, hurry it up. I need my bartender. We're short-staffed as it is!"

I closed my eyes, reality beating me like a

bullwhip. We *were* short-staffed, and we were going to stay that way for a good long while if I didn't do something about it.

Standing up, I snatched my phone and shoved it into my pocket. I didn't want to think about hiring someone new. The weight of Rachel's terse farewell sat heavy on my shoulders. She was gone...and maybe Brock was right. Maybe she was never coming back.

How the hell did she expect me to be happy about that?

TWELVE

RACHEL

The painful call with Josh really soured my mood. I spent the rest of my day in the hotel, ordering room service and watching movies. I couldn't even play my guitar. I went to bed on a sugar high, feeling like a whale after all the food I'd stuffed into my face.

On Saturday morning, I woke up with a tummy ache and tried to get rid of it by going for a really long walk. I got lost quicker than I expected, but I did find a postcard, a real pretty one of the sun setting over the Pacific. I bought it and shoved it into my bag, hoping that I'd be able to write something pleasant.

Josh's words still hurt.

I mean, I guess I understood how he was feeling and it was nice to be missed. I just really wanted him to be happy for me. This whole experience was a dream come true but he was tainting it, and I didn't think that was fair.

Thanks to a lovely couple, I managed to find my way back to the hotel in one piece. I wasn't sure what to do with myself, so I ended up playing my guitar and singing until my voice was hoarse. I wasn't used to having so much time on my hands. It was a luxury that I quickly tired of. When Parker knocked on my hotel door that evening, I stumbled over myself trying to get to it.

"Hi." I chuckled, flicking a wayward curl over my shoulder.

"Good evening." He grinned, his brown gaze traveling down my body.

I'd decided to go a little fancy and was wearing the black dress Millie gave me for my birthday. It had thin shoulder straps and kind of flared out 'round my knees. It made me pretty...at least that's what Josh said, although he was hardly a reliable source. I could be wearing a trash sack, and he'd think I looked good.

"You are perfect." Parker's voice sounded a little in awe, which made me blush...again!

"Thank you," I murmured, grabbing my purse and following him to the elevator.

We drove, with the top down, to Helium. It was a club on Sunset Boulevard that had a line of people going 'round the corner. My lips parted as I approached the dazzling purple sign. Gorgeous girls and handsome guys were lined up waiting to go in. Parker led me straight past all of them and murmured something to the bouncer who took us straight through. It was like being a celebrity. A heady giddiness rumbled my insides as I played with the idea that one day I might actually *be* a celebrity! I was on my way!

We climbed the stairs and entered through the big black doors. Behind those was a set of thick purple curtains. A man in a tux pulled the curtain aside, and I gasped as we walked into a plush-looking club. Live music pumped from the stage as a singer with a crew of expert back-up dancers performed. The guy was amazing and so talented. His voice was like chocolate—smooth and creamy. My heart near-melted at the sound.

"This way." Parker took my hand, laughing at my expression as he led us to a table in the corner.

"This is unreal." I giggled, squeezing his arm. "So, you're telling me this is like Aren's club?"

"Yeah." Parker nodded. "Really similar. There's tables dotted throughout and a dance floor at the front, not quite as big as that one."

He pointed down to the space and I nodded, smiling at the fans who were jumping around on the floor in front of the stage.

"But the stage is a similar set-up. Depending on what Aren thinks is best, and the performances that you guys put together, you'll get a live band some nights and back-up dancers and singers."

A thunderous applause filled the room as Mr. Amazing finished.

"Thank you, Helium!" he shouted into the mic, causing a second wave of cheers and applause.

He loped off the stage as the next act teetered on. She was in heels and a flowing gold dress that was stunning. Her tight black curls were teased high and her glossy red lips drew my eye when she smiled. She did a spin, her dress sparkling under the spotlights as she came to stand in front of the microphone. I was entranced. She had a smooth, husky voice that reminded me of KT Tunstall. When she started singing "Suddenly I See," I hooted with laughter.

Parker gave me quizzical look.

"I was just thinking she sounded like the woman who originally sang this song."

Parker grinned. "Yeah, she does."

"This place is so cool."

He leaned toward me with a twinkle in his eye. "If you ask me, I think Club Liberation's cooler." He winked, making me giggle.

I sat back in my chair and soaked it all in—the buzzing crowd, the stage lights, the beautiful costumes. It was all so magical, and then there was the song she was singing. It spoke to me somehow. In that moment I was exactly where I was meant to be, and if Aren was willing to give me a contract, I would most definitely sign it.

*****

"I have a contract for you." It was the first thing Parker said when I opened my door to him on Monday morning.

I squealed and jumped out of his way to let him in.

He chuckled, sliding the bag off his shoulder and taking a seat at the small table. Pulling out a thick pile of papers, he then placed it on the table and gave it a tap. "Here you go."

My eyes bulged before I could stop them. "That's my contract?"

"Yep." Parker winked. "I spent yesterday afternoon going over it with Aren and making sure you're getting the best deal possible. It's pretty standard and exactly the same as the contract that his previous singer signed in February, so as long as you're happy with it, we can move forward."

I sat opposite him and flicked my thumb through the pages. "It's like a book."

He grinned. "Aren likes to cover all the bases."

"I can see that." The stack in front of me must have been at least thirty pages. The writing was small, making the 'book' seem like an epic novel. I scratched the side of my neck and tried to smile at Parker.

"Don't be overwhelmed, I do this for a living. Let me walk you through it." He shuffled his chair around so he sat closer and lifted the first page. "This is a standard industry contract, and most of it will seem like mumbo-jumbo, but basically what it's saying is that you agree to let Aren train and prepare you for a recording contract while working at Club Liberation. You'll perform six nights a week and will be required to practice daily, as well as be available for any marketing and promotional requirements. Aren is obligated to train you and invite producers to watch you perform. If they like what they see, Aren will set you up with an audition and help you with that process." He pointed at his chest. "I will also be available to help you negotiate any contracts, and I'll be working to get you auditions, as well. If Aren, or I, can't secure a label for you within twelve months, then you are free of the contract. However, we've never had that happen before."

My insides were buzzing so fast and strong I could barely hear what he was saying.

He flicked through the pages, briefly going over things, pointing out paragraphs here and there.

"This just says that you'll take Aren's advice with performances, song selections, and wardrobe. Think of him like a coach or tutor." Parker flicked over to the next part. "This is your income."

My eyebrows rose as I looked at the figure. *Someone pinch me!*

"Minus, of course, the housing Aren provides and other necessities, like utilities, clothing for performances, travel, things like that."

I nodded, still too stunned stupid by the idea of earning close to eighty thousand dollars in a year.

Parker turned the page before I could read more. His finger breezed down the paper. "This is just legal jargon to protect both parties," he mumbled.

I scanned the paper, trying to absorb the words, but I barely understood the two sentences I read. I was not a *top of the class* kind of gal. Hell, I missed close to a year of school when I was homeless and then recovering. Josh's uncle made me do twelfth grade at the school just out of town. It was torture, and I barely scraped through with straight Cs. I'm not necessarily proud of that fact. School just wasn't for me. Music was the only class I did well in and even then, I only got a B, because the teacher had it in for me. Stupid wench.

"Okay, the final page is for you to sign." Parker pulled a pen from his inside jacket pocket.

I gazed at the fat ballpoint in his fingers.

"Unless you have any questions."

"No, I don't think so. I mean, it's hard to understand all the phrasing, but I get most of what you're saying."

"It must seem overwhelming, and if you want to keep this for a few days and read it over, you're more than welcome. Do you have a lawyer you want to show it to?"

"Do I need to do that?" I wound a curl around my pointer finger.

"Well, no, but some people like to." Parker placed the pen on the table and threaded his hands together, resting them lightly on top of the contract. "This document is here to protect all the parties involved. If you sign it, you're giving yourself the opportunity to become the singer you deserve to be. When we sign, we are committing to helping you reach that goal. It's mutually beneficial. If we succeed, then you succeed, and if you succeed, we're all going to make ourselves some music and some very sweet cash." His wink and sassy smile settled my nerves. "Trust us, Rachel. We're going to make your dreams come true."

"Okay." I nodded, reaching for the pen.

"Just sign here." Parker pointed to the page, and I scrawled my John Hancock with a flourish.

He then collected up the pages and knocked them against the desk to straighten them before sliding them into his bag.

"Congratulations, Rachel. I know Aren's really excited about working with you."

"Me, too." An unexpected laugh popped out of me.

"Fantastic." Parker rose from his seat. "Why don't you get yourself packed up. I'll go check you out of the hotel, and we'll head to your new place."

"Sounds good."

He walked out of the room. Once again, I waited for the door to click shut before jumping from my chair with a squeal.

"Mama, I'm on my way!"

I thought about calling Josh right then, but I was worried his silence or cynical remarks might kill my euphoric moment. I'd call him later once I was settled into my new apartment.

Snatching my stuff together, I proceeded to shove it into my bag and then collect my guitar. Ten minutes later I was down in the lobby, just in time to see Parker strolling toward me with a grin. He took my suitcase and ushered me out to his car.

"I asked the hotel to scan the contract for me, so it's already on its way to Aren. He'll sign this afternoon and it's a sealed deal."

"All right." I slid into the car and buckled up while he closed my door and walked to his side. "So, where's my new place?"

"Downtown. We house all our girls there."

"Your girls?" My nose wrinkled.

He laughed at my scrunched up expression. "In training. Singers who are doing a similar thing to you. It's just easier for them to be near the club and gives you a sense of family, knowing your neighbors are in a similar boat to you."

"Aren't they my competition, though?"

Parker grinned but kept his eyes on the road. His aviator shades took over half his face anyway, so I couldn't really tell what he was thinking.

"We select our clients very carefully." He raised his pointer finger. "We only take on those we know we can promote successfully and who have the talent to make it." He raised his next finger. "We like to have variety in our mix, so while we're trying for a country-pop label for you, we're looking for other things for our other clients. Don't think of it like competition. You're all there to help each other succeed."

"I like that." I nodded with a smile, a thrill buzzing through me. I couldn't wait to meet the girls.

*****

The drive took some time, thanks to insane traffic, but eventually Parker pulled into an underground parking garage and led me to the elevator. We went up to the fifth floor, and I followed him down a dimly lit corridor. It was a far cry from my swanky beach hotel, but at least it was clean.

Parker stopped outside door 505 and wrestled a key from his pocket. The door was a yellow-white kind of color, and the handle was a little rickety. I didn't say anything, of course, and my insides didn't start deflating until I walked into the cramped studio. There was a single bed in the corner, a dusty lamp perched on the floor beside it. A small kitchenette with a two-seater table taking up most of the floor space sat in the corner of the room.

The TV, perched on top of a broken bookshelf, looked like it came straight from the 1980s.

"The bathroom's through that door." Parker pointed.

I opened it to find a shower over a bathtub. The sink had yellowy-brown stains around the plug hole and the mirror was scratched. I opened the medicine cabinet and found a few supplies on the narrow white shelves.

"Nice." I forced out the word.

I caught Parker's brief smile in the mirror. "I know it's not the Hilton, but you're going to be so busy, you won't be spending much time here anyway. Most of the girls get ready at the club each night. The dressing room's huge, and there's always drinks and snacks available."

"Okay." I nodded.

Parker pulled out his phone while running his gaze over the paisley wallpaper. "So, I'm going to leave you to get settled in. I'll come back and get you at eight, and we can head over to the club. Aren wants to show you around."

"Sounds good." My smile was tight, but Parker didn't notice. He was too busy texting on his phone as he walked out the door.

I gazed around the room, my face crumpling. Flopping onto the bed, I nearly jumped at the loud squeak of the springs. The mattress was kind of lumpy, and it made me miss my bed...I mean, Josh's bed.

Clearing my throat, I shook the thought aside. So what if I had to make small sacrifices. This was hardly that anyway! I'd had much worse.

"Whatever it takes," I muttered.

With a determined huff, I rose from the bed and hefted my suitcase off the floor. I flung back the lid and Josh's postcard fluttered out of it, landing upside-down on the floor.

I collected it up, running my fingers over his address. That was as far as I'd gotten. I didn't know what to say to him.

A loud siren wailed outside, making me flinch. Looking over my shoulder, I turned and walked to the window. The view outside was a brick wall. If I opened the window and leaned out as far as I could, I might have been able to touch it.

The card in my hand started to feel heavy, so I placed it on the table.

I'd write Josh later.

I wasn't sure what I was supposed to say to him in that minute.

THIRTEEN

JOSH

I was worried about Rachel, but I couldn't peg why. I'd been haunted by our last phone call, and something about that particular day was making me uneasy. I wanted to hear from her, to know she was okay, but my stubborn ass couldn't find it in me to call her. I had to wait until I could pretend happy, but I just wasn't there.

"Well, this night sucks." Brock swigged his beer and pointed his glass at the stage. "Talk about drowning in sorrow. What's this guy's problem anyway?"

I looked to the guitar-playing soloist. He was

from a few towns over and came to play every now and then. I didn't mind so much. He had a great voice, and his music usually soothed me. So he sung about heartache a lot. I could relate!

Unlike my best friend, we didn't have ourselves the perfect life.

"Would you go home," I spat. "You've got a pretty woman waiting for ya."

"She does the late shift on Mondays. I don't got anywhere else to be."

"It's only Monday?" I drooped my head. "I feel like it's been a year since she left."

"Would you stop? It's been less than a week, and I'm already sick of hearin' ya." Brock slapped his beer down and swiveled on his seat so he could stare me down proper. "You have to get over her."

"I can do twelve months. We're just going long distance for a while."

"Yeah, sure. Long distance. That always works for people." Brock rolled his eyes, scratching the backwards cap on his head.

"We're different," I muttered.

"Right, because your last phone call went so damn well."

I clipped him over the back of his head. I would have done more if I hadn't been forced to fill an order.

With a tight smile, I took the money from a lady I'd never seen before and poured her and her husband a couple of beers. She waited by the bar to take them back herself. Even though it was a quiet night, Harriet was still rushed off her feet. I had to give her the next day off, there was no two ways about it, but I couldn't run the bar on my own.

Maybe if I rang and told Rachel that, she'd come home.

She knew how much I loved this place, how much it meant to me. She'd hate for it to go under. Maybe I could guilt her back.

Yeah, it was cruel to even think it, but I was a desperate man.

The guitarist finished his song with a final strum and received a pitiful round of applause for his efforts. He smiled anyway. "Okay, folks, I've just got one more song in me for tonight."

"Praise be to God," Brock muttered.

"This is a favorite of mine by the legendary Keith Urban."

A soft cheer went up from table nine and then he started strumming. I closed my eyes, knowing the song immediately.

"Stupid Boy"... of all the songs. My fingers pressed into the wood of the bar, and I couldn't take my eyes off the guy.

The song dug into my very soul, crippling me.

Was I that man? The stupid boy clinging for all the wrong reasons?

I sure as hell was acting like him.

Brock tried to say something to me, but I couldn't hear him. I hated the idea that I'd been holding back a treasure. My beautiful Rachel was finally seeing her dreams come true, and I couldn't even be happy for her.

I felt like shit.

The song mercifully came to an end, and I was pulled out of my stupor...well, mostly. I couldn't raise a smile for anybody, and maybe that's what emptied the bar out so fast. I was plagued by my bad behavior. Rachel had struggled so hard and long to get to this point. She deserved it.

The jukebox clicked over and "Smile" by Lonestar began to play. A wry grin crested over my lips. The bigger man. That's what I needed to be.

I pulled the phone from my back pocket and dialed Rachel's number.

It rang seven times. I don't know why I counted, but she never answered. So I listened to her sweet voice.

"Hey there. I can't take your call right now, but please leave me a message. Say something that'll make me smile."

I grinned and I was glad for it, because I'm sure it came through in my voice. "Hey, baby. I was just calling to tell you—I guess I want you to know that—" I squeezed the back of my neck, feeling like a prize idiot. "Hell, I'm not good at this." I huffed. "Baby—I—I want you to be happy. I know how long you've dreamed about this kind of thing happening and I...I'll support you, okay? I guess...I...Yeah, I'll support you." My voice petered off, and I couldn't think of anything else to say, so I hung up.

In spite of my rambled message, I felt better for leaving it. Rachel would appreciate the call. I'd done the right thing. Picking up a chair, I set about stacking them onto the tables so I could sweep up and head to bed. The idea was lonely, but I had to get used to that.

Duke's claws scraped against the wood as he trotted into the main bar. He'd been trained to wait for the noise to die down, and his body clock seemed scheduled to wake from his evening nap at just the right time.

He wandered over to me, still looking a little sleepy as he nuzzled my hand.

"Hey, boy. At least I still got you, right?"

I scratched his oversized skin and he snuffled.

"You ain't thinking of leaving anytime soon, are ya?" His response was to lean against my leg, his long tail whipping back and forth like crazy.

I grinned. "That's my boy."

FOURTEEN

RACHEL

Parker knocked on my door at eight sharp. I scuttled over in my heels. Since we were going to the club, I dolled up again. I was wearing a sleek red dress that I'd bought on Sunday. Parker had handed me a wad of cash and told me to go snazzy up. I wasn't comfortable taking the money from him, but he assured me it was a loan and I could pay him back with my first paycheck. It still felt weird but I couldn't resist, so I went a little crazy.

My red dress looked perfect with my sparkly, new pumps. It was a little strange getting used to strutting around in the higher shoes, but I figured I could do it. Parker had let me know what kinds of clothes to look for.

"You have to dress to impress in this town," he'd said.

I think I'd done a pretty good job.

My ankle rolled when I got to the door, but I managed to hide my wince behind a friendly smile.

"Hey there."

"Wow, Rachel, you look beautiful." Parker's dark eyes drank me in, an appreciative smile on his lips.

I dipped my hip. "Why thank you, sir."

He chuckled and held out his hand. "Shall we go?"

"Of course." I took it and he led me out of the building.

My day had been spent battling doubts as I unpacked in my tiny, bleak apartment, and I was looking forward to seeing Club Liberation. Hopefully it'd make me feel better. If it was anything like the club Parker took me to over the weekend, it would be amazing. I couldn't wait to see the stage I'd be performing on and get a feel for the place.

Butterflies made from fairy dust and electricity purred in my stomach, making me giddy and a little lightheaded.

I squeezed Parker's hand as he led me down the street, my grip loosening when we rounded the corner and came face to face with a security guard who was as wide as he was tall.

"Hey, Murphy." Parker greeted him with an

easy smile.

"Evening, Mr. Stewart." His huge chin bunched when he nodded.

Parker pointed at me. "This is one of our new girls."

Murphy gave me a tight, closed-mouth smile, which I mirrored. I didn't like being referred to as one of Parker's girls. It didn't sit right with me.

I ignored the niggle inside, reminding myself to make the most of this. Worrying about niggles wasn't going to get me a recording contract. I had to do whatever it took to get me where I wanted to be.

Murphy pulled back the big, black door and let us in.

"I thought I'd bring you in the back way." Parker grinned. "The line out the front is always so long, and I don't like getting heckled when they let us waltz right through."

I nodded, only half-listening. I was too busy concentrating on not breaking my ankle as I tottered up the darkened stairwell. Parker let go of my hand when we reached the top, stepping aside so I could walk in front of him. We moved into a dazzling dressing room. It was empty, but I smiled when I saw the row of mirrors with makeup splayed across the counters in front of it. I took in the glittery material draped over backs of chairs and the bright lights surrounding each mirror. It was like real Hollywood behind the scenes stuff, and I was going to be getting ready in this room.

"Nice space, right?" Parker touched my lower

back.

"Yeah, this looks amazing." My chuckle was breathy and a little too fan-girlish for my tastes. I swallowed it back and pulled a confident smile.

"Come on, let's go find Aren."

"Okay." My glee was on a high, my dancing butterflies breaking into a frenzy as I walked out of my future dressing room and down the corridor to the main club.

I could hear cheering and whooping then a loud, "Why thank you, boys." The woman gave a flirty laugh and wolf-whistles ensued.

My forehead crinkled, my butterflies being eaten alive by my previous niggle.

"That's the stage entrance." Parker pointed to the right. "But tonight, we're going to hang out in here."

He took my hand and pulled me into nothing like the club he'd taken me to on the weekend.

I walked into a seedy, dark-lit room that gave me the creeps. My panicky gaze flickered around the big space, taking in table after table of men. There were a few women, but not many. The occupants varied in size, shape, and age, but they all had one thing in common—hungry leers on their drooling faces. Every eye in the room was glued to the stage, and my warm buzz evaporated when I saw what they were staring at.

A woman, looked to be just a little older than me, wearing a sparkly miniskirt and silver tassels on her nipples, was gyrating to the beat of some sexy song I didn't recognize.

I heard the words "Kiss you all over" and swallowed.

Her sexy, husky voice and her body moving that way was hypnotic, but...but all I could see were silver tassels.

I hoped to God they didn't think I'd be wearing something like that. What kind of record deal was she hoping for?

I couldn't hide behind a smile that time.

Parker glanced over his shoulder at me and did a double-take.

"What's the matter?" He leaned forward to yell in my ear, as that was the only way he could be heard over the thumping beat.

"This is not at all like the club you took me to on the weekend. This is no Helium!"

"It's not that different." His reply was sharp and had a snap to it that told me not to argue. "Come on, let's go." He tipped his head and pulled me through the crowd.

Eyes tracked me as I trailed behind Parker, and I turned to give out a few scowls. The fat one in the business suit two sizes too small chuckled at me and wiggled his eyebrows, rolling the cigar in his fingers as his gaze went straight to my ass.

I picked up my pace, nearly crashing into Parker as he stopped at a round booth table in the upper corner of the room.

"Aren!" He let my hand go, spreading his arms wide before ushering me forward.

Trying to smile was impossible. All I could think about was Josh, Clark's Bar, Duke. In other words—comfort, warmth, safety.

"Good evening, Rachel." Aren's smile was charming as he stood from his seat and extended his hand. "Come, sit."

I took his hand. His fingers were sweaty and hot, as if he'd been sitting on them or something. As soon as I'd climbed the two stairs and was seated, I slipped my fingers out of his grasp.

"Welcome to Club Liberation!" he bawled into my ear.

Forcing a grin was an effort, but I managed. It was a tight, noncommittal one, but at least it was something. Aren's probing gaze made me uncomfortable.

"So, I'm excited you chose to sign the contract. It's official now. You're one of my girls. We'll start training tomorrow."

I pointed at the stage, faking a bright laugh. "I'm not going to be one of *those* girls though, right? You signed me for my country voice and charm." I thickened my accent, really trying to sell it.

His leering smile and narrowing gaze slashed at my hope—the back of his finger running down my arm didn't help much either. "You're going to be whatever I want you to be."

I flinched at his dark tone, my face hardening as I stared at him. "I didn't sign up for that." Damn that my finger shook when I pointed at the stage again.

Aren's sigh was so short I nearly missed it, but then his lips pressed against my ear. "I think you'll find that you signed up to let me guide and coach you. That contract states that you *will* take my advice on performance, song selection, and clothing. If I think I can sell you as a tassel-wearing temptress, then that's what I'm going to do."

"I'm not doing that," I muttered.

"Yes, Rachel, you are, because I have your name in ink."

His words were a kick to the guts. My eyes stung with fire as I blinked, looking back to the stage as Miss Sexy took a bow and twirled her tassels one last time before skipping off.

The hollers and cheers following her made me sick to my stomach. I didn't mean to sign up for that.

I didn't mean—

Shit!

What the hell was I going to do?

FIFTEEN

RACHEL

I sat like a stiff-legged statue for the rest of the night, panic coursing through me. I had to get out of that contract. Sure, I'd signed, but those kinds of things were broken all the time, right?

It hurt my heart to think I'd come so close only to fail, but I couldn't make myself go up on a stage and do that. Josh would be horrified, and I'd hate myself forever. I didn't get saved from the gutter only to throw myself into a new one.

Having the conversation in a deafening nightclub was pointless. I had to wait until the morning. When dawn came, I could say my piece and head on back to Payton. The very idea reeked of humiliation, but Josh would forgive me. He always did eventually.

At midnight, Parker offered to walk me back to my apartment. I jumped at the chance. After suffering nearly four hours of bikini-clad betties strutting the stage, I'd had my fill. I was nauseous with the very idea of having to do something like that.

Parker held my hand as we stepped out into the dark street. I tried to wiggle free, but his grip only tightened.

"You have a good night?"

"Of course," I lied.

It was not the time to complain. I had to perfect my speech, pick my moment. I didn't want to make them angry. I had to come up with a nice, easy explanation for my change of heart. Fingers crossed I could pitch it just right and they'd tell me they understood and then send me on my way. I had enough money to buy a bus ticket to Payton. I'd have to head straight back. I didn't have the money to stay in LA, and I wasn't about to ask Parker to look for any more jobs for me.

He held open the building door.

"Thanks, Parker. I can make my way from here."

"No, that's okay. I'll walk you up."

I turned away to hide my eye roll. I wasn't in the mood for small talk and evening chatter. As soon as the elevator doors opened, I strode ahead of him down the corridor and pulled the key out of my purse.

He caught up to me easily and placed his hand on my lower back. "I'll be here by nine tomorrow morning."

"What for?" I kept my head down, focusing on the lock.

"You're booked for a photo shoot tomorrow. We want to get some publicity shots organized so that we're ready to go as soon as you are."

"Right." My head bobbed way too fast. Hopefully he didn't notice.

"Don't be nervous. You're going to fit right in at Club Liberation, and I'll spend this week putting together a nice promo package for you. Kind of like a résumé with professional headshots. I'm going to make you look so good people will be begging to sign you."

I couldn't help turning with a huff. "I thought you wanted a wholesome country girl, not some slut like was up on the stage tonight."

Parker snickered, stepping into my personal space and sliding his hand around to my hip. "With a body like this, we can turn you into both. The men are gonna love you." He leaned forward, his fat mouth aiming for mine.

My eyes bulged, my head pulling back so fast I whacked it on the door. "What are you doing?" I pushed at his chest.

"Sorry." He took his sweet time stepping away, a cocky smile on his lips. "I thought I felt something."

"You thought wrong."

He raised his hands and backed off. "Maybe I can make you change your mind." He winked.

"I don't think so." I wrestled my door open and slammed it shut behind me, leaning against the wood and fighting for air.

Oh my Lord, I couldn't handle that, too.

Josh would die if he knew Parker had tried to kiss me.

"I can't believe you let him do that, Rachel."

"Colby was only having a little fun! You know what he's like. It didn't mean nothin'!"

Josh grunted, the broom in his hand moving so fast, I thought the dust at our feet would turn into a hurricane.

"I was trying to be friendly. He's a customer! We were just dancing."

"Dancing," Josh grumbled. "He nearly kissed you!"

I rolled my eyes. "Come on, honey, he was pecking my cheek! You know it wouldn't have meant anything. He's completely in love with Doris what's-her-name."

"I didn't like the way he was looking at you when he was touching you."

"You don't like the way anyone looks at me, you jealous old hog!"

His razor glare could have stripped paint. I met it head-on, crossing my arms and sticking out my chin.

He let out an irate snort, throwing the broom toward the kitchen before spinning away from me and stomping up the stairs.

With a heavy sigh, I trotted up behind him.

"Leave me alone," he shot over his shoulder.

"You're being ridiculous!" I followed him into our

bedroom, trying to hold my tongue while he jumped around the room, yanking off his boots.

My guitar was sitting in the corner behind him. If anything could butter him up, it'd be a sweet melody from me, so I brushed right past him as he hopped around and found myself a spot on the edge of the bed.

The perfect song rested on my lips, and I strummed the first chord of "Trust Me" with a smile.

Josh's furious undressing routine slowed in pace, but he still wouldn't look at me. I kept singing to him anyway. I meant every word coming out of my mouth. I was in love with him; I had been for months. We'd been sleeping together for a while, and I'd whispered the words in the heat of passion, but I'd never outright said them straight to his face, let alone sung them.

I was halfway through the second chorus by the time he was naked, and rather than plucking the guitar from my hands and laying me down on the bed, he damn well walked out of the room.

A string of curses swept out of my mouth, cutting my song short. I laid down my guitar and stomped into the bathroom. The hot shower spray was beginning to steam up the room, and I saw a flash of Josh's tight behind before he flicked the curtain closed.

With a huff, I snatched the material and flung it back.

"You are as stubborn as a mule, Joshua Clark!" My fists landed on my hips.

"Get out and let me shower in peace," he yelled straight in my face before flicking the curtain between us.

My eyes narrowed to tight, determined slits and I ripped off my shirt and jeans, kicking my pile of clothes *toward the toilet before stepping in behind him.*

"I'm sorry if me dancing with Colby made you uncomfortable. I know you don't like that kind of thing, and I should have respected that, but you have to forgive me, and I ain't leaving your side until you do."

Josh whipped around to face me, a deep scowl marring his perfect features. Flicking his wet locks out of his face, he licked the water off his lips and glared at me. "I do not have to forgive you."

"Yes, you do!" I felt small beside his bulky, hard body, but I raised my chin anyway.

"And why is that?"

"Because we're in love with each other and that's what couples do. They fight, they forgive, they make out, and they get over it!"

His eyes narrowed, his expression pinching tight for a second. "You love me?"

Pointing behind me with an exasperated eye roll, I hollered at him, "I just sang you a song saying I did. I haven't changed my mind in the last five minutes."

"Say it." His demand was short and terse, but it still made a smile jump onto my lips.

I placed my hand on his hips, just above that dang triangle that turned muscles into marshmallows. "I love you."

"Say it again."

"I love you. I love all of you, including that stupid, jealous head on your shoulders and that great big heart in there." I tapped his chiseled chest before gazing down at his erection. With a grin, I wrapped my fingers around it. "This ain't bad either."

His eyes rolled north, and he tried to hamper that

sweet groan he made whenever I touched him, but he couldn't do it. I still heard that faint sigh.

A triumphant smile kissed my lips. "Say you forgive me, Josh."

"I ain't ready." He practically squeaked the words, giving away his big, fat lie.

I squeezed him tighter, yanking hard and purring, "You ready now?"

His large hands landed on my head as if he needed help to stand, my furious stroking making his stomach muscles quiver and jerk.

"Say it, Joshie," I sing-songed. "Or I'm getting out right now."

He pressed his lips together, another moan rumbling in his throat.

"Okay, have it your way." I let him go, flicking his hands off my face and turning to leave.

I didn't get very far. Before I'd even finished my swivel, Josh grabbed my arm and turned me back to face him. Plucking me up off the bathtub floor as if I weighed nothing, he pressed me against the wall with just the right power to get my insides dancing.

My back smacked against those cold tiles, and I couldn't help a breathy giggle. I wrapped my legs around his waist and gripped his shoulders.

"I forgive you," he whispered, planting a hard kiss on my lips. Our hungry tongues wound together, the heat of the kiss rivaling the hot spray pelting our skin. Josh pulled back, his breath sharp and hot on my lips. "I'll always forgive you."

He entered me then, so fast and hard I cried out, tipping my head to the ceiling as my insides did a triple *back-flip. His wet lips massacred my neck while he drove into me, pounding me against that bathroom wall and giving me every reason in the world to fight and make up with him over and over again.*

I gripped the back of his hair, pulling at the thick locks as he took me to that place only Josh could...a special kind of heaven reserved for lovers. The only place you could truly bare your soul and know you were still safe.

Heat pooled between my legs just thinking about Josh inside of me. An intense ache for him permeated my very core, making my stomach hurt. Snatching my purse, I yanked out my phone and went to dial his number. My thumb hovered over the screen. I'd missed a call from him. I frantically dialed voicemail and pressed the phone to my ear.

His deep, rich voice made me smile, but my lips soon dipped, my forehead crinkling. His sweet, awkward words had my legs buckling. I sank to the floor, sliding down that dirty door and hitting the hard wood beneath me. His voice petered out quickly and he ended the call.

"Sweet man," I whispered, sucking in a shaky breath.

He was going to support me.

I shook my head, wriggling on the floor and tugging at the dress. It was so dang short, it couldn't even cover my butt sitting the way I was.

With puffy breaths, I tore at the material, struggling to pull it off while not dropping my phone. I bunched it in my hands and threw it across the room before wrapping my arms around my legs. Resting my chin on my knees, I relished my curtain of hair, hiding me from the outside world as I gazed at my phone.

I couldn't call him back.

There was no way he'd support what I'd done. He'd be madder than a mule chewing on bumblebees...and he had every right.

I was so ashamed.

"Acting like a damn fool, Rachel Myers!" I scolded myself. Tears near choked me. My dream had become ash before it'd even had a chance to flourish. I'd been gullible and careless, and I wanted to take back my signature with a fury.

Talk about humiliating.

"I'm sorry, Mama," I sniffed. "I thought this was it. My lucky break. I should have known it was too good to be true. It was all just too easy, wasn't it?" I stared up at the ceiling as if Mama was up there gazing down on me. "I can't do it. I know you said whatever it takes, but this ain't right. I'm not a show girl, I'm a singer."

I had no idea what Mama was thinking right then. I'd be disappointed if I was her and that hurt real bad, but I'd hate myself even more if I let someone stick silver tassels on my nipples.

I gripped the phone in my hand, tempted to call Josh and tell him I was heading back to him.

But I couldn't.

He'd want to know why, and then I'd have to explain. I couldn't lie. That boy knew how to break me without even trying. Then he'd be all riled that they fooled me and annoyed that I didn't take my time to do my research. No, I wouldn't have it. I had to fix this and return with my head held high.

Josh wasn't my savior, and I didn't want to make him one.

He was my lover, my friend—maybe even the man I wanted to spend my life with—and I wouldn't have a snowball's chance in hell of that ever happening if I didn't get out of the dang contract.

SIXTEEN

JOSH

Sitting at the piano usually soothed me, but it didn't seem to be happening. I tapped my pointer finger lightly on the keys so they didn't make a sound. I didn't know what to play. I was hardly in a honky-tonk mood, and the idea of playing a slow, melancholy tune was kind of depressing.

The bar was due to open in an hour. I'd already set everything up and was hoping for a quiet night. Poor Harriet was exhausted. I'd given her a night off, but even so... I really needed to cut her some slack and hire me a new girl.

My fingers dipped on the white keys, and I

started playing the opening riff to "Walking In Memphis." And then my voice joined in. Before I knew it, I was singing the song with gusto. It ended like it started, and the buzz I got from playing disappeared.

Rachel hadn't called me back.

It'd been less than twenty-four hours, so I was possibly overreacting. I just thought she'd be on that phone in a heartbeat—all excited, happy that I was finally on board. I admit my message was poorly executed. I was a mumbling oaf when it came to feelings, but at least I'd tried. I wanted her to acknowledge that effort.

"Don't be afraid to bare your soul, Josh." Aunt Lindy's voice was down to a hoarse whisper. Her days were numbered and we all knew it. She was the only one not afraid to talk about it, and whenever she tried, I cut her off at the pass. Her watery eyes glistened as she clutched my hand. "How you gonna love completely if you don't give them all of yourself?"

Those words stuck with me for some reason. Rubbing a hand over my face, I rested my elbows lightly on the keys. The piano let out an off-key groan, but then went silent. I'd given Rachel all of myself, but I'd never told her how much I loved her. I might have said it when sex was involved—I couldn't be sure. It was easy to mumble anything when she made my brain soft with her tiny hands and silken center.

But I'd never had it in me to look her in the eye

and say it real gentle. I don't know why, I guess it made me feel vulnerable somehow, like lifting back the cover on my soul. I'd never given anyone full access to that place. Not since Dad died. It seemed too risky. Like if I did, they'd find my weakness and destroy me.

The only way I managed to survive losing the people I loved was to put up a shield to keep me safe. But Rachel wasn't dying, and if I ever wanted her back, be it tomorrow or in twelve months' time, maybe she needed to hear those words from me.

Rising with a sniff, I adjusted my jeans and clomped over to the bar, snatching the phone off the counter before I could change my mind.

I dialed her number and blew out a breath as I raised it to my ear.

It rang once, twice, three times…and then went to voicemail.

My head jerked back with a frown, and I checked the screen to make sure I hadn't done anything wrong.

But no.

Had she just ignored my call?

With a scowl, I pressed redial.

It rang once, twice…and went to voicemail again.

I wasn't a fool. I'd counted the last time I'd called, and that phone had rung seven dang times.

Slapping the phone down on the counter, I muttered a curse. She'd cut the call twice, which meant she was either hiding something or she didn't want to talk to me.

Both options were blades to my bones. Clenching my teeth, I resisted the urge to throw the phone across the room. I would have lost the battle, too, if Duke hadn't started barking to let me know someone was coming in the back door.

Thank the Lord for Denny, 'cause I don't know what I would have done if he hadn't arrived when he did.

SEVENTEEN

RACHEL

"You don't want to get that?" Parker pointed at my phone.

My head could barely shake a no as I buried the phone in the bottom of my bag. It was real mean to ignore Josh's call, but I was determined not to talk to him until I had the whole mess ironed out.

Parker had picked me up on time, just like he said he would, and we were driving to the photo shoot. I should have said something before we even left the apartment, but courage failed me, and he'd ushered me into the car before I had a chance to say anything. I'd practiced my speech, muttering into the darkness until I had it damn near memorized.

"You feeling okay today?" Parker glanced over at me.

"Just nervous, I guess."

"First photo shoot. I understand. You're going to be great."

My nose wrinkled. "You know what? About that...I'm not sure I'm the right girl for this job."

"We think you are." Parker was wearing his damn aviator shades like he always did, so I couldn't tell what he was thinking. "You're everything people are looking for—that wild beauty and stunning voice. You're a luscious combination, and I don't think we're going to have any problems finding you some type of deal."

"I appreciate that, I really do, but I'm just concerned that Aren is going to lead me down a path I don't want to take."

A muscle in Parker's jaw jerked, his Adam's apple bobbing in his throat. "You signed the contract, Rachel. You have an obligation to see things through."

"But I didn't know what I was signing! You made it all so—"

"We're here," Parker cut me off, pulling the car into a sparsely populated lot. The wheels screeched when he braked, and I jolted forward in my seat. "Let's go."

He didn't open the door for me this time, instead clipping toward a small warehouse-looking building. I followed after him, determined to say my speech.

"Parker, please wait," I called after him. "I just want—"

"You can't get out of it." He spun to face me. "If you weren't sure, you shouldn't have signed."

I had no comeback. He was right. I shouldn't have signed that damn thing! My cheap butt should have hired a lawyer instead of trusting the jerk-face in front of me.

"Lose the scowl." Parker snatched my arm and pulled me into the building.

I wrenched my arm free, huffing at his manhandling. He ignored my daggers, a charming smile taking over his features as he strolled into the studio. I peered around me. The walls were white. It was a cavernous, empty space with no soul. I glanced at the camera gear. It was an impressive array of stuff, all very expensive and professional by the looks of things. The photographer had a mammoth beast of a camera in his hands and was going ga-ga over whoever he was shooting.

"Yes, that's it! Perfect. Give me those sexy eyes. Uh-huh and lick your top lip."

I frowned, going on tiptoes to look over his shoulder.

That's when my stomach plummeted, sank right down to the tips of my boots. The girl he was photographing was wearing nothing but a thong. Her long, tanned body was stretched across a pile of pillows, and she was hugging a microphone stand, pretending to lick the mic like it was a lollipop.

"I ain't doing that." I backed toward the door,

fear near blinding me.

I hadn't even gotten two steps when tight fingers grasped my upper arm and pulled me to his side. "Where do you think you're going?" Aren's hot whisper scorched my ear.

"I want out." I glared into his steely eyes. "I don't care what it takes. I am not doing this. I didn't sign up to be no porn star."

His smarmy smile made my skin crawl. "This is just promotional material for the club. The men like to know who's singing for them. This isn't going into a magazine. It's simply flyers for the club."

"I'm *not* doing this!" I yelled.

The room froze as if God was pausing us all with his big remote control. Everyone stared at me. A few mouths popped open, but I only glimpsed them for a second. Aren's stormy look was keeping me in my place. Fear laced my belly, but I lifted my chin to try and hide it.

"Come with me." He yanked me out of the room, nearly snapping my head off.

"Let me go." I tried to wriggle free, but his grip was relentless.

Towing me down the hall, he shoved me into a chair and snatched a pile of pages off the shelf behind him. "Your contract." He slapped it onto the round table. "The one *you* signed, telling me that you would accept my advice and guidance."

"But I didn't know that this is what you were going to advise me to do. You made it sound like you were training me for the stage."

"That's exactly what I'm going to do."

"No, I mean, a *real* stage, not some cheap, nasty club where I'm gonna be leered at by drunken men! Parker lied to me when he took me to that Helium place. There's probably not even a potential recording contract, is there!"

"Keep your voice down," Aren snapped. "Of course there'll be a potential recording contract. These things take time, that's why you're giving me twelve months."

"I ain't giving you anything."

Aren's gaze, although pale compared to Parker's, grew dark and ominous. I shrank away from it, my nerves not settling one bit when Parker waltzed into the room.

"Everything okay in here?"

"Miss Rachel wants out," Aren snapped.

"You two conned me. You made it sound very different." I slapped the rickety table, making it wobble on its uneven legs.

"Believe what you like, but we have your name in writing."

"You can't make me do this." I sat up in my chair. "I can just walk away."

"Okay." Parker nodded, looking far too nonplussed for my liking. He leaned his elbow on top of the water cooler and stretched out his hand. "That's fine, just pay us what you owe us, and then we can deal with the breach of contract situation."

My face bunched with a perplexed frown. "I don't owe you anything."

"You—" Parker's head shot back in surprise. "Excuse me?" His comical expression didn't even make my lips twitch.

A heavy foreboding pressed me right through my chair.

"This is just off the top of my head." Parker flicked his hand in the air, moving away from the wall and slowly walking toward me. "There's three nights at the hotel, including all your room service charges. That came to just over two thousand dollars."

I lurched in my seat. "What! I thought—"

"There's the clothing and shoes you purchased on the weekend, the night out at the club, and then the first month's rent on your apartment, plus the security deposit. I think you're getting up to nearly seven thousand dollars now."

"I don't have seven thousand dollars!"

"Oh no." Parker touched his chest, his mock sympathy making me feel like a worm. "That is really not going to help your case when we take you to court for breach of contract. How are you going to afford a lawyer?"

"I—You—"

"Hmmm." Aren played thoughtful. "I guess you're going to have to ask your family for help."

"I'm not..." I shook my head. "I haven't seen my family in years."

"Well, there's always that boyfriend of yours." Parker tapped his chin. "What was his name again? Josh...something. Oh wait!" He snapped his fingers. "Joshua Clark. That's it. Hey, hang on a second, *Clark's* Bar. Does Josh own that place?"

Anger was clogging my airwaves. I could barely

breathe let alone talk.

"I wonder how much that's worth?" Aren murmured.

"Probably enough to cover compensation and legal expenses. May not stretch to what she already owes us, though."

"You leave him out of this!" I shot from my chair, pointing at them both.

"Oh, so you don't want him to know?" Aren's mocking tone was like a slap in the face.

"That bar is everything to him. You will *not* take that! He has worked too damn hard!"

"Rachel." Aren raised his hands as if trying to calm a bull. "We don't have to take it from him. We're just guessing that if he finds out you need the money, he'd be willing to do anything to help you out. He's just that kind of guy, right?"

"I wouldn't go to him!" I seethed. "He doesn't need to know!"

"Okay." Parker nodded, sliding his hands into his perfectly pressed slacks. "So, how are you going to get the money then?"

My mouth went dry. I couldn't even swallow.

He made a face, his long nose crinkling near his left eye. "Looks like you're in a bit of a bind. If you want out, you're really going to need Josh's help."

"I can't do that." I shook my head.

"Then I guess you better fulfill your contract."

"This is—This is blackmail!"

"No. It's business." Aren glanced at his watch. "Now get yourself to makeup. We're shooting your stuff next."

It was like the fight had been yanked right out my throat. I had no words, no venom to throw at them. I was stuck. How could I possibly put Josh in the position to bail me out of my own stupid mistake? He couldn't lose the bar over this.

My jaw worked to the side, my lips quivering as I willed myself not to lose it. I crossed my arms over my chest, holding myself together. I guess I deserved nothing less. Roy McGarrett was probably right. I was a worthless whore. Josh had tried to make me something different, but stupid ol' me had ended up right back in the same place.

"This way." Parker flicked his head, and I had no choice but to follow.

I had no choice but to sit in that makeup chair and become something I wasn't—false eyelashes, plumped-up lips, teased hair that made me look like a scarecrow.

But that wasn't the worst part.

The worst part was having to strip off every inch of my dignity while manipulative men stood by with smirks on their faces.

My only safety net was a guitar, which they made me treat like a teddy bear. They also gave me a floppy straw cowboy hat that I used to cover myself whenever I could.

Trying to pose for photos was a nightmare. It didn't take long for the photographer to get madder than a bull seeing red. He started yelling just the way my daddy used to, and my old instinct forced me to jump to submission. I put on a show, and by the end of the session I'd become the girl they'd wanted me to be.

Stage names were thrown over my head while the camera snapped, and I was soon Sissy Hancock—the sexiest cowgirl in the west.

I wanted to hurl.

Puke my guts out all over those silk pillows, but I held it in.

I knew what it was to throw my self-respect away. I'd had to do it before to survive.

At least this time I was doing it to save someone I loved.

EIGHTEEN

JOSH

The phone rang.

I raced toward it, leaping over a chair to grab it in time.

"Hello, Rachel?"

"Hey, Josh. Sorry to disappoint. It's just Uncle Amos here."

My lips twitched with a smile in spite of my chagrin. I'd been waiting almost a week for Rachel to call me back. My stubborn streak had kicked in big time, and I didn't care how much it hurt. I wasn't dialing her number again. She could damn well call me. I'd left my first message and that was enough. If she was going to ignore me, then fine!

I tried to hide all this from my voice as I forced out a chuckle. "How's it going, traveling man?"

"I'm having such a great time."

"Where you up to?"

"I'm back in the States now. Crossed the border from Canada last week, and I'm heading down the coast now. Hoping to get to Mexico by the end of the summer."

"Sounds great. You should look up Rachel when you're passing through California."

There was a sudden pause and I squeezed my eyes shut, wishing I hadn't said anything.

"Rachel's in California?" Uncle Amos's voice curled high around her name.

"Yep." I cut the word short, giving everything away.

"Well, what happened, son?"

I clenched my teeth, picking at the counter top.

"I can't imagine you two fighting big enough for her to go that far west."

Joining in his chuckle was an effort. His hearty laugh was loud compared to my dry snicker.

"She got herself a singing opportunity. An agent was passing through town and offered her the chance to audition. She was singing for the bar and he saw her."

"Wow." Uncle Amos laughed again. "Oh, wow. She must be over the moon."

"She sure is."

"So, did she pass? I mean, did they want her?"

"I think so. She called to say it went real well

and uh, that they'd be working with her for a year, training her up and everything."

"Did she get a recording deal?"

My jaw worked to the side as I struggled to make my voice ring with cheer. "I don't know all the ins and outs of it. She's been real busy, so it's hard for her to call."

Uncle Amos paused. The weight of his silence felt like a ten-ton truck. "But she's okay though, right?"

I swallowed. Shit, I didn't know! She'd have to actually call for me to find that out. I kicked at the board running beneath the bar and turned to survey the empty space. A soft light shone through the windows, the thick rays highlighting the dust dancing in the air.

I turned my back on it, a sick dread nestling in my stomach. My initial worry for Rachel came charging back through me like the cavalry.

"I'm not sure where she's up to with everything. I know she's in LA and being taken care of by this agent—Parker Stewart. She sounded real happy last time she called."

"Okay, well as long as she's doing all right." He snickered. "That girl. She deserves it, you know. She was like a ball of yellow sunlight, could brighten up any room she walked into."

"Yeah, yeah, she could." My voice sounded small and distant.

"I bet you're missing her."

I cleared my throat, jerking tall. "I'm being supportive."

"It's okay to be hurting, too."

I shook my head, my lips pursing to the side.

Uncle Amos waited for me to fill the empty space, but I couldn't do it. My eyes roved the bar, taking in the line of clean glasses and the liquor bottles on the top shelf. I thought of a million things to tell him, but none of them would come out.

"Well, I guess I better get going then." My uncle could always sense a lost battle. "Why don't you send me her details, and I'll look her up when I'm passing through."

I nodded. "Will do. You take care."

"You too, son."

I hung up before more could be said. I was never one for long goodbyes anyway. The phone felt slick in my sweaty palms. I didn't have any details to send the man, because I didn't know any damn details.

A thought came to me, making me break for the stairwell and charge up to my room. Flicking aside the contents on the cluttered desk, I pulled a business card from beneath the edge of the keyboard.

I hated making phone calls to people I didn't know. Hell, I could barely make 'em to people I *did* know. My thumb twitched over the buttons while I hesitated, pacing to the unmade bed and back.

"Just do it, you fool!" I cursed and pressed the buttons, holding the phone to my ear as if it were infected.

"Parker Stewart."

I felt like a guard dog listening to an approaching stranger. It was an effort not to growl into the phone. "Hi there, I'm looking for Rachel Myers."

"And who is this?"

"It's her boyfriend."

"Oh, Josh, how's it going?"

"Where's Rachel?"

"She's doing really great. We're setting up promo work for her already, and she's got her first performance tomorrow night. It's just for a small crowd at a club downtown, but we're all very excited. That girl is a hard worker, and her passion for music is second to none."

"So, she signed the contract then?"

"Oh, have you not spoken to her?"

I pressed my lips together, holding in a string of vile curses. "We keep missing each other," I lied.

"I get it. It's a busy time. I'll make sure to tell her that you're trying to reach her, though, okay? Expect a call from her sometime soon."

"All right. Thank you."

"No problem. Don't you worry about your girl. We're taking good care of her."

He hung up, and I listened to the dial tone for a good half-minute before hanging up myself. Something didn't feel right. That pretty boy's smooth voice grated on my nerves. He was like a greasy, slimy bowl of fries that left a bad taste in your mouth.

My insides wavered with indecision until I finally did something I'd never done before in my life. I made my third phone call in less than ten minutes.

NINETEEN

RACHEL

The dressing room that I initially thought was so magical ended up being cramped and smelly before a performance. Girls wearing next to nothing fussed around with their makeup and bitched about everything from bad sex to chipped nails. It was an experience, one I was sure never to forget.

"Okay, Sissy, you're up next!" The lady with the manly voice and an ever-present look of disapproval hollered at me. "Sissy!"

Damn, I hated that name.

"Got it," I called back, tinkling my fingers in the

air.

I wanted to puke again. That feeling seemed to live inside me, no matter what I was doing. It was my first performance, and I was nervous as anything. I'd been practicing all week, so I knew the moves down pat. I didn't like most of 'em, but I was going to do 'em anyway.

"For Josh," I mumbled, rising from my chair and grimacing as I caught my reflection in the mirror.

I had on the tightest pair of shorts I'd ever worn. They came just past my butt cheeks and they had little tears in them, exposing the highest part of my thigh. My legs were slicked with fake tan, as was my exposed tummy. Adorning my top half was a string bikini that only just covered my breasts. It felt three sizes too small, and I couldn't help adjusting it for the millionth time as I walked to the stage door.

Josh would hate me for doing this. He'd hate that I was doing it for him, but if I thought about it any other way, I felt plain dirty.

Miss Frowny Face batted my hands away from my final bikini adjustment and plopped a hat on my head as I walked past her. My boots—the only comfortable thing I was wearing—sounded loud on the hard floor, and I rose to my tiptoes for the rest of the trip. I waited behind the curtain, rolling my eyes when Aren appeared behind me. His hot breath tickled my ear.

"Make me proud, sugar." His fake accent was pathetic, and I nearly told him so but didn't have time.

Candy—the microphone-licking Barbie doll—pranced off the stage while Aren smacked my ass and pushed me into the limelight.

I froze on stage for just a minute. Having no guitar made me feel naked, but no amount of fighting throughout the week had gotten them to change their minds.

"The only way we'll let you have a guitar is if you're naked," Aren told me, all matter-of-fact, like it was no big deal.

A wolf-whistle from the back of the room made me flinch. "Looking good, honey! Ow!"

"Strut!" Aren snapped at me from behind the curtain. My hips moved as if I was some robot and my new boss held the controls. Placing my hand on my hip, I sashayed up to the mic, the catcalls and whistles growing with each step I took.

My fingers shook as I curved them around the stand.

Think of Josh and just do it!

My command was strong and forced my voice out of me. "How y'all doing, tonight?"

More cheers and whistles.

"I'm Sissy Hancock."

"The sexiest cowgirl in the west!" they shouted back at me.

"Yee-haw!" I lifted my hat and waved it in the air like I was having the time of my life.

The sound man took my cue and "One Way Or Another" started up. I moved my hips and dipped low, flicking my butt out as I stood back up. The men cheered me on and I grabbed the mic, throwing everything I could into the song.

The words pumped out of me, and I dove into the melody and rhythm. I hid myself inside it, pretending I was standing in a room of my own...pretending that there weren't hungry eyes tearing off my meager clothes and making me feel completely naked.

I made myself think about the only set of eyes I wanted on me. I pretended I was doing a sexy little dance for him, a precursor to a lovemaking session that would have me seeing stars.

As sick as it may have sounded, I was doing it all for Josh. I couldn't let them take Clark's away, and they knew him well enough to know that's just what he'd do to save me, because he was that kind of guy...and I didn't deserve him.

I shimmied my way to the end of the song, gyrating and swaying my body as if I'd been doing it for years. The men loved it. They were all over their sexy little Dixie Chick.

A fine sweat glistened on my skin and I raised my hand. "Thank y'all! What a crowd."

Their cheers were lost as my next song started—"Shake It Up."

It was a true country piece and easy to get lost in. I think I actually smiled when I was singing it, until my back-up dancers skipped onto the stage and started shaking their tassels. I spun away from them and swallowed back my grimace, pasting on a cheesy, white smile just like Aren wanted me to.

The men loved it, drooling like wolves as the half-naked girls pranced off the stage.

"You sure are a fine-looking crowd tonight." I held the mic, gripping the stand and forcing myself to keep up the charade.

"Not as fine as you, sugar. Shake that bootie!" someone shouted from the back.

Much to my disgust, I gave it a little shake. A raucous cheer went up, and I launched into my next song.

I did three more after that, dancing around that stage and flicking my mass of curls until I had their tongues hanging out. The applause was thunderous. I walked off, throwing my hat into the crowd before disappearing behind the curtain.

Aren pulled me into a hug before I could even make it down the stairs. I didn't have it in me to hug him back, in spite of the fact a thrill was racing through me. I hated what I'd done to get that applause, but I couldn't deny the sweet sound of praise.

This was what Mama wanted for me…sort of.

"You were so hot and amazing. The crowd loves you!" Aren laughed. "They're gonna be lining up around the corner to check you out. This is perfect!"

I let him have his moment. Hell, I even patted him on the back.

Dropping me to my feet, he held me at arm's length with another chuckle before pulling me to his side and marching me down the stairs. His arm felt like an anaconda over my shoulders, but I couldn't flick it off because rather than steering me back to the dressing room, he led me out into the crowd.

It's ironic, ain't it? In that moment, the man who was manipulating me and making my life hell became my protector. I wanted that anaconda on my shoulders, because I was swimming in a shark pit, and they wanted to eat me alive.

I wrapped my free arm around Aren's waist and snuggled into him, pressing myself away from wandering hands. It didn't stop the odd slap and tickle from the ballsy guys, though. I kept my chin up and even stopped and talked sweet to Aren's bigwigs, but it was torture.

I blessed their hearts, of course, muttering the words with a sickly sweet smile, figuring none of them knew that when a southern girl said that to you, she was politely calling you a jackass.

The bile in my stomach burned so hot and strong I didn't think I'd be able to contain it.

But I did.

Because I was a fool.

And I deserved nothin' more.

TWENTY

RACHEL

The threadbare curtains—damn useless at blocking the sunlight—combined with the wailing of a police siren woke me early. I squinted and groaned, pressing my shaking fingers against my skull and wishing for a few more moments of oblivion.

I felt like shit.

Used trash.

And the feeling was all too familiar.

I hated myself for being back in that place. The amount of times I swore I'd never return yet there I was again, letting men use me in order to keep myself safe.

Parker had walked me home the night before telling me how amazing I was. Everyone had loved me. I'd put on a brave smile but didn't say anything as I clipped home in my boots, a Sissy Hancock flyer stuck to the bottom of one of them. When I got in the door and pulled the ripped piece of paper off my boot, I gazed down at the grimy image with a hopeless frown. The main picture had my back to the camera, the side of one of my breasts showing beneath the arm that was holding back my hair. They'd made me stick my ass out and look over my shoulder like I somehow was hungry for it.

I'd torn that wrinkled flyer to shreds, throwing it like confetti around my bed before collapsing onto my pillow and cursing myself until I couldn't keep my eyes open anymore.

Sleep hadn't dulled my self-loathing. Picking up a shred of flyer, I squeezed it between my fingers and threw it to the floor.

"Right back where you started, ain't ya."

My whispered muttering took me back to my sixteenth birthday...the day I set out to fulfill Mama's promise.

Marty's arm was around my shoulder as we drove out of Roderick, his promise to take me away from that small hick town making me grin from ear to ear.

"Run away with me." He'd whispered the words only that morning.

So, I'd snuck out of school and raced home. The house

was empty, but I hurried anyway. I grabbed my guitar from its hiding place in the shed, stuffed a few things into a small bag and jumped back into Marty's truck.

He was a senior who hated school, too. We'd met a few months back in detention and had been flirting up a storm ever since. I'd convinced myself I was in love with him...or maybe I just knew he was my ticket out.

We'd driven one hour out of town before stopping at a rundown motel.

"Let's sleep here tonight. I want to be fresh for a good long drive tomorrow."

I'd nodded, like a stupid girl, and followed him into a seedy, dark room where I let him screw me twice. After all, he was driving me to Nashville—he must love me some, right?

It'd hurt, both times. A burning pain I'd never forget, but I gritted my teeth as he moaned and grunted, knowing I needed to make sacrifices in order to get where I wanted to be.

At ten that night, he'd left me to clean up while he went in search of some food and drinks.

He never came back.

I'd waited up all night, worrying and fretting until the dawn brought with it the realization that he'd been after only one thing—a sixteen-year-old's virginity.

I didn't have enough money to pay for a second night, so I'd been forced to call my daddy.

He chewed my ear out, calling me a halfwit among other things. His checklist of punishments was long and foreboding, so I'd hung up on him and split. Managed to hitch me a ride out of nowhere and so began my downhill slide.

I knew what men wanted, especially horny teenage boys, and I used that to my advantage.

I wasn't proud, but I had my guitar and a promise.

I was on my way, and I was going to make it.

It was hard not to scoff at my pitiful ambition, especially when I found myself right back where I'd started.

Flinging off the covers, I gripped a fistful of hair, tears scorching my eyes. I sniffed them back. It was pointless giving in to them. I was stuck now. I had to protect Josh and I could do it.

"Twelve months. One little year," I muttered.

I used the bathroom, brushed my teeth and took the thick gunk off my face, accidentally ripping the false eyelashes. I cringed and threw them in the trash, wondering how much they'd cost me. A thick bitterness seared my insides.

Those assholes!

They conned me—a clueless country girl who didn't know any better.

"You *let* them con you." I glared at my reflection. "You dumbass."

My face crumpled, tears threatening once more. I gripped the sink, my knuckles popping white as I tried to hold myself together. Stripping off my clothes, I jumped into a hot shower and tried to wash off the leering gazes I spent the night enduring. It sort of worked, I guess. It felt good to be clean, anyway. I walked back into my bedroom wearing a towel turban and threw on my comfy pair of jeans—the ones with the holes in the knees—and an old T-shirt that smelled like Josh. I lifted it to my nose and inhaled deeply before slipping it on.

On impulse, I reached for my phone. I wanted to hear his voice in my ear, listen to that awkward message again, knowing it would make me smile. I frowned at the screen, seeing I'd missed another call from him.

Pressing it to my ear, I bit my lips together and listened.

"Hey, baby. It's me again. I just wanted to call and make sure you're all right. I'd love some details of what you're doing. You signed a contract yet? You working? What's it like? It'd be really great to hear some news. I— I... Okay, I'll see ya."

I couldn't hold back the tears after that. He wanted news! What the hell was I supposed to tell him?

I scoffed and started talking out loud. "Yeah, I signed a contract, all right! I locked myself into performing like a showgirl for the next year so I can protect you from losing your bar to those weasels. But don't worry, honey. I'll grit my teeth and do it, and just pray that when I come back in a year, you might have it in your heart to forgive me."

He wouldn't.

How could he possibly?

"He said he always would." I rubbed my thumb over the phone screen.

I had to call him back. If I ever hoped to return, I had to keep the lines of communication open, but...

"I can't," I whispered, my breath shaky as panic rocketed through me.

My face bunched tight, and I squeezed my eyes shut for a second before pulling in a breath and taking the chicken's way out by texting him.

Hey, honey. I'm great!

I nibbled my lip.

Contract signed, already started training and working. Been real busy.
I'm on my way to making it!

I nearly wrote *with love forever more*, but wanted to save that up for my postcard. I glanced at my bag. I had to fish that thing out and send it already. Although, Lord knows what I was going to write on it. I couldn't tell him the truth. Josh was a warrior at heart. He'd storm down here in a rage at what they were trying to pull, and then they'd give him their smarmy smiles and throw legal jargon at us so fast we wouldn't know what to do with it. We'd be up to our eyeballs in legal bills faster than we could blink, and Josh would lose Clark's.

That could not happen.

Frowning, I ended my text with a double kiss and an R. I felt like a no-good girlfriend as I pressed send. Josh deserved better. Why the heck he'd ever asked me to stay still baffled me. I don't know what he saw in me.

Throwing my phone onto the bed, I turned for

the only comfort I had left.

I sat in the kitchen chair and placed the guitar on my lap, strumming out a tune I'd been working on since I arrived in LA. It was pretty damn lousy. My songs were never good enough, yet I still played around with them anyway. I mumbled out a few words about my dreams coming true and felt like a fraud.

With a heavy sigh, I cut the song short and began strumming a Michelle Branch tune that I knew by heart. It was a melancholy song that somehow seemed the only choice for that morning—"One Of These Days."

The mournful words oozed out of me, and in spite of their sad tone, I felt better for singing it.

Josh's face filled my mind, my ache for him growing to a deep-seated longing that I'd never be rid of.

I'd always been too afraid to call Payton home, worried I'd end up feeling trapped there, my promise to Mama slowly disintegrating as I turned myself into a career waitress.

But maybe I'd been blind to the truth.

As I strummed and sung, I had to wonder, because the little apartment in downtown LA felt like prison, and I was pretty sure that was not what Mama had in mind when she made me swear I'd do whatever it took to make it.

TWENTY-ONE

JOSH

A text.

She sent me a damn text message!

I wanted to call her back and give her a piece of my mind, but I didn't have the words for it. Silence always accompanied my anger. I wasn't one for shouting unless I had to. If anything, I'd rather use my fists to unleash my fury, but I ain't never hit a woman. I saved my fists up for the odd man who deserved it, and that wasn't going to change, ever.

I made do by smashing my phone down on the counter. I heard a crack but was too riled to care.

I'd poured out my heart to that girl, asking her

how she was doing, trying to be supportive, and I got a two-sentence text that told me nothing!

My teeth were clenched so tight, I thought they might shatter under the pressure.

Damn it!

I wished I could take back my previous message about being supportive. I was a dang liar. I didn't want to support her at all. I didn't want her to make it. I wanted her home!

"She ain't never called it that."

Brock's words punched me in the gut again.

I slammed my fist into the counter, hissing as my knuckles crunched into the wood. Duke barked out back, and then a soft tapping on the main door had me shaking out my hand. I was forced to get over myself as I swung it open and spotted Melody Piper. She'd been a family friend my entire life and was home from college on her summer break. A few nights back, her daddy had mentioned she was looking for some work, hinting that I should seriously think about it.

He'd been right, of course. I'd had several complaints from customers throughout the week about slow service, and Harriet's tips were dropping thanks to picky patrons.

"Hey, Josh."

"Afternoon, Mel. Come on in."

She stepped past me, tucking a fine lock of dark hair behind her ear. It was a nervous habit she'd always had. I grinned, trying to ease her disquiet. She'd always been a jittery one.

"Why don't you come on through and I'll show

you around."

"Thanks." Her sneakers squeaked on the floor, and it made me miss the sharp tap of Rachel's boots. I held the thought in, guiding Melody through to the kitchen and explaining where everything was.

She nodded and listened real carefully. She was one of them studious A-plus kids at college. Her wide eyes were intent on my face as I talked and she was all serious, as if I was giving her the most important job in the world. It made me miss Rachel's playful fire, and I had to glance to the floor several times while I was talking.

It wasn't exactly rocket science, but she asked all these questions, and I was pretty sure after our half-hour conversation that she'd probably be a damn sight better at waitressing than Rachel ever would.

But heck, that wasn't the point.

"Thanks so much for giving me this chance, Josh." She tipped back on her heels, giving me the sweetest smile. "It'll be great to earn a little cash this summer."

"Hey, you're doing me the favor." I shrugged, digging my hands into my pockets.

Her gaze turned soft and sympathetic. "I bet you miss her."

"Who?" I put on a brave front, thinking feigned ignorance would get me out of the conversation, but it didn't work. She looked at me like I was as dumb as a load of bricks. Clearing my throat, I glanced across the bar and shrugged again.

"Rachel's doing real well. I'm proud of her."

"It must be so excitin'. I always thought she had an incredible stage presence. I'm glad someone else could see that, too."

Her comment made my mouth go dry.

Here I was being a stupid boy again, wanting to trap Rachel in my little cage. She deserved to fly free. The world deserved to see her soar.

Swallowing down my pride was going to be harder than I thought, but I could feel my iron grip slipping.

Melody slid her hands into her back pockets and scanned the empty bar floor. "Do you want me to stick around? I can work tonight if you need me."

My smile was tight when I nodded. "Sure, why not. You can start by taking them chairs down and setting them round the tables."

"Sure thing, boss." Melody winked, forcing me to smile at her again.

Once she was working, I headed back to the bar, delicately picking up my phone and assessing the damage. A jagged crack scarred the glass. I muttered a curse, unlocking the screen to make sure it still worked. Thankfully, it did.

Rachel's text jumped out at me again, and my eyes damn well started smarting.

I blinked a couple of times and deleted the text, deciding not to call her back.

What would it achieve anyway? She was on her way to making it. She didn't need a backwater barman anymore.

Rachel had never claimed to be mine. I just

made her that because I wanted it so bad.

Grinding my teeth together, I sniffed and slid the phone into my back pocket. It was time to put that girl out of my mind. Because whether I wanted to or not, I had to face the reality that sooner or later, I had to let my Rachel go.

TWENTY-TWO

RACHEL

It'd been six weeks since I texted Josh, and I hadn't had one phone call or message back. I was being stubborn, too, I guess. But communication was a two-way thing. You send, he replies, you send, he replies! I was just waiting on his damn reply! That was all.

Truth was, I didn't really want to talk to him. I didn't want him knowing what I'd become. It was as good as it would ever get for me. I should have known, but having to admit that to him was too much. It wouldn't matter how I explained it. I didn't think he'd ever understand.

To him, I'd always been something special.

But I wasn't.

Deep down, I'd forever be that homeless wretch. It didn't matter how much makeup I wore or even if my voice was like an angel. I couldn't change who I was, and working for Aren was proof of that. I could fight and pretend until the day I died, but I belonged in Club Liberation…I was just that kinda girl.

Gazing at my made-up reflection, I ran a finger over my eyebrow and leaned forward to check my lipstick. I was due on in ten minutes, and it was going to be a really big night.

Over the previous month or so, Sissy Hancock had become a hit. Aren, in his eternal greed, decided to dedicate one night a week to his new favorite country girl. I guess I didn't mind it so much. At least I got to sing the kind of music I enjoyed the most. Sometimes he even let me have my guitar.

Not every time, though.

That particular night, I was on full display—wearing the shortest damn miniskirt you'd ever seen and the tiniest bikini top with white tassels on it. At least I had my hat and boots, a small comfort.

I was getting used to the club. The longer I stayed, the easier it was to slip into the routine. I'd learned to tune out the catcalls and pretend the hands on my ass belonged to Josh and nobody else. I'd been slapped, petted, leered at and I could take it all.

"Rach, you're up in five."

I nodded at Susie. She was on programming tonight. I liked her better than sour-faced Annette, that was for sure.

Pulling in a breath, I stood from my chair and checked myself one last time. I'd lost weight…or maybe my waist just appeared tiny with absolutely no fabric to cover it. My fingers shook just a little as I ran them over my naked torso.

"You can do this," I muttered.

Aren said I had to put on a good show. He had some bigwig from a recording company coming along. I nearly fell off my chair when he told me.

If he hadn't been so damn smug about it, I probably would've said thank you. Instead, I told him I'd do my job and walked away.

Maybe part of me was excited. It might be my ticket out. If the guy liked me, I could move on to greater things. Surely anything had to be better than this, right?

"Rach, time to go!" Susie called.

I hopped to, prancing over to the stage stairs and putting my happy face on. I raised my hand to give Loretta a high-five as she ducked off the stage. Her ear-to-ear grin disappeared the second she was behind the curtain. She slapped my hand and then squeezed it. "Good luck, sister. This is your night. You go get that deal."

I grinned and had to resist the urge to pull her into a hug. She'd turned out to be a real sweetheart. Taking a quick breath, I arranged my expression to the sexy smirk Aren made me practice all the time, and swayed my hips onto that stage. A cheer went up, punctured with wolf-whistles and hoots.

"Hey, boys," I purred into the microphone, wiggling my eyebrows and increasing the noise in the club ten-fold. "How about we do us some singing."

"These Boots Were Made For Walking" started up and I did my thing—butt swaying, body moving like liquid as I danced around the microphone and flicked my hair.

The crowd loved it. I crouched low and flirted with the front row while hungry hands grabbed for me. I'd learned to trust the bouncers, and it gave me more confidence to be the girl Aren insisted on. Jumping back, I teased the crowded dance floor and hoped Aren wouldn't make me walk through after my set was over.

Back-up dancers joined me on stage as the song reached the second chorus. We performed the sexy little line dance we'd choreographed a few days earlier, sending the men into a frenzy. The song came to a finish, and I ended with my standard hair flick and chest thrust.

The thunderous applause and hollers gave me a minute to catch my breath. I swayed to the mic and looked across the stage to see what my next song would be. Aren had decided to make it a request night, so other than a few pre-planned songs, I was singing on the fly.

I gazed at the sign Susie held up for me and read, "Country's Written All Over Me." That song always made me think of Josh. I nearly shook my head, pretending I hadn't heard of it before, but dang, I knew the song by heart, and as much as I didn't want to bring Josh into that place, I hated the idea of not singing that tune. So I nodded and then actually smiled when Susie lifted up a guitar and held it out for me.

Yes! I raced for it and swung the strap over my head. Nestling the instrument against me, I strutted back to center stage.

"I love country," I purred into the mic and started strumming.

It was an effort to sing the first line, but I did it...and then I saw my man—an apparition in the back of the club, and I sang that song just for him.

It made me miss him something fierce, but I got through it, belting out the lyrics to the back wall and grinning from ear to ear. Country was written all over me. People in that club would never be able to see it, but I'd tattooed Josh's name on my heart years ago. It was there in permanent ink, and no matter what my future held, he'd always be a part of me.

That thought closed up my throat, and I skipped the final chorus, cutting the song short. No one seemed to notice or mind, and thankfully the next song had nothing to do with sentiment. I did have to lose my guitar after a fierce look from Aren, but when "Life Is A Highway" popped up on Susie's sign, I nodded a quick yes. The beat started, and I pranced that stage and actually had me some fun. I got the crowd joining in for the chorus just like I used to in the bar.

I couldn't help throwing my head back with a

laugh as the song came to a finish. The rest of my set went real well, and I danced off that stage a happy girl. I got nights like that occasionally. They'd see me through and make me believe that a year wasn't so long.

But then Aren was waiting for me at the bottom of the stairs, ready to ruin it all.

"Amazing." He kissed my cheek, snatching my hand and pulling me out into the bar.

People noticed me right away, reaching out for me like they always did. I stayed close to Aren, ignoring the fingers brushing my skin as I walked past.

"Walter really liked your show." Aren wiggled his eyebrows as he led me to a raised table in the back corner.

I'd been prepped for the meeting—sort of. I knew Walter Spence owned a company that recorded music videos and whatnot. Aren had invited him along to check me out, and I'd been told exactly what to say and do to impress him.

"Hello, Mr. Spence." I put on my sexy voice and upped the drawl a little. "It's a pleasure to meet ya."

Aren said he'd love it.

"Believe me, the pleasure is all mine." He kissed my knuckles and pulled me around to sit beside him.

I plopped into the seat, sitting way closer than I meant to. I shuffled away, but he pulled me back to his side. He had short, fat fingers. They pressed into my thigh, giving it a little squeeze under the table. It took everything in me not to flinch away. He was acting like he owned me.

There was nothing I liked about the man. Even his expensive clothing and cologne couldn't make him appealing to me. He was broad across the chest and shoulders...and belly. He had a big face, too, with jowls that reminded me of Josh's bloodhound. He had a fine head of speckled hair, but he'd gone and ruined it by shellacking it down with a greasy-looking gel that made it shine.

My nose wrinkled before I could stop it.

"So, what'd you think, Walter?" Aren's honey-coated voice was sickly sweet.

"I think I like what I see." Walter's pale gaze wandered my body, lingering on my breasts while his hand inched a little higher up my thigh.

I swallowed, resting my arm lightly on the table. "So, Aren tells me you're in the recording business."

"I am...and I'm after a girl just like you."

"So, you liked my voice then?"

"Uh-huh." He looked like the devil with an ace up his sleeve. I didn't like his smile. I didn't trust it.

"What would you have me singing?"

"I'm picturing a country theme, obviously. I have a team of writers who work for me, and I'm confident we can put something together that's going to suit your style, Sissy."

I should have found that encouraging, and I suppose part of me did, but I was nervous.

"You looked pretty fine up there with your guitar, like you were having a good time."

"I love my guitar." It wasn't hard to smile when I said that.

"Perfect." His grin was broad and fooled me into thinking that maybe he did have something to offer me. "I love talented ladies."

His thumb caressed my thigh and I pressed my lips together, trying to hide how much it bothered me.

"The money's good, Sissy. I could make you a rich lady."

That part sounded nice. Maybe I could get myself enough to buy my way out of the contract with Aren.

"What kind of contract is it? I wouldn't be locked into any kind of time frame, would I?" I couldn't help glaring at my boss. His eyes rounded with warning, but I turned away from his furious gaze to listen to Walter.

"It's per recording, so a case-by-case basis. The time frame is as long as it takes us to record the music and film the video."

"Video?" I frowned.

"Music video." He grinned.

Wow. He was offering me an album and a music video. That sounded pretty darn good.

"How much are we talking here?"

He leaned forward and whispered a number into my ear. The figure made me slightly dizzy. I jerked to look at him, making sure I'd heard him right.

"That's right, Sissy." He turned into me, crowding my space and using his free hand to caress my cheek. "I can make you a rich woman. I can make all your dreams come true."

My lips quivered. They were shaking as I tried to reply, but all that came out was a little squeak.

He chuckled, leaning back and looking over his shoulder at Aren. "Let's set something up. I'd like Rachel to give me a private performance so I can see her without all this crowd in the way. I'll send you a list of songs I like, and she can work on those. Let's aim for Wednesday. That'll give her a few days to practice."

"Will you want to meet with her afterward?" Aren tapped away on his smart phone.

"Definitely. If you can clear her schedule for the night. That way, if I like what I see, we don't have to hurry through any discussions." Walter turned to me, his pale eyes sparkling. "I'll be able to show you exactly what you'll be doing and give you a sample of the songs."

"Sounds great," my voice trembled.

"Done." Aren placed his phone back on the table and grinned at me. He looked damn happy. I figured his finder's fee was pretty sweet. There was no way he'd be giving me a night off if it wasn't for something good. If the numbers Walter whispered in my ear were anything to go by, then I could understand why.

Aren would do everything in his power to make this happen for me, and I needed to do everything in my power to make it happen for myself. That much money would hire me a lawyer, and maybe he'd be able to find me just the right loophole to get me out of this thing. Maybe I *was* on my way.

Or maybe I was just the world's most gullible idiot.

TWENTY-THREE

RACHEL

I was.

I was an idiot. A stupid, naive, *didn't know shit* idiot.

Of course I didn't realize this until I waltzed back into the dressing room, feeling kind of smug as I imagined how I was going to spend my money. First things first, I was going to get out from under Aren's thumb, pay back all his damn bills, and set myself free.

It didn't earn me the right to go back to Josh, but at least I'd be in control of my own career. Even when I was homeless, I'd had some say. I was in control of who I chose to approach for 'help.' I wanted that control back.

Slouching into my chair, I looked up at the ceiling and blew out a relieved sigh.

Walter Spence made me nervous, but for that much money, I'd be willing to work with him. Especially if it was per recording. As soon as it was done, I could hightail it out of there if I wanted to. Unless I enjoyed the work and he wanted to offer me more.

A music video.

What would that be like?

I grinned.

"Why are you smiling?" Loretta flicked my curls as she walked past me. They landed in my face, and I blew them off before sitting up and turning to her with a twinkle in my eye.

"I have a private performance on Wednesday to audition for Walter Spence."

"Really?" She spun with a skeptical frown.

"Yeah, why not?"

She wriggled out of her skin-tight tank top and reached for her bra. "I just didn't think you'd be up for that kind of thing. According to Hazel, Walter likes it rough." Her eyebrows shot north as my gut plummeted south.

"Excuse me? What are you talking about?"

"Sex. He likes it rough." She shimmied out of her skirt and stood there in her underwear, eyeing me. If I looked as pale as I felt, then I could understand why.

"I ain't sleeping with him. I'm recording a music

video."

She placed her hands on her hips, her long hair cascading over her shoulder as she tipped her head to the side. "I thought you just said he booked you in for a private session."

"Yeah, an *audition*. I ain't no whore. He's not getting underneath this skirt."

Her face folded with a look of pity. "Oh, Rach, you really don't know anything, do you?"

My scowl was deep as I glared at her. "Excuse me?"

"Prepare yourself, sweetheart, because if you want that contract, you're going to be doing a hell of a lot more than singing."

"He can't make me do that."

"No, you're right. He can't. But if you want that music video, then you'll need to. Small sacrifices, right?"

"*Small sacrifices*? Are you kidding me?"

Loretta shrugged.

"How do you know this stuff? Who's Hazel anyway?"

With a soft sigh, she moved to my side, settling into the seat across from me. "She used to work here...but she's made it to the next level, if you know what I mean."

I grimaced. "Why would she want to do that? Walter Spence is a fat, ugly man."

"A *rich*, fat, ugly man."

"But...ew!"

Loretta chuckled. "This is just what she told me and she was prone to exaggeration, but Walter gets what Walter wants, and if you want any shot at getting out of this dump, then you should seriously consider it. You know, short-term pain for long-term gain."

I made a face. "That's disgusting."

"You should be grateful he's even noticed you. I've been stuck here for nearly two years."

"You didn't sign for twelve months?" My eyes bulged wide.

"Sure I did...and then I signed for another twelve."

"Why?"

"This business is hard to break out of. Once you agree to do one thing, it leads you to another and then another. I've accepted that, and I'm okay with my role here. It's better than being on the streets. Paying Aren off what I still owed him would have put me right back where I started, and I wasn't willing to do that."

I frowned, turning away from her. "He's going to trap me here forever, isn't he?"

"He's *already* trapped you." Loretta stood from her chair but paused to squeeze my shoulder before walking away. "And don't forget, Aren arranged this for you. You screw up this audition with Walter, and he's going to make you pay."

Her warning tone gave me the willies, and I had to look away from her so she didn't see the fear riding over my expression.

What the hell was I going to do?

"You sure Hazel was telling you the truth about Walter?" I croaked.

Loretta slid on her skinny jeans and zipped the fly. "You could never be sure with Hazel, but I'd be prepared if I were you."

I winced, gripping my hands together and praying Hazel was wrong.

Prancing around on a stage was one thing, but having sex with Fat Fingers...I didn't know if I could do it.

I mean, yes, I'd slept with strangers, but that was before Josh...and that was for survival!

This was for...

Breaths punched out of my mouth, uneven and erratic.

What if Aren tried to use that damn contract against me again? What if he went after Josh?

Small sacrifices! That's what Loretta called them.

But how much was I really willing to sacrifice?

TWENTY-FOUR

JOSH

"Duke, come on, boy. Get inside." I clicked my fingers and slapped my thigh, grinning when my bloodhound came running.

He galloped across the backyard and barreled past me into the kitchen. Stopping at his water bowl, he guzzled loudly while I petted his back. I'd made him run a little farther than usual that morning, but I'd needed it. Running seemed to soothe me in a way other things couldn't. Once I'd set my pace, I was able to zone out, the world going into soft focus for a while.

I liked the world that way—it didn't sting so

bad.

Aunt Lindy had gotten me into running as a kid. Every time my dad deployed, she'd force me to go exercising with her. At the time, I loathed it. I wanted to wallow in my room, missing and hating my dad for leaving me, but she got me out on those country roads and forced me to run...and it had been exactly what I'd needed.

I'd never broken the habit, although having Rachel in my bed in the mornings had me cutting my runs pretty short. But she wasn't there anymore, and the more time passed, the longer my runs became.

Nearly seven weeks and I still hadn't called her back.

I was a stubborn fool, or maybe just a really smart man.

Pulling my hair free of its ponytail, I flicked my curls out before splashing water on my face. It dripped off my chin as I gazed in the mirror. I didn't know what my reflection was trying to tell me. People kept saying I looked tired. Mrs. Watters down the road was a mite worried. She kept on dropping off meals for me, muttering about that heart-breaking wench who left me. I didn't like that part so much. Yeah, Rachel had left me, but I was the only one who was allowed to complain about it! And she sure as hell wasn't the slutty whore everyone claimed she was. She'd done those things out of pure survival, plain and simple.

Duke trotted over to me but stopped halfway, his head jerking for the back door. His bark was gruff, but the way his tail wagged told me this was no guest. Whoever was walking in that door was coming home.

"Rachel?" I whispered, hope soaring through me until I rounded the corner and saw my uncle rubbing Duke's head.

"Hey, boy!" He chuckled, crouching down and getting a fair lick to his ginger-speckled beard. He laughed and kept rubbing, throwing me a broad smile.

"What are you doing here?" I leaned against the doorframe with a grin.

His gaze remained on Duke, and he finished his petting session before standing tall and coming toward me with a cautious expression.

My face wrinkled, instant tension knotting my shoulders. "Everything okay?"

His nod was too short and sharp to be sincere, and dread spiked through me. Uncle Amos did not deliver bad news well. I would never forget the day he told me Dad had died. He'd just blurted it out, and I'd gone into a state of shock.

Aunt Lindy had taught him a thing or two since then, but it was still taking all his constraint not to slap me with it.

I had no idea what could possibly be wrong. The guy was away traveling, living a life full of adventure. Aw crap, he was here to tell me he was dying. Cancer, just like his wife.

I took a step away from him, digging my heels into the hardwood floor and bracing myself. "What is it? You dying?"

His thick eyebrows popped high and he shook his head. "No, nothing like that."

"It's not good news."

"No." Amos shook his head. "It's not. You might need yourself a drink."

"Just say it!" I swallowed after my hollering outburst, my heartbeat loud in my ears.

With a sigh, Uncle Amos brushed past me, sliding the pack off his shoulders as he sauntered into the main bar. My muscles were wound so tight it was hard to walk. I had no idea what it was about...absolutely no clue, and that was damn scary.

His pack landed with a thump next to the bar and he pulled two shot glasses down, filling them with bourbon and then sliding one my way. He looked at home back there, like no time had passed at all. The comfortable pre-opening silence in the bar, the patter of Duke's paws on the wood as he danced around my uncle's feet. I hated that the sweet moment was being tainted by something...something bad.

Uncle Amos tossed back his drink and placed the glass down before finally looking at me.

"You're not going to like it." He scratched his long whiskers.

"I'm going to have to throttle you if you don't spit out this damn news already!"

His sigh was deep and heavy as he yanked something from his back pocket. "I know I could've called, but I thought it'd be better if I showed you this in person."

He slapped a flyer onto the bar. The shiny paper slid my way, and I caught it with the palm of my hand before collecting it up. My heart failed right there on the spot. It turned to custard and slid into my belly, the thudding in my ears replaced with a high-pitched ringing.

"Rachel?" I choked out the word, running my finger over her glossy image.

She was wearing nothing but boots and a thong, perched on silky pillows looking like a porn star. A guitar and straw hat were resting beside her supple body, and her hair was teased into a mountain of curls that she had clasped in her hands. Her perfect breasts were on full display, her pink nipples erect, and her tongue was peeking out the side of her mouth—a smoldering temptress.

Written in fancy letters across the bottom was:

Sissy Hancock—the sexiest cowgirl in the west.
Performing nightly at Club Liberation.

I threw the flyer down as if it was infected and muttered a string of curses. I could barely see past the rage blurring my vision.

"Have your drink, son."

"I don't want a drink," I growled. "How the hell could she do this!"

"We don't know the full story."

"Did you see her?" I thundered, my voice sounding ten times louder in the empty bar.

"I tried to get in, but the line was around the corner. By the time I finally reached the door, security told me she'd already performed. When I asked to see her, he said I had to book a private session or come back the next night. He handed me a card and that was it. I called the number the next day, and the lady told me a night with Sissy was a flat rate of eight hundred dollars."

My chin near hit the floor. "A night with Sissy?" I could barely spit out the words.

"I think it just means a private performance," he mumbled, neither one of us buying his lie.

I wanted to hurl. Gripping the bar, I leaned against it and fought the stars dotting my vision.

"Where'd you find that thing?" I pointed at the flyer.

"They were handing them out on the street in downtown LA. I was just out walking one night and it was shoved at me." Uncle Amos ran a hand through his shaggy locks and scratched the top of his head. "I thought you said she was doing okay?"

I scowled, turning away from that chastising tone of his. "I tried calling her to check in, but she only texted me back with minor details. I had no idea she was—" I pointed at the flyer with an agonized frown.

"I tried to go and see her the next day, but they said I had to wait for the evening and line up like everybody else. I tried calling her, but it just went to voicemail." My uncle's lips bunched, making his round cheeks puff out. He reached for the flyer, looking at the image with a sad pensiveness. "I'm worried about her. There's no way she would have gone if this was the offer. You don't think they tricked her somehow, do you?"

My white-hot shock snapped into hiding, anger

coursing through me at the idea of that Parker guy forcing her to do this against her will.

"I'll kill him," I muttered.

"Now don't get ahead of yourself." Uncle Amos raised his hand. "This is exactly why I wanted to come back and see you. I am worried for her, but charging in there guns-blazing ain't gonna solve this. We need to think it through."

"What am I supposed to do?"

"Call and talk to her. Tell her no promise to her mother is worth this."

"She won't call me back, and she sure as shit won't be telling me about this, you can guarantee it."

Duke whined, his tail thumping on the floor as he stared up at me with his big eyes. I glanced away from his loyal concern. He'd always been able to sense my moods, and right now there was nothing he could do to make it better. There was nothing *anyone* could do!

"Maybe you're right," Uncle Amos murmured. "She needs to see your face."

My head snapped up, and I caught his steady gaze. "You telling me I should go, bring her home?"

"That's exactly what I'm telling you." He slapped the flyer on the bar again. "I don't think our Rachel would want to do this. There must be something keeping her there. You need to head to LA and tell her you love her, and she doesn't have to degrade herself this way to make it."

"What if she doesn't listen to me?"

"Boy, don't be a fool." He threw the flyer at me. "She loves you. She needs to see your face and hear you tell her how much she means to you. She won't be able to resist coming back after that."

I swallowed, suddenly doubting if I was up for that task. I'd never been good with words, and the way my heart was thundering, I didn't know if I could pull it off. Of all the times in my life to get it right, it had to be then.

The thought of other men seeing my girl that way made me sick.

I had to get her out of whatever hole she'd crawled into.

"I'll stay and watch this place while you're gone." Uncle Amos scratched Duke's head, grinning down at my dog. "We'll take care of things, won't we, Dukey-boy."

The bloodhound's tail smacked against the wood.

I crossed my arms with a sigh. "Okay, I'll get going, but can you not say—"

"I won't be telling nobody about this." Uncle Amos flicked his gaze my way. "I'll just say you've gone to visit your girl to cheer her on."

I winced. The very idea made me want to crumble. If that was the flyer advertising her performance, what the hell was she doing *during* a performance! Bile ate at my insides as I clambered up the stairs, snatching my wallet and keys before making for my truck.

"Stop for the night." Uncle Amos patted me on the shoulder as I hugged him goodbye. "You'll do her no favors by dying trying to get to her."

"Got it." I rubbed Duke's head then spun for the door.

"Josh."

I paused with my hand on the knob and glanced back.

"It's going to be okay."

I wanted to believe him, but as I ran for my truck, I couldn't stop the doubts. What the hell had Rachel gotten herself into? And why hadn't she ditched it all and come back to me?

TWENTY-FIVE

RACHEL

The club was empty. Wednesday mornings were usually for sleeping and having some time out, but not for me. I was doing my final practice before having to perform for Walter later that night. Aren had me in full dress-rehearsal mode, and it was hard to hide my jitters.

I was damn near naked in a transparent dress. It was a black, sheer concoction that most definitely belonged in a bedroom. The only thing I had underneath it was a red, lacy G-string. But worst of all was that my boots and hat were nowhere to be seen. Instead, I was wearing red heels that were impossible to move in. My ankle rolled as I tried to sashay across the stage. I caught myself and carried on like I hadn't nearly fallen on my ass.

I hated the song—"Sexy Love."

I mean, it wasn't a bad song. It was actually really catchy, but slather it in the fact Walter Spence wanted me singing it just for him while I pranced near-naked on a stage, and it suddenly became the dirtiest, filthiest piece of smut I'd ever had to perform.

It wasn't my style at all, and I didn't understand why I had to do it. I thought I was Sissy, the country sweetheart, not some lace-wearing slut!

"No, damn it! Sway your hips more," Aren barked at me from the back of the room. "The song's about sex! You're supposed to be a siren, not a wooden pole! You're too stiff. Loosen up and shake that booty."

I wanted to curse him right then, but I knew it'd be pointless. He'd just make me run through the routine until I gave him what he wanted. I tried to think 'liquid' as I moved back to the center of the stage and "Sexy Love" started playing again. Singing the song in the husky voice Aren wanted, I threw my all into putting on a good show. I became the sultry feline he'd asked for...well, Walter had asked for.

A shudder quivered my belly as I dipped low and licked the edge of my mouth as if I wanted it.

I didn't! I *so* did not want it, but when I told Aren that, it didn't go down too well.

Hazel had been right.

Walter was a dark man who liked dark pleasure, and Aren had booked me in for a night.

"I want you to impress the pants off that guy. You've got him for a night, so make it count."

"The night? I thought it was just a private performance."

"Yes, and after that performance, you'll accompany him for the evening."

"To do what?"

"Whatever he wants you to."

The smirk on Aren's face shot through my head again, making my vision blurry. My voice faltered, and I tripped over the line about wanting him in my bed.

"Shit, Rachel! Would you get it right? We don't have all day!"

Aren was mean when he was hung over. He turned away from my vicious glare.

"Start again!" he shouted over his shoulder.

I pressed my lips together, sucking in some much-needed air through my nose. "I need a break."

"You'll get one when you've got it right."

"I—" I swallowed back my protest. I couldn't argue. He'd just go on about the contract and threaten me with destroying Josh's livelihood.

Damn my foolish ambition!

The song started up yet again and Aren pointed his finger, silently commanding me to go back to the beginning *again*! I cleared my throat and strutted to my starting position, trying to keep my chin high, but it was damn hard. The music kicked in with a cheerful beat, but I stood my ground until the lyrics started, then I moved across the stage, doing all the things Aren told me to. The song was going well, and I thought I might get through it without having to stop, until I glanced up and noticed a shadow at the back of the room.

I didn't have to see his features to know who it was—those broad shoulders, the way his feet were planted. I knew every curve and ridge of that body.

I froze, the air in my lungs becoming quicksand.

Josh.

What the hell was he doing here?

"Rachel! What the fuck is wrong with you today!" Aren growled at me, but I didn't even flinch.

I couldn't take my eyes off Josh. He moved further into the room, his features illuminated as he stepped into the center of the dance floor.

Damn, he was still as hot as ribs on a barbecue.

The ache for him, the one I'd been trying so hard to ignore, surged within, followed quickly by a spike of fear...then a deep-seated shame.

My cheeks burned, my eyes shifting over every inch of Josh's disgusted, sorrowful expression.

I caught Aren's glare out of the corner of my eye. He spun to see what had me paralyzed.

"What the hell is he doing in here?" Aren pointed at Josh and thundered toward him. "I don't know how you got in here, buddy, but get lost. The club doesn't open until six, okay? You can pay your entry fee then and see as much of my girls as you like."

"I'm only here for one, and I ain't leaving without her." Josh pointed to me.

"Excuse me?" Aren flicked back his jacket, placing his hands on his hips. "Look, I don't know who you are, and I really couldn't give a shit right now, but my girl needs to practice and you're—"

"She's *my* girl." Josh stepped across the room, towering over Aren and looking ready to pummel him.

That un-froze me.

I flinched, scooting to the edge of the stage and clambering down the stairs before Josh did something that could put him in jail.

"Security!" Aren hollered.

"Josh." I raced to his side, nearly breaking my damn ankle. He caught my elbow, that look of confused disgust marring his expression again.

"Josh?" Aren stood back. "As in Joshua Clark?" His gaze narrowed, his eyes dancing with a dark malice that made my skin crawl.

"He's leaving." I grabbed Josh's arm, trying to spin him around and push him to the door.

"I ain't going anywhere." Josh crossed his arms, making my hand look small and pathetic on his bulging forearm.

"Get him out of here, Rachel!" Aren snapped.

I dug my fingers into Josh's arm, near desperate as Murphy and Boxer strolled into the room. Josh could take them, but that didn't matter. He couldn't pick me up and carry me out of here even if I wanted him to. There was too much at stake...too much he didn't know.

I had to get him out safely and send him back home before Aren took everything from him.

"Josh, please, just go."

His head whipped toward me. He looked tired, his anger not having the same spark and flare it usually did. The poor guy had probably driven all damn night to see me, and I was kicking him out before he'd even had a chance.

But he didn't understand.

"Come on, I'll walk you out." I yanked on his arm, pulling him to the door.

He resisted me, flicking my hand off.

"I can have one of my guards assist you, if you'd prefer." With a smug smile, Aren pointed at the two burly guys behind him.

Josh's chest puffed out at the challenge and he growled, "I'd like to see them try."

"Josh, please." He ignored my quiet warning, standing his ground like a towering redwood.

Boxer moved first, stepping into Josh's personal space.

Bad idea.

They didn't call my man Grizzly Bear for nothin'.

Josh's fist fired without warning, knocking Boxer clean off his feet, which was a pretty big coup. Boxer was a large man, although it was more fat than muscle...unlike my Grizz.

A flash of pride swept through me, and I was fighting a smile until Aren pulled a phone from his jacket pocket.

"Josh!" I snatched the crook of his arm, yanking hard so he couldn't be throwing any more punches. "You gotta go! This ain't worth it. He'll call the police, and this is LA. There won't be no Sheriff Tolsen walking in here with a friendly smile."

My warning made him feel small-town. I could tell by the way the tendon in his neck pinged. He slowly turned back to face me while Boxer struggled to stand behind him. The guard's expression was thunderous, but I could tell he wasn't about to take Josh on unless Aren ordered him to.

"Come on, let me walk you out. Please."

Josh's jaw clenched tight, making his powerful face look even more commanding. My belly quivered with heat, and it took everything in me not to jump into his arms. I fought my desire, digging my heels into that floor and trying not to fold. Eventually Josh turned, firing a nasty glare at Aren before letting me guide him from the room.

"Follow her. Make sure she doesn't go anywhere," Aren muttered to Murphy.

Josh flinched, his fingers bunching into two tight fists.

"Don't!" I warned him before calling over my shoulder. "I'm not going anywhere. I'll be back in just a minute."

Josh stiffened at my words. It was like walking a damn scarecrow out of the club. His body resisted me the whole way. He had yet to say anything, and I kind of dreaded what was coming when we stepped into the street, but at least I would have him out of the club and hopefully in a few short minutes heading back to Payton...safe and sound, where he belonged.

TWENTY-SIX

JOSH

We stepped into a back alley that smelled like trash. I scanned the grimy surfaces and cringed. It seemed to sum up what Rachel was doing and it made me sick.

"Josh, what are you doing here?" Rachel's question slapped me in the face, turning my insides to stone.

How could *that* be the first thing she said to me after I'd hauled my ass over a thousand miles to see her?

A hard bitterness I hadn't counted on twisted my gut into tight knots. I ran a hand through my hair, looking away from her and clenching my jaw. I wanted to thunder and scream—ask her what the hell she was doing up on that stage, dancing like some hooker. I wanted to grab her by the shoulders and shake her until she snapped out of it.

I thought she'd be relieved to see me. I expected her to run into my arms, maybe trembling just a little, and beg me to get her out of the place. I definitely did not expect her to be standing in a garbage-can alley asking me why I'd come, in that accusing tone of hers.

I turned back to face her, barely getting out the cutting words through my clenched teeth. "I came to make sure you were okay and weren't being forced into something you didn't want to do." I yanked the flyer from my back pocket and flicked it at her. It landed on the ground between us, her naked photo on full display. "I guess I understand now why you never called to update me."

Rachel's expression crumpled and she stood on the image, kicking it away with the tip of her pointy, red shoe.

"What the hell are you wearing?"

She closed her eyes, crossing her arms over her chest. "It's just a costume."

"I can see everything!" I didn't want to, but I couldn't help running my eyes down her body—a body I knew so well. She was damn sexy, but I wasn't turned on like I usually would be. Rachel didn't wear slut well, or maybe she did and that's what was killing me. I turned away from her. The idea of other men ogling her in that thing made my muscles so taut I thought they might snap.

Grinding my teeth together, I sniffed, wondering what I was supposed to say to her. I didn't exactly feel like opening up my heart anymore.

"I'm sorry I haven't called." She swallowed, tucking a springy curl behind her ear and staring at the pavement. "It's been busy here. I..." She sighed, closing her eyes for a second. "Josh, you have to go."

"I came to bring you home," I spat, hardly sounding inviting, but I was on a mission. Although Rachel wasn't begging me to take her, maybe Uncle Amos was right. Maybe she was at Club Liberation against her will. I softened my tone. "It's okay, you know. You can come back. There's always a home for you in Payton."

"I can't." She shook her head, a brief anguish flashing over her face before she lifted her chin in my direction. "Payton's not my home. I'm... It never has been."

Her words hurt so bad I almost forgot how to breathe. Why was she doing this? Why was she choosing this over us? I was here for her, ready to rescue her from this hellhole, and she was saying no. Anger scratched at me, a bitter resentment turning my tone toxic. "You're becoming the girl your ma wanted you to, huh? On your way to making it." I couldn't help my mockery. "I bet she'd be real proud if she saw you right now."

Rachel's nose twitched the way it always did when she was holding in her words. I had no idea what she wanted to unleash on me. I kind of wanted her to get mad. Maybe a good argument would set us right. We could shout it out and get back on track. I wanted to poke her again, see if I could rile her enough to break, but her lips started wobbling and I lost my nerve.

"That's not..." She blinked a couple of times, gazing at the grimy wall to our right.

A whiff of stinky trash wafted in the air around us. I wrinkled my nose and bit my lips together.

Rachel's voice trembled when she finally spoke. "It's not what you think. I—"

"Do you want this?" I stepped into her space, gently touching her cheek with the pads of my fingers. "Do you really want to be here right now?"

She wouldn't look at me, in spite of the fact my thumb was coaxing her chin up. She sniffed sharply then finally turned her head to face me. "Yes. This is what I want."

She said the words with such conviction I had to let her go. I stepped back from her like she was diseased or something. She wanted this? She wanted *this* over me?

"Is that all our relationship was worth to you? I thought we had something." I choked out the words, taking another step away from her.

"We do!" She reached out, her voice pitching in alarm before dipping low. "We...did." She gazed down at the pavement, her long curls hiding everything from me.

Did—I hated that damn word. I mean, I guess I knew we were over, but I thought if only we could see each other, it'd make it all good again. I wanted to save her from this place and she wasn't letting me. Anger coursed through me in black, suffocating waves. It was hard to talk, to see straight. As much as I wanted to throw Rachel over my shoulder and march her to my truck, I couldn't. She didn't want that. She wanted to stay here, dressed in nothing and singing on some stage.

I never thought she'd lower herself to that. She'd done things she wasn't proud of before, but that was to survive. This time around she had a home, a safe haven, and she wasn't choosing it. I couldn't understand why.

I made one last attempt, desperation lacing my voice. "You're honestly choosing this over us?"

She closed her eyes with a heavy sigh, her voice soft and broken. "Just go, Josh. Go home."

The words burned me, turning my insides to ash. Bitterness coated my mouth, unleashing a harsh growl that I'd never used with her before. "I can't believe you ran off and became the slut everyone thought you were." My eyes narrowed into tiny slits. She pinched her arms, refusing to look up at me. "And to think *I* was the one who was wrong."

With a shake of my head, I spun away from her, marching back to my truck in a fuming rage. She didn't call out my name or chase after me. My words probably had her nailed to the spot. They were pretty damn mean, and I guess I regretted them, but I wasn't about to turn around and take them back. I had to get the hell out of there.

I was dog-tired, but I didn't care. I wanted home. I needed to get away from that club as fast as I could. I needed to get away from the girl I loved, who'd turned herself into something I couldn't stand.

TWENTY-SEVEN

RACHEL

Josh's closing statement tore me in half. I stood in that alley, splintered and rigid, fighting my tears. Murphy came out and found me, took me by the arm, and silently hauled me back inside. I didn't fight him. I was numb.

"Is he gone?" Aren snapped at me.

I nodded.

"Good, now get back up on that stage and finish practicing. And Rachel…" He pointed at me. "If he comes around here again, it's not going to be pleasant, for either of you."

I turned away from his warning, resisting the

urge to give him the finger as I walked back to the stage. I got up and did my thing, going through the motions like a robot. Aren made me do it five more times before finally letting me sit down for a drink.

He placed a whiskey in front of me. "Drink up. We need to loosen those limbs. You're still too stiff."

I sipped at the burning liquid to appease him.

"Walter's going to be here in about five hours. You can rest in the back today. I don't want you going home. Have a sleep, a shower, and then get dolled up. This has got to be the best performance you have ever given, you understand me?"

"How much will you be making?" I muttered.

"What?"

"You're hankering for me to sign something with Walter, which means you must be making a pretty penny."

Aren gave me a smarmy smile as he leaned toward me. "Whatever figure he whispered in your ear last night, I get forty percent of it."

"Forty?" I slammed my glass onto the table.

"It's in the contract. You read that paragraph, right?" He sniggered and snapped his fingers at Murphy. "Take her upstairs and make sure she doesn't leave."

The round guard went to help me up, but I flicked him away. "I can walk on my own." Then, of course, my ankle rolled in those damn shoes! I kicked them off and clutched them to my chest, padding out of the room and away from the one man set on ruining my life.

MELISSA PEARL

But I was the one who signed, wasn't I?

I was the one who sealed my own damn fate.

The look on Josh's face before he walked away nearly killed me. He believed every lie I told him. It hurt that he'd bought it all so easily. He'd come all this way to get me, and I'd had to turn him away.

Murphy opened the door for me, and I stepped into a small, hotel-like room. It had a double bed, a vanity, and a bathroom off to the side. Plain and simple.

"I'll be just outside the door," Murphy mumbled before closing it behind him.

The click made me flinch, the sound having a finality to it that was heartbreaking.

I'd lost Josh. My knees gave out on me and I crumpled to the floor. The one man who'd taken me in, in spite of my past, had just turned his back on me. He'd always looked at me differently, but for the first time ever, he wore the same judgmental scowl as every other person in Payton. Even if I wanted to, I couldn't go back. He said he'd always forgive me, but I didn't think he could forgive me for this.

The tears I'd been fighting burned my eyes, a few trickling free. I let them run down my face. They tickled my cheeks, but I didn't bother brushing them away. I was having a black hole moment. I'd had them before, when my world started crumbling around me and I didn't think I was going to make it.

My lowest point had been the day Josh found me. The only thing I'd had left to my name was

Mama's guitar, and I didn't have it in me to sell it. I hadn't eaten anything in four days. I was starving, sick, and a thunderstorm had been following me for at least a day. I hadn't been able to outrun it anymore, so I'd snuck through an open gate into a square backyard and huddled in a doorway, trying to stay dry. It hadn't worked. The freezing rain had pelted me until I didn't think I could stand it. Mercy found me and sucked me into oblivion, and then Josh opened his back door and I was redeemed.

He'd saved my life that day, and he'd driven all the way to California to do it again.

And what had I done?

I'd thrown him away. I'd lied to his face so he'd leave me.

I sucked in a shaky breath, my body quivering. I'd been in survival mode since that first photo shoot, fooling myself into thinking I could do this, but I couldn't. I didn't want to.

The idea of having rough sex with Walter Spence was unbearable. Who gave a shit about a music video contract anyway? I couldn't do it! I wouldn't.

Roy McGarrett was right about me. I was a *past* whore, and I'd never give myself to anyone like that again. I had to find another way to survive.

I didn't know how I was going to get out of it, but if I didn't do something to change my circumstances, I'd never get Josh back.

My sweet grizzly bear.

I'd probably never get him back anyway, but I

had to try.

It wasn't until I saw him walk away from me that I realized how badly I wanted him. I'd been trying to ignore my yearning, pretending I was doing this for all the right reasons, but I was a damn fool. He was the *only* thing I wanted—the only thing that ever really mattered in the first place.

*****

"Time to go." Aren stood behind me with a gleaming smile. I scowled at his reflection in my mirror, but he just laughed and squeezed my shoulder. "Lose the frown, sweet cheeks. It's show time."

I was made up like a Barbie doll. A professional artist had been brought in to do my hair and makeup. I barely recognized myself as I rose from my chair and followed Aren out the door.

My nerves were on fire, dancing through my body wearing tap shoes with spiky heels. I wasn't sure I had the courage to go through with my plan. The repercussions would be bad. I was a fool to think otherwise. All I could pray was that they wouldn't affect Josh too much. That was the most flawed part of my scheme—I didn't know how to protect him. I was hoping it'd come to me sometime that afternoon, but it hadn't. All I knew was that I wasn't going to be sleeping with Walter.

Josh was the last man to ever touch me that way, and I never wanted that to change.

Aren opened the door for me, and I walked into a dimly lit room. I'd never been in there before, but I'd heard about it. It was the plushest room the club had and was only used for special events. It was decked out in velvet pink fabrics with dark hardwood floors. A huge shag pile rug lay in the middle of the room, held down by a wide leather couch. Large silk pillows lined the back, shuffled around by the monstrous Walter Spence.

I pressed my lips together and looked away from his leering smirk. Glancing at the low-rise stage, I noted the pole and wanted to barf. Swallowing for the millionth time that day, I turned at the sound of Walter's voice.

"Pretty nice, isn't it, Sissy?"

I'm sure he was trying to be sexy with that husky question, but I found it repulsive. Forcing a smile turned out to be an effort; I could tell by the sharp frown pulling his eyebrows together. I blinked twice and tried again, telling myself to relax. I managed to flash him a grin. "Hello, Mr. Spence."

"Please, call me Walter."

His gaze was hungry, roving my body, making me feel like Little Red Riding Hood. He was the wolf salivating over me, but there was no woodsman to come to my rescue. He'd already been that day and I'd sent him packing.

"Shall we get started?" Aren clipped across to the stereo.

"Actually, Aren, I spent my afternoon preparing a special piece, an extra song I'd like to start with." I held out a flash drive for him. He looked suspicious, reluctantly taking it from me. I leaned into him and whispered. "It's to make up for this afternoon. I don't want you doing anything to pay Josh back for visiting. I'll make this night what it needs to be and you leave him alone. We clear?"

A smug grin tugged at his lips. "Clear."

I wanted to slap at his triumphant expression but held my anger in check. If he'd known what I was about to do, he never would have slid the flash drive into the sound system. Thankfully, Murphy had been too dumb to question me when I'd asked him to get me a laptop that afternoon. I'd lied my way through that one, too, and nearly passed out when he'd returned with what I'd asked for. My plan had fallen into place so easily, but it was going to have consequences, big ones, that weren't going to be pretty.

TWENTY-EIGHT

RACHEL

I clipped to the stage, stepping up and throwing a flirtatious smile over my shoulder before facing the back wall. I'd rehearsed my moves, and as soon as the backing track for Taylor Swift's "I Knew You Were Trouble" started playing, I spun and faced the men, flicking my hair back and putting on the sexy show Aren wanted. Although, this one was different...this was *my* sexy show, and I spat each word at the man who'd conned me, glaring at him intensely as I gave him the proverbial finger through a kick-ass song that said it all.

Aren's smug smile fled pretty damn fast, and I

was soon facing off with a thunderous look of warning that nearly hindered my mission, but I lifted my chin and stayed strong, singing through the rest of the song and pointing my finger right at him as I sang the last word, "Trouble."

The only sound to follow my performance was the air streaming out of my nose in angry puffs. Aren was giving me the darkest glare I'd ever seen while Walter gazed at me in confusion. Eventually, his fat fingers slapped together in an awkward clap.

"Well, that wasn't exactly what I expected, but still damn sexy. Shall we keep going? I'm pretty keen to see the first song I asked you to perform—'Sexy Love'."

My eyes snapped to the large man on the couch, and I flashed him a tight smile. "I'm sorry, Mr. Spence, but I'm not going to be doing that song tonight. There's no point auditioning for a role I don't want, so rather than wasting your time, we should probably just cut this meeting short right now."

I moved to the edge of the stage, ignoring the tycoon's gaping confusion.

"Give us a minute, Walter," Aren gritted out between clenched teeth before storming toward me and snatching my arm. His fingers dug in so tight, I could feel the bruises forming.

"Ow!" I yelped as he hauled me to his office. He ignored my protesting, practically throwing me through the door. I stumbled and caught myself against his desk.

"What the hell was that!" His bellow nearly shook the room.

I fought my quivering lips and tried to stand strong as I turned to face him. "It was a statement. I want out."

"We've been through this. You can't get out."

"That's bullshit! I want to see this contract again. Show me where it says I have to have sex with some dirty old man!"

Aren muttered a string of curses as he headed to his filing cabinet, ripping it open and snatching out my file. Smacking it onto his desk, he yanked my wrist and pulled me to his side.

"Read it! You have to follow my guidance and do as I say! And I say you don't fuck up this chance with Walter Spence! You screw his brains out and you get us that money!"

I leaned toward the small print, squinting to read it properly. It was damn hard with Aren breathing in my ear, and the legal jargon was enough to stew my brain. Curse it! I didn't understand what the hell it said on that paper.

Aren's hot breath scorched my ear. "You do *not* want to breach this contract, you understand me? I will take you down and destroy everything you hold dear. You seriously think some pathetic lawyer from Hicksville can save you from this? I will annihilate you." He grabbed my arm again, spinning me around to face him.

"I'm not some whore you can sell!"

"Then tell your little boyfriend he can kiss his bar goodbye, because that'll be the first thing to go when he tries to bail you out!"

Rage fired through me, hot and ripe, and I couldn't stop myself. I slapped him—hard. My fingers cracked across his face, stinging something fierce. My only satisfaction was his initial look of shock, and the red handprint left on his cheek.

However, my triumph was short-lived. He got over his surprise damn fast and slapped me back, knocking me clean off my feet. I cried out. My elbow hit the ground hard, pain shooting up my arm, but that was nothing compared to the agony of being hauled back up by a handful of hair. Aren's fist clung tight, shaking my head as he yelled at me.

"You think you have any say in this! You are *mine* now, and you are *not* going to ruin this for us. You don't say no to a guy like Walter Spence. He could turn his back on this entire club. That's a lot of business, Rachel! So you are going back into that room, and you are going to give him whatever he wants!"

"Go to hell!" I spit in his face and earned myself a backhand slap that hurt worse than the one before. He followed it up with a punch to the gut that had me fighting for air. I coughed and gasped, clutching his arm to hold myself up. He yanked on my hair again, making my eyes water. Fear pulsed through me. I'd never been beat like that before. The one time my daddy went after me in a rage, my mother had stepped in to stop it. There was no Mama this time. Just me and an angry bull who wasn't going to let me walk away.

"Now, I'm going to give you a minute to compose yourself, and then you're going to walk back into that room and—"

I shook my head. "No. Beat on me as much as you like, but I am *not* going back in that room."

I must have been damn crazy, because he took my permission and went for it. He didn't just slap me the next time, he thunder-punched me in the face and threw me across the room. I'd never felt pain like it. My body hit the floor and slid a couple of feet before smacking into the thick, wooden sofa leg. Pain coursed through me in such thick waves I couldn't even cry. Terror was blinding me as I pressed my fingers into the wood and watched Aren's shoes approaching through my blurry tears.

He was going to kill me.

No, he wouldn't do that. He was going to keep me alive and make me pay.

His fingers wrapped into my hair again and he jerked my head back, wiping the trickle of blood from my lip.

I wished for Josh so bad but he was on the road, heading home to Payton, thinking I didn't love him anymore. I willed him to change his mind, to storm through that door and unleash his grizzly. Whether he hated me or not, if he saw what Aren was doing, he'd kill him…and I'd let him do it.

Aren's breath was hot on my skin. "You do not want to take this further, Rachel. Now be a smart girl and do as you're told."

Part of me wanted to give in. I didn't think I could handle another round of pain. I'd be useless in a torture chamber, I knew that much, but I just could not make myself say yes to that man. I wouldn't do it.

Now that might have been the wrong decision. I'd already proven myself to be a fool, so it probably was, but I was determined. Walter Spence was not laying a finger on me.

Shaking my head was impossible with Aren gripping my hair like that, so I had to suffice with a glare. Luckily for me, he took that as compliance and let me go. Standing tall, he straightened his jacket and I clambered to my feet, slipping off my shoes as quietly as I could. Aren walked for the door.

"I'll explain to Walter that you needed a little persuasion. I'm sure he won't mind; he's kind of dark that way."

How I didn't faint, I wasn't sure. It must have been the sheer doggedness coursing through me, but the second Aren opened that door, I lunged for it, driving my fist into his balls when he tried to grab me. He let out a feeble cry and I shook out of his grasp, my flimsy dress tearing as I fled.

"Stop that bitch!" he roared.

I kept running, slipping down the stairs and making for the outside door. Footsteps scuttled and clomped behind me, but I didn't look back. I had to get out of there. The emergency exit came into view and I slammed into it, shouldering the door open and stumbling into the alley. I fell to the hard ground, scraping my knee. It was a struggle to get up. Pain still radiated through my body, fear near-blinding me.

"She went this way!" Boxer yelled from inside.

I scrambled to my feet and ran down the alley, my bare feet slapping against the hard stone. I heard a crash behind me and glanced over my shoulder to see Boxer giving chase. He was surprisingly fast for such a bulky guy. Anger was no doubt fueling him on. Josh had left him with a pretty fine shiner that was probably pulsing with pain as he ran.

Skidding around the corner, I nearly tripped but found my feet just in time, avoiding a painful face-plant into the concrete. The cold, stone alley was getting dark, dusk stealing what little light was left and replacing it with ominous shadows. I scampered over the concrete, panicked breaths shooting out of my chest.

My body was tiring fast. I couldn't outrun Boxer, and there was no way I'd survive being dragged back into that club. I had to hide and just wait it out.

I scanned my surroundings, my brain a frenzied mess as I tried to look for a good hidey-hole. I couldn't see anything except a dumpster. I wasn't above flopping into that smelly thing, but I didn't think I'd have time before Boxer came charging around the corner. I pushed forward, the alley opening up into a street. Human traffic would keep me safe. It didn't matter that I was half-naked. I could hide in the crowd.

Relief at the idea flooded through me until I barreled into the open, only to find the street empty. It was a back road for delivery trucks and such, not exactly a thoroughfare.

"Hey!" Boxer shouted at me.

I flinched, spinning to make out his bulky form before darting to my left. I squeezed in between two parked cars and crouched for a minute. The hiding place wouldn't cut it for long. I pressed my palm against the bumper of the car and looked around the street. Boxer would be there any second.

A friendly voice from behind me caught my attention.

"That's fine. Don't worry about it, man. I can do a late delivery."

"You're a savior, Jack. Thank you."

"It's no problem."

I glanced over my shoulder to see a guy sliding up the back door of his truck. He placed something inside and turned to jump down from the truck bed.

"There's just one more piece."

"Got it." The man landed on the concrete and followed the other guy inside.

I took my chance. Leaping from my spot, I darted over to the truck and scrambled up just as Boxer came around the corner. Ducking behind a set of dresser drawers, I squished myself into the darkness and started praying.

Boxer hadn't seen me get into the truck. I could tell by his cursing and then the retreat of footsteps in the opposite direction.

Thank the Lord.

I stood from my spot with a wince, but had to quickly duck down when the two men returned carrying a bubble-wrapped coffee table. I bit back my hiss as I squished into my space, pain shooting up my spine as I scraped it on the rough panels of wood within the truck.

"Okay, I'll drop this off on my way home."

"I so appreciate it. This customer's a piece of work, so be warned."

They both chuckled, and then the screech of metal filled the truck. I gasped as the door locked into place.

I had no idea where the delivery van was going...but did I really care?

In that moment, getting away was the only thing that mattered.

TWENTY-NINE

JOSH

I rubbed my eyes then blinked against the tiredness dragging at me. I hadn't stopped driving since leaving downtown LA. Glancing at the clock on my dashboard, I quickly worked out that I was six hours down and had about fifteen to go. There was no way I could pull a second all-nighter. I had to stop for some rest.

I hated that idea.

I was worried that stopping would bring it all back home, make me feel stuff I didn't want to accept.

Would I ever be able to forget that look on

Rachel's face when she told me to *just go*?

It cut worse than anything. At least when my dad and Aunt Lindy died they weren't leaving me by choice. I hadn't asked them to be taken from me. If bombs and cancer hadn't been involved, they would still have been there.

Rachel had the chance to come back...and she didn't take it.

I gripped the wheel, wanting to yank the damn thing off.

Why! Why didn't she want me!

Flicking on the radio, I turned up the volume then rolled down my window. I wanted to get one more hour under my belt before finding a place to rest. The music and air would keep me awake for that much longer. It was a dangerous way to play, but I didn't care. I couldn't stop yet. Not yet.

A woeful song about heartache was playing. I rushed to change it and was pleased to hear Jack Ingram singing "Love You." Perfect. That was exactly what I needed to hear right then...a song that basically told my woman where she could stick it.

The anger spiking through me felt good. I pressed down a little harder on the gas, wanting to put as much distance between Rachel and me as possible. She could have her damn club and demeaning career if that was what she wanted.

I drove on, into the darkness, trying to convince myself that I was better off without her...trying to pretend I didn't notice how skinny she'd gotten while she'd been away and the slightly hollow look in her eyes.

I gave her an out and she hadn't taken it. That wasn't my problem.

Turning up the volume, I blasted the final chorus, fighting myself the entire way. Part of me felt justified for thinking like that, while another part of me wanted to yank on the wheel and drive back, throw Rachel over my shoulder, and bring her home where she belonged.

But she didn't want me to, so I gripped the steering wheel a little tighter and kept moving forward.

THIRTY

RACHEL

It was a bumpy, painful ride in the back of that truck. I had no idea where I was going or how long it would take, so I closed my eyes and clenched my jaw. I hugged my knees like they were my favorite teddy bear and fought tears the entire trip.

What was I going to do when the truck stopped?

Would the man haul me to the police station? Who would I say to come get me?

I couldn't call Josh. I'd seen his face as he tore me to shreds with his bitter words. I couldn't call Uncle Amos either. I was too ashamed to admit what I'd done. That only left Parker or Aren, and I definitely couldn't call them.

I'd messed up so bad. There was no out.

The truck slowed, I assumed for traffic lights. It'd been stopping and starting a lot as it traveled through the city, but then a high-pitched beep sounded and the truck shifted backwards. We were stopping.

I tensed, fear injecting my muscles with renewed vigor. Still crouched behind the drawers, I awkwardly shifted to my toes and waited. The breaths pumping out of my nose sounded noisy as the beeping stopped and the air in the truck went still. The cab door opened then slammed shut. The man started talking, and I assumed he was on his phone. I couldn't make out what he was saying, but he was moving to the back of the truck.

Should I just shoulder him out of the way as I dashed past?

What was the better move? Attack first, or hide in the shadows?

The latch on the door clicked and the metal screeched as the door shot up. I held my breath, squishing myself against the wall.

"Not a problem, ma'am. I'll bring that up for you right now." He hung up on the call. "Geez, a piece of work all right," he muttered to himself, shifting the coffee table and walking further into the truck. He was going to turn around and spot me at any moment. What the hell was I going to do then?

I gripped the edge of the dresser, ready to launch myself at him if he turned, but he didn't.

He snatched a bubble-wrapped piece of artwork and tucked it under his arm, turning for the door without glancing my way. My body shook with relief as he jumped down from the truck. A new voice started speaking, a lady this time. Her staccato words and demanding tone told me she was the piece of work the guy had been referring to.

With my breath on hold, I eased out of my spot and inched toward the truck door. They were still chatting, but when I glanced out, they were moving into the house. I took my chance. Jumping down from the truck, I landed with a hiss. My feet were scraped raw from running barefoot, and they weren't appreciating the impact of the hard road.

Bracing myself against the truck, I limped away from discovery, breaking into an awkward run once I no longer had the truck to rely on.

I didn't know where I was. There was a hint of salt in the air that I couldn't figure out. Nipping to the right, I stumbled along, not sure where to go or what to do. Buildings loomed on either side of me, and I was transported back to the first night I ran away...that feeling of utter desolation as I second-guessed my every move. All I'd had was my guitar, a small bag of clothes, and a pitiful wad of cash.

I didn't even have those things now.

I'd never felt so vulnerable.

My body throbbed, my face swollen and aching. It was hard to see out of my left eye. It'd puffed up during the truck ride. I gingerly fingered it when I stopped to catch my breath against a brick wall. In spite of the fact it was summer, the air had a cool nip to it. I was wearing next to nothing, and when the breeze tickled my naked skin, goosebumps rippled over me.

I had to find shelter.

I had to think like I used to.

Closing my eyes, I forced my brain to focus.

Maybe sheltering behind a dumpster in an alley would be enough to get me through the night. I couldn't think about the morning. I just had to survive the darkness.

Sucking in a shaky breath, I eased off the brick wall and limped a little further down the street. A road was ahead, the whine and buzz of traffic shooting past. Maybe I could hitch a ride somewhere.

The thought made me pick up my pace until another, scarier thought stopped me.

Whoever picked me up would see my face, my torn clothing. They'd no doubt figure I was beaten, possibly raped, and force me to a hospital. The police would be called in. They'd ask questions.

Most normal people would probably think that was a good thing.

But it was no normal situation. Aren was the kind of man who could lie his way out of assault charges. He had the charm of a prince. The police would give me straight back to that asshole, and I didn't even want to think about what he'd do to me once I was in his clutches again.

I spun away from the road, darting right and discovering a narrow alley. There was no dumpster in it, but I walked down it just the same. Music played from the building on my left, wafting into the air and dancing softly around me. The building on my right was silent, dark…empty. Trailing my fingers along the wall, I finally came to an old wooden door. The handle was a little rickety when I tried it. To my despair, the door was locked. I tried the handle again, desperation making me stupid. Tears shook my belly as I rattled the knob, begging it to open. It didn't, so I had to walk away. Stumbling down the alley, I figured I might as well get as far from the street as possible and huddle in the corner for the night.

That's when I saw the window.

It was small, but so was I.

Frantically running my hands around the edge of the frame, I saw no easy way to open it…unless I smashed the glass. I couldn't exactly crack my elbow through that thing, so I dropped to my knees and searched the area for anything to help me. I got lucky and snatched a fist-sized rock off the ground. With a grunt, I threw it at the window, guilt spiking through me as the glass smashed. I didn't wait to see if any lights came on behind me. I didn't want to deal with shouting voices and questions. Instead I launched myself through the narrow space, slicing my shin on a jagged piece of glass. I ignored the sting, hauling myself through and falling to the floor. Blood dripped onto the concrete. I wiped my leg with my finger. The slice wasn't too deep but would still bleed a little. I needed to find something to stop the flow.

Clutching the wooden shelving beside me, I groped my way off the floor and hobbled across the room. I'd landed in some kind of junk area. It was piled high with rejected furniture and boxes that smelled like they'd been sealed for years. It was hard to find my way in the dim light, and I stubbed my toe a couple of times but eventually found the door.

I discovered a bathroom across the hall and wiped myself up with some paper towels. I didn't want to turn any lights on and give myself away. Probably a good thing. I was guessing my reflection was an ugly one. I wasn't ready to come face to face with it.

Backing out of the bathroom, I crept down the corridor, took a couple of turns and eased out a side door that led me into a cute little theater. It looked old but smelled freshly painted, like someone was trying to revive it to its former glory. Running my hand along the edge of the stage, I supported myself around the curved structure, trying to find a good place to hunker down for the night. Everything felt too open and exposed, so I ended up dragging myself back to the junk room.

Exhaustion tugged at my shaking limbs and I fell to the floor, shuffling back against the wall and using my bent arm as a pillow. In spite of my weariness, I doubted sleep would find me quickly. A cool breeze wafted through the shattered window, so I eased myself out of its draft and closed my eyes.

That was when I picked up the faint tune from

above me. It was coming from the apartment across the alley, sounding way louder than it should have and piercing my very soul.

Tears eased out of my eyes as I listened to the words of a song I'd heard a few times before— "Best I Ever Had." It was impossible not to think of Josh then. His beautiful, Thor-like face, so strong and in command. I'd broken it. His bitter words couldn't hide the pain radiating out of his eyes. He'd never look at me the same again. He wouldn't be able to forgive me.

I'd left him to turn myself into something I hated. I'd always thought there was something better for me, but there wasn't. Josh *was* the best, and I'd walked away from it.

And now I'd left Aren, and Josh was going to pay for that, too.

I wanted to crawl back so bad and beg Josh to forgive me. He said he always would, but why should he?

I couldn't.

THIRTY-ONE

RACHEL

My head pounded in my sleep, making me dream nightmares throughout the dark hours. As the sun lit the edges of the room, I finally dropped into a dead slumber. I don't know how long I slept for, but a soft whistling pulled me from the darkness, slowly rousing me…but not fast enough.

The door flew open, along with my eyes.

The whistling was cut short, replaced with an expletive. "Bloody kids," a man muttered in an accent I ain't never heard before.

He stepped further into the room and my time was up.

His eyes hit me, rounding with shock as I scrambled up against the wall and pressed my back into it.

Breaths were spurting out of me, fear-induced ones that sounded loud in the room.

"Whoa, okay." The man raised his arms, his gaze softening as he took me in. "I'm not going to hurt you, all right?"

I nodded, swallowing quickly. My eyes darted to the broken window as I calculated whether I could make it through without the guy catching me. I had no idea what kind of man he was or what he'd try doing to me. He had a rugged, unshaven look about him. He was wearing board shorts and a worn-out T-shirt, a pair of flip-flops on his tanned feet. I didn't know what to make of him, although there was a kindness in his eyes when he smiled at me.

"Don't worry about the window. We can replace that."

I frowned at him. Why wasn't he yelling at me?

"I'm Leo. I run this theater, and you need help." He pointed at me.

I shook my head, sucking in a sharp breath and flinching when my tender back scraped on the rough, concrete wall.

"Are you running from someone dangerous?"

My lips trembled and I tried to shake my head again, but it didn't really work. Tears built in my eyes, blurring my view of the nice man.

He crouched down in front of me, gently touching my knee. I jerked and shuffled away, knocking into a shelf that started to waver and tip.

"Whoa." He jumped up and steadied it before it could tumble on top of us. "You're like a skittish rabbit. I'm not going hurt you. I promise."

I wrapped my arms around my knees and pulled them against my chest. The movement made me wince, my throbbing body feeling the effects of my previous night.

"It's okay." Leo crouched down again but didn't reach out for me. "Let me take you to the hospital."

"No," I gasped. "I can't... He can't find me."

Leo's head drooped. "Aw, shit, you really are in trouble, aren't ya?"

I slashed at my tears, my vision clearing in time to see him run a hand through his hair and blow out a slow breath.

"So, I'm guessing the police are out of the question, too, then, huh?"

"He'll lie," I croaked. "He'll make me go back."

"Is he, ah, your..." Leo ran his thumbnail over his bottom lip. "Your pimp?"

"I ain't a whore," I snapped. But my fervor quickly faded, and I admitted in a broken whisper, "But he wants me to be...and I can't do that. He hired me to sing and dance, nothing more."

"Okay." Leo nodded. "Okay, well, I still think you should go to the police. He's obviously beaten you pretty badly. You need to get patched up."

"I'm not going." I struggled to my feet and made a move for the window, despair creeping through me as I thought about climbing the shelves.

"Wait, don't go. Let me help you."

A spike of old fear charged through me. I'd had that offer before. Nice boys putting on a show and then expecting me to do things for them...to them. I scowled at him, shaking my head and gripping the edge of the shelving. No, there was only one man I trusted on this earth and he lived in Payton.

"Leo! Where are you?" A female voice made me jerk.

My head snapped toward the man and he lifted his hand again, calling over his shoulder, "In the storeroom, foxy."

That's when I noticed his wedding ring. That shouldn't have necessarily made me feel safer— married men could be assholes, too—but it was the way he said the word 'foxy' that got to me. There was a soft affection in his tone that froze me to that shelf.

"Da-da!" a little voice squealed.

Leo's face lit with a grin. I understood why the second a chubby baby with golden curls and bright blue eyes toddled into the room. "Hey, cherry blossom." He lifted her high before kissing her cheek and nestling her against his side.

"So, I've only got an hour before Angel's due at playgroup. What do you want to—" A gorgeous blonde stepped into the room, her words disappearing when she saw me. "Oh my gosh."

"Day-dee boo boo." The little girl pointed at my face.

Her mother gave me a shaky smile before gently taking her daughter's hand. "That's right, cupcake, she's got a boo-boo. Should we put a Band-Aid on it?"

The little girl nodded, looking very solemn.

My eyes welled with tears again. "I should just go. You shouldn't have to—"

"No, it's okay. Let's, um, get you cleaned up." She stepped toward me, stretching out her arm like a mother hen, ready to gather me to her side. Her sweet expression reminded me of Mama, in spite of the fact this woman looked to be around my age. I had to resist the urge to crumple against her and start howling like a newborn.

I let go of the shelf and turned to face the little family.

"I'm Jody." She smiled.

"Rachel." I choked out my name and sucked in a shaky breath.

"Well, our apartment is only a few blocks away. I can take you there and…get you some clothes, and some painkillers."

"Dan ban-ai," the little girl piped up.

Jody giggled. "That's right, Angel, and a Band-Aid." She winked at me then took my hand and gently guided me out of the room.

"I'll keep Angel with me." Leo trailed us out of the room.

"Good idea." Jody looked at him. "Don't worry about playgroup. Let's just skip that today. I'll come back and get her soon."

"No, don't worry about it. We'll do some cleaning and be home in time for lunch. Isn't that right?" He bounced his daughter in his arms. She giggled, an infectious sound that had me grinning until a pain tore through my lip and I was forced to put my bland face on.

Leo started humming then broke into a gusty rendition of "Do You Love Me," starting with the line about working. He danced to the stage, wiggling his hips and making the girl cackle with laughter again. It was the sweetest sound I'd ever heard.

Jody squeezed my hand with a chuckle and pulled me up the main aisle of the theater.

I followed her out to the car, unable to speak as I slid into the passenger side. It was impossible not to wince. Jody gave me a sympathetic smile as she started her car.

"So, what got you so knocked around?" Her eyes stayed on the road, and I was grateful for it. I didn't want anyone looking at me. I hadn't seen a mirror, but I was a mess. It was taking every ounce of willpower not to fall apart on the spot.

I couldn't find any words, so I ended up shrugging. Tears were clogging my airways anyway. I sniffed and gazed out the window, flicking my hair over my shoulder to hide my face from the passing pedestrians.

"I know you probably don't want to talk about it. I'm just trying to figure out if I'm putting my family in danger by helping you."

"No." I spun to face her. "I won't stay. I just need some clothes and maybe a little money, and I'll be gone. I swear, I'd never do anything to hurt you or your precious family. You three are like…you're beautiful."

"Thank you." She beamed. "I never thought I could possibly get this lucky."

"How long you been married?"

"About three weeks." She chuckled at my surprised expression. "We just went to a local courthouse and did it quietly, but we're going to Australia for Christmas so I can meet Leo's family, and we'll have a proper celebration then."

Australia. So that's why he talked so funny.

Jody's lips were still playing with a smile. "It's weird. I always thought I'd want a big wedding with the white poofy dress, but when you meet the right guy, you'd be willing to get married in a sack, you know what I mean?"

I did. I mean I think I did.

I'd never been that romantic about marriage. My daddy was an awful husband to Mama, and I didn't know why anyone in their right mind would choose to enter into a binding agreement like that. I cringed.

You mean like you and that contract? I berated myself.

A fresh wave of tears stung my eyes. I blinked and sniffed, trying to deny them.

"You must feel like total shit," Jody murmured.

A pitiful laugh shook my belly, and I rested my head back against the seat. "Yeah, I really do."

Jody patted my knee. "I know you're not ready to talk about it, but everything's going to be okay."

"No, it's not," I whispered. "I chased the wrong dream, and now I'm going to lose it all."

The car slowed to a stop outside an old brick building. Jody walked me inside, a pained expression on her face as we rode the elevator to the top floor. She let me into her house, and I followed her through to the bathroom where she turned on the shower and placed a towel on the vanity.

"Throw those rags out the door, and I'll bring some fresh clothes in for you." She laid her hand on my shoulder. "Once you're clean, I'll patch you up, and you're going to tell me everything."

The command was a strong one, but it was said in such a nice, soft voice that I wanted to do it. I wanted to spill my guts to the woman, because there was something about the look in her eye that told me she'd get it.

THIRTY-TWO

JOSH

I ended up pulling into a truck stop and snatching a few hours' sleep before lumbering on. I staggered in Clark's door sometime mid-morning, dumped my keys on the bar, and slumped onto a stool.

Duke started barking, his claws clicking on the wood floor as he bounded from the back room. He jumped up, his front paws landing on my knee as he tried to welcome me home. His tail wagged like crazy, and I scratched his ears before pushing him off me.

Uncle Amos appeared from the kitchen, drying

his hands on a towel. His hopeful expression was dashed by my gloomy, resigned smile.

"What happened?"

I shook my head.

Duke whimpered and settled at my feet. His weight against my legs was a small comfort, reminding me that even though I'd returned alone, I was where I was meant to be.

Without a word, my uncle moved behind the bar and poured me a shot. I downed it in one fluid motion, slapping it onto the bar with a grimace. He poured me another. I spun the glass between my fingers, not quite ready for the second burn.

"She must have had her reasons, son."

I shrugged.

"What'd she say?"

"She told me Payton wasn't home." I cleared my throat. "She told me to go."

"Did she look happy?"

I kept my gaze on the glass of bourbon, biting my lips together and shrugging again.

"She didn't want to come with me," I grumbled before touching the glass to my lips and gulping back the liquid.

Uncle Amos knew better than to push me. I glanced up at his concern then had to turn away from it. He understood loss, but this was different. This was plain old rejection, and it stripped me bare, stealing my words.

With a sigh, he took my glass and replaced it with a beer.

And that was how I spent the rest of my day—

sitting at that bar, nursing my beer, and not saying a word.

Brock showed up at lunchtime. He moved me to a table, and Uncle Amos slapped a beer and burger in front of both of us then left us to it.

My best friend was wise enough to keep his mouth shut. He'd never one hundred percent trusted Rachel, but he'd backed off when he'd seen how much I wanted her. She'd done everything to prove him wrong...until she'd left me and turned herself into a showgirl whore.

I closed my eyes, trying to ward off the bile burning in the pit of my stomach. The image of her in that black excuse for a dress was stark and devastating.

The silence, which had been a comfort up to that point, was trying to suffocate me. I lurched out of my chair and over to the jukebox. It was a stupid thing to do, but I picked a mournful song that said everything my mouth couldn't.

I walked back to my seat, the soft sound of "Goodbye In Her Eyes" following me. Plonking my butt into a chair, I ran my thumb over the condensation on my glass before lifting it to my lips.

Brock smiled sadly beside me—I saw it out of the corner of my eye. Looking at him was impossible.

He'd seen me like this before. He knew what to do—keep his damn mouth shut and let me wallow. He'd kick my butt in a few days and pull me out of my stupor, but until then, woebegone music and wordlessness would reign.

THIRTY-THREE

RACHEL

I took my time in the shower, crying as the hot water hit my wounds. I patted myself dry, hissing and wincing as I discovered fresh bruises. My naked body was a beat-up wreck. I wiped the steam from the mirror and made myself look. My back was peppered with bruises from hitting the floor and smacking into the sofa in Aren's office. I had finger-shaped bruises on my upper arm, and my legs were scraped and cut from my dash for freedom. I cringed and leaned toward the glass so I could get a good look at my face. It was an ugly business.

My lip was cracked and swollen, and my cheekbone had puffed up like a marshmallow that someone decorated with black-and-blue permanent marker. The swelling bruise was pushing at my eye, making it a little hard to see. I pressed at the puffy tissue and whimpered, tears glistening in my eyes. If Josh could see me, he'd go feral...and then once all the fight had died out of him, whether he hated me or not, he'd cradle me in his arms and tell me I was safe.

I sucked in a shaky breath, my chin trembling as I fought a fresh wave of tears.

A knock at the door made me flinch.

"It's just me," Jody said. "I've got some clothes for you."

I wrapped the towel around myself and eased the door open. Her smile was the first thing I saw, and it settled my insides a little.

"I've got the first-aid kit out, so just come through to the kitchen when you're ready. Oh, and if there's anything you need, like maybe a comb and a toothbrush? I'll get Leo to pick it up on his way home."

"Why are you being so nice to me?" I croaked.

Her smile was soft as she held out a pile of folded clothes. "Because I know what it feels like when your entire world falls apart and you can't see a way out."

I frowned. Her? With her perfect husband and daughter? How could that be possible?

"Get dressed and I'll tell you my story, then you can tell me yours." She winked.

My smile was crooked and tentative as I closed the door and shimmied into a pair of sweats and a loose T-shirt. It felt good to be dressed in something so comfortable.

Shuffling out to the kitchen, I followed Jody's directions and sat on the stool next to the counter. Her fingers were gentle as she examined my face, rubbing antiseptic cream onto my wounds.

"So, what's your story then?" I flinched when she touched my swollen cheekbone.

"Sorry." She winced. "Are you sure you don't want to go to the hospital?"

"I'm sure."

She sighed, obviously seeing she couldn't budge me. Reaching for my ankle, she lifted my leg and placed it on the opposite stool before rolling up my pant leg and tending to the gash on my shin. I tried not to jerk and squirm, but it hurt real bad and my foot was twitching in spite of my efforts.

Jody glanced at me and was then nice enough to distract me with her story. "I was nineteen when I left home to chase my dreams. I was going to become a Broadway star, but..." She sighed, pulling a wide bandage from the box. Her lips pursed to the side while she flipped it over and peeled off the back. "I got pregnant. The guy was my college professor and didn't want to know. I was kicked out of school and came home very shame-faced. My father could barely acknowledge me. It was awful." She leaned over my leg, her brow furrowing as she gently laid the bandage on my skin.

"So, Leo isn't your daughter's father?"

"He is in every way that's important." Jody smiled. "He came into my life at just the right time and was everything I needed."

"You're lucky."

She pressed down on the bandage, securing it over my wound, and then stood tall to look at me. "I know...and I try to remind myself of that every day."

Collecting up the first-aid debris, she scrunched it in her hands and threw it away before lowering my leg and nestling into the stool beside mine.

"Do you have any other wounds I should know about?" Her blue gaze searched my face.

I looked away from it, dipping my head. "Just some bruises on my back."

"He didn't, ah...he just beat you up, right? You weren't..."

"No, just a beatin'." Thank God! I sighed. "It was a damn thorough one, but I don't feel like I've got broken ribs or anything."

"Okay." Jody patted my knee. "So, how about your broken heart then?"

Tears glassed over my eyes as I looked up at her, my entire body trembling as a sob shot out of my mouth. I covered the sound with a shaking hand and bent over. "Oh, Jody, I don't know what I'm going to do."

Another sob hiccupped out of me. Jody laid her hand on my back and gave it a soft rub.

"It's okay. I'm going to help you in any way that I can."

Jumping up, she rushed over to the living room and brought me a box of tissues. I pulled one free and dabbed at my face. "Thank you."

Gathering up my right hand, she gave it a gentle squeeze and rubbed her thumb over my knuckles. "So, tell me. Why is your life falling apart?"

I sucked in a quaking breath. It punched back out of my chest and I started talking. I blubbered out my story—every dirty, grimy detail until I felt stripped bare and hollow on the inside.

She didn't say much, just prompted me with questions at the right time. Her scowl grew deep when I told her about the contract and what Aren was expecting me to do, and then at the end she made it all better by pulling me into a delicate hug and whispering, "Shhhh, it's okay. Everything's going to work out."

I didn't believe her, but it was nice being held just the same. The way she stroked the back of my curls made me think of Mama.

*****

"Surely, he can't get away with that! There's got to be something we can do."

Jody's voice stirred me from my sleep. She'd put me down to rest in her bed after my confession had drained me. I'd fallen into a fitful doze only to be woken a few hours later by voices in the kitchen.

"Does she have a copy of the contract?" The

accent told me Leo was home.

"No, you saw her. She barely had clothes on!"

"Yeah, yeah, I saw her." I couldn't figure out if he was disgusted or sad. I strained to hear more.

"Bobby's bound to have a lawyer. Surely he can help her. That contract has to be a crock, right?"

"It sounds pretty dodgy to me, yeah. I can't believe she signed it."

"She's eighteen. She was following her dream. You think you're invincible, and then you realize that people are full of shit!" Jody's riled voice had a breathy chuckle spurting out of my nose. Oh yeah, she knew.

I didn't hear Leo's reply. I was distracted by a pair of wide baby blues staring at me through the crack in the door.

"Hello, sweetness," I softly drawled.

Her eyes danced with a grin before she swung the door open and toddled inside.

"Boo boo." Her chubby finger pointed at my mangled face.

"It's getting better already. Your mama fixed me up real good."

"Mama." She said the word with a grin, her round cheeks looking way too cute and kissable.

I ran my finger down her cheek and she giggled.

"Angel," Jody whispered from the door. "I told you Miss Rachel was sleeping."

"That's okay." I eased off the bed, swallowing down my groan. "I was just getting up."

"Well, don't rush, but there's food and drink here if you'd like something."

"Thank you," I murmured.

Jody moved to the bed and helped me stand. I clutched her shoulder, letting the pain run through my stiff body before finding my breath again. Shuffling out of the room, I tried not to trip over Angel as she tottered around my feet like an excited puppy.

"C'mere, you." Jody snatched her up and placed her on her hip, giving her neck a raspberry.

The little girl giggled sweetly. Angel was the perfect name for that child.

Leo walked through the front door as I eased onto a stool. His smile softened when he saw me.

"G'day." He nodded. "How you feeling?"

"Like I've been run over by a combine harvester."

He chuckled, his face crumpling with a sympathetic smile. His flip-flops squeaked on the wooden floor as he approached me. "So, I've just spoken to a mate of mine, and he's going to contact his lawyer, see if we can't get you out of this contract."

My eyes rounded. "But I don't have money for a lawyer. If I did, I would have tried to get out of this weeks ago."

"Don't worry about the money." Jody flicked her hand in the air. "We just need to get you safe, and we can figure out the rest later."

"But I…"

"Jody's right." Leo stepped up to his wife and laid a hand on her lower back. "Don't worry about it. We're here to help you."

"Why?"

He just grinned at me, shaking his head before snatching a turkey sandwich off the plate and taking a mammoth bite. Angel giggled at her daddy's funny faces while Jody rolled her eyes. She was fighting a smile, though, and lost the battle pretty quick, her halfhearted reprimand landing on deaf ears.

I watched the exchange, the way her expression heated with color as her gaze locked with Leo's. They had that thing. The one Josh and I used to have. That silent bond...the one I'd severed.

THIRTY-FOUR

RACHEL

Five days passed, and I could finally walk without wincing. Jody and Leo had set me up in their apartment across the hall. It was actually a music studio, but there was a bed in the spare room. I spent most of my time in there, catching up on sleep and letting myself heal. I didn't feel too isolated and alone, though. Leo would often be at the piano playing, and there were singers coming in and out, auditioning for some kind of musical.

Leo was a composer and Jody could sing. Lord Almighty, that woman had a voice. It was the perfect place for me to heal...surrounded by love and music. It was the kind of home I always wanted.

I nibbled the edge of my lip as I walked to Leo's car then slid into the passenger's seat.

"It's going to be okay," he repeated for the hundredth time that morning.

He was trying to soothe me every time he said it, but it never helped my nerves. We were heading to my apartment in downtown LA to collect my stuff. Leo's friend Bobby got my key when he visited Club Liberation the day before. He went with his lawyer friend who demanded to see my contract. Apparently, Aren tried to fight him on it, but after a few well-worded threats, according to Leo, the guy jumped-to, rushing to comply with their demands. The lawyer had entered into negotiations with Aren, trying to terminate my contract. Thankfully, it was full of holes and Leo was confident the matter would be resolved quickly.

"Aren will want to keep this under wraps. If this goes public, he's toast," Bobby had assured me.

"But what about the other girls?"

"Let's set you free first, and then we can give the other girls the information they need to help themselves."

"Thanks, Bobby." He'd patted my back, real gentle-like, and then handed me the key to my apartment.

I fidgeted the whole drive there, panic and relief taking turns inside my stomach. It was a fierce battle, a foreboding dread raining over both sides. When Leo followed my pointing finger and pulled to a stop against the curb, I thought I might pass out.

Leo reached for my hand and gave it a little squeeze. "Hey, you're safe. He's not going to hurt you again."

I nodded, unbuckling my belt and following Leo across the road. I led him up the dingy stairwell and down to my door. My fingers were shaking so bad Leo had to take over and unlock the door for me. I walked into an overturned room that broke my heart. The apartment had been ransacked, Aren's spiteful punishment no doubt.

"Those bloody wankers!" Leo looked around the mess, stepping over piles of torn clothing and pulling a bag out from under the bed. I didn't care about the clothes...or the shoes...or the makeup strewn and smeared across the room.

All I could see was Mama's guitar, snapped and broken on the living room floor.

Dropping to my knees, I collected it into my arms. The strings only just held the damaged instrument together. Wrapping my fingers around the neck, I leaned it against my forehead and cried. It was my last connection to a woman I'd adored, the woman who'd told me there was more to life than serving my ungrateful father.

I cried like a baby, tears trickling down my injured face as I cradled that thing and mourned the loss of my mama and the pitiful wreck I'd let myself become.

After I don't know how long, Leo gently coaxed me off the floor, letting me bring my snapped guitar with me. I didn't want much else, just my bag and the few belongings I'd originally brought with me.

I left the key on the table and walked out of the room, never looking back. Leo placed my guitar in the backseat and buckled me in before running around to his side of the car.

Once we were safely on our way, I laid my head back on the seat, my curls piled high on one shoulder.

"How long have you been playing?"

I closed my eyes. "Mama gave me that guitar for my eleventh birthday. It's been the most precious thing I've ever owned."

"It can be replaced."

I glanced in the backseat and shook my head. "No, it can't."

Leo pressed his lips together, letting me have my self-pity, but not for long. "You don't need her guitar to feel connected to her. Every time you play and sing, she's near. Your talent…I assume that came from her."

Blinking at the sting in my eyes, I licked my bottom lip and nodded. It did and I liked his thinking.

"I wish I hadn't failed her," I murmured.

"Who said you did?"

"Oh, come on." I looked at him in disbelief. "Quit being so nice to me. I was an idiot to sign that contract! I left the best thing that has ever happened to me to come out here and make something of myself, and I screwed it up. I settled for the easy option, and it turned to total shit."

"I'm not saying you didn't make a mistake, but what did your mother really want for you?"

I gazed out the window, watching a large white cloud amble across the blue sky. "She wanted me to sing. She thought I was so good the world deserved to hear my voice. She wanted me to make something of myself."

"Who says you weren't something before?"

I frowned, forced to look at him after that weird question.

He gave me a wry grin. "I used to want the big lights, a grand stage, and important people telling me how brilliant I was. I was so focused on achieving that, I nearly missed out on where I was meant to be. Life is full of shitty circumstances that you can't avoid. You just have to go with it. And you know what always surprises me?"

I shook my head.

"The most amazing, beautiful things often come out of those totally shit-arse moments. It's like a light finally flicks on in your brain, and you see the world differently. You realize what you really needed all along, and it makes you appreciate what's important. Suddenly, you don't give a rat's arse about what anyone else thinks, because you know in here," he pointed at his chest, "that you're doing what's right for you."

"I've been chasing Mama's dreams for me since the day she died. I'd never wanted to settle until I'd made her proud...until I'd become a success."

"What does success really mean?" Leo ran a finger across his lower lip while keeping his eyes on the traffic.

It was a stupid question, so I didn't bother answering. Everyone knew what success meant...and I was so far from reaching it, it was a joke.

He glanced at my frown, a half-smile tugging on his lips.

"Because to me, success is living a life that I love, *being* with someone that I love. Money and fame are worthless. They can be there one day and gone the next, but love—that's there through thick and thin, and that's the only thing you should really be fighting for. Being happy with what you have...that's success."

My heart stopped beating for a second, my dry mouth taking a minute to find its voice. "I've never heard anyone talk that way before."

He shrugged, throwing me a rueful smile. "Believe me, it took me a long time to figure that one out."

"All I ever wanted to do was make Mama proud. I thought being rich and famous would do that."

"Look, I didn't know your mum, Rachel, but I'm sure she was proud."

I scoffed. "I doubt she'd be proud of my recent choices."

"She'd be proud you're getting out of it. Now that I'm a parent, I know that feeling of just wanting your kids to be happy. That's all you want, really. If you're happy, she's happy."

"I ain't happy yet."

"You'll get there. You just need to figure out what makes you shine...and follow that dream." He snapped his fingers and pointed at me. "I've got a song for this moment."

I didn't know what he meant by that, but kept my mouth shut as he pulled out his phone and plugged it in. He waited until we were stopped at the lights before he found the song and pressed play, grinning at me like an excited schoolboy.

I'd never heard it before, but I liked the sound.

"What song is this?"

"'Permission to Shine' by Bachelor Girl."

Closing my eyes, I let the words seep into me, enjoying the soft, hopeful melody. I wasn't sure if the song fit me perfectly, but I liked the idea of shining...and shining *my* way, not half-naked on a stage but holding my guitar and strumming out a song to people I cared about.

My eyes popped open, that lightbulb coming on so bright it was blinding.

I'd had that.

I'd had my stage, my love...a life I wanted.

According to Leo—success.

If only I'd realized at the time that it was enough.

THIRTY-FIVE

JOSH

The bar had been quiet the last few weeks...or maybe it was just me. I couldn't crack a smile if I tried. I was dead on the inside, and nothing could pull me out of the slump I'd fallen into. Brock was trying to kick my ass out of it, but I wasn't ready. I'd never felt sadness like it. A weight sat within me, dragging me down while images of my girl dolled up like a prostitute ran on repeat in my brain. She chose that over me. I'd been such a fool, believing she'd loved me all along, but I'd just been a stop along the way.

I rubbed the glass clean and popped it on the

shelf behind me. It was close to closing, but the bar already sat empty. It was a Wednesday—my quietest night of the week, so I wasn't that surprised. Rachel usually sang on a Wednesday, and I had yet to replace her. I just couldn't bring myself to do it, and the jukebox didn't seem to be cutting it on that particular night either. There was no big game on, so my few regulars went home early. I guess my morose mood brought them down, and they trickled out the door an hour before closing. I let Melody go early, too, leaving me to do the clean-up on my own. I didn't mind. I wasn't enjoying the company anyway. I'd even sent Uncle Amos off traveling again. He'd been pretty reluctant to go but I'd barked him out the door, and he knew he wouldn't budge me. I was the kind of man to heal on my own, and in my own sweet time.

Duke grumbled at my feet. I'd let him back in, seeing no one was around anyway, but then he stood and barked, letting me know someone was on their way. The main door opened, and I was about to turn and tell the patron we were closed, but that would have been a lie...besides, when I saw her walking in, I lost my voice anyway.

I had no idea who she was, but she had a look about her that had me intrigued. I clicked my fingers and sent Duke out back. He whined but did as he was told, smacking his lips together as he went.

The girl was dressed in skinny jeans and a black leather jacket. She wore thick, army-style boots and carried a black motorcycle helmet under her arm. Her long, dark waves of hair were a tangled mess, her large brown eyes soaked in sadness. She was cute though, with her round face and her button nose with the little silver piercing. There was a sweetness about her, but it was tinged with an overriding despair I connected with immediately.

She was a skinny thing, reminding me a little of Rachel as she slid onto the stool and gave me a tight smile. I figured she must have been a teenager. Her face was too fresh, her skin too young to be much older than twenty.

"What can I get for you?"

"A drink," she muttered, digging into her jacket pocket and pulling out some rumpled bills.

"You got ID?"

"It won't do me no good."

I gave her a half-grin, trying to figure out where she might be from. Her drawl wasn't as thick as most folks around Payton. She almost had a city twang marking her words. It had me curious.

I pressed my palms against the counter and shook my head. "I can't serve you liquor."

Her eyes flashed with defiance as she met my gaze head-on. "I ain't asking for liquor. Just give me a Coke."

Keeping my eye on her, I snatched a glass and threw some ice in before filling it to the brim with Coca-Cola. "How old are you?" I placed the glass in front of her.

She took it with a heavy sigh. "Nineteen."

"And what are you doing in Payton?"

Her eyes grew distant for a second, that despair swamping her for a long moment before she finally shrugged. "Just passing through."

She looked lost...alone, and I understood the feeling.

Leaning against the counter, I rested my forearms along the beveled edge. "I'm Josh."

Her smile was soft and fleeting. "People call me Ness."

"Is that your real name?"

"It's the one I like." She sipped at her Coke.

"So, Ness, where are you passing through to?"

She shrugged. "I've got no idea."

"You from around here?"

"I grew up in Mississippi, but moved to Chicago when I was thirteen."

"That where you coming from?"

She shook her head. "I've been in the City o' Angels."

I scoffed. I couldn't help it. As far as I could tell, I ain't seen no angels in LA.

A spike of anger burned through me and I leaned away from her, tapping my fingers on the counter. Part of me wanted to leave her to her drink, head back into the kitchen and finish off the last of the cleaning, but I couldn't do it.

She looked so sad. She needed to talk, and I was the only one around to listen.

With a sigh, I ran my fingers through my hair and asked her, "So, what are you running from?"

Her big brown gaze hit me for a moment, all glassy and wet before dropping back to the drink in her hand. Her jaw clenched tight, and she swallowed then whispered, "Love."

THIRTY-SIX

RACHEL

I spent the afternoon playing with Angel until she went down for a nap, and then I casually chatted to Jody about everything from music to the fact her sister was marrying a film star. Leo popped through the door mid-afternoon and beckoned me to follow him. I shot Jody a confused frown, but she just shrugged and tittered, turning back to the pile of laundry I'd been helping her fold.

I followed him to the studio apartment but didn't close the door behind us. Angel tottered through every now and again, and I knew she'd want to check things out when she woke.

Leo grinned at me before jogging across the room and lifting a shiny guitar from behind the piano.

"Here's a little gift from me to you." He held it out, and I stood there like a frozen fool.

He chuckled. "Aren't you going to take it?"

"You can't be buying me a guitar. You've done too much already."

"Would you just accept it, please? I can't have you living without a guitar after seeing you weep over the last one you lost. I know it's not from your mum, so it can never mean as much, but..." He sighed. "Look, we both know your mother wants you to have it."

I narrowed my eyes at him, wagging my finger. "Don't you be pulling out the mama card. That ain't fair."

He gave me a cheeky grin and stepped toward me. "If it makes you feel any better, it was Jody's idea. Now don't be stubborn. You know you have to take it."

"I thought it was too quiet in here this afternoon. Jody said you were working."

"I was. I was *working* on finding you the perfect guitar."

I tried biting back my grin, but it was pointless. Stepping forward on hesitant feet, I gently lifted it from his hands, a sense of awe riding through me as I ran my fingers over the shiny black exterior.

Resting on the arm of the couch, I pulled it against me and found my fingering. A smile brushed my lips as I strummed a few chords. It was pretty well tuned, and I only had to tweak one string before I was happy.

"You're smiling." Leo grinned. "It's a great feeling, right? Getting lost in the music."

I tucked a springy curl behind my ear and gave him an impish grin. "I love it." I brushed my nails over the strings, the comforting sound making me warm down to my toes.

Leo rested his butt on the piano stool. "I get that same sensation every time I press down on these ivories." The piano trilled as he raced the back of his fingers up the keys.

I chuckled. The expression on his face was adorable. He settled properly into his seat and started playing a sweet tune. For some reason, I recognized it. I don't know where I'd heard it before, but it seemed to suit him perfectly. I think the song was called "Music," and his voice sounded fantastic rising and falling over the melody. I shuffled my guitar and got ready, grinning widely when the faster pace kicked in. I strummed along with him. He called out the chords to me, and we laughed together as we fluffed our way through it.

The song was cut short by tottering steps we only just heard. In fact, I saw her before I heard her. Blond curls and ruddy red cheeks appeared beside me. Angel's wide blue eyes were sparkling. She gave me a cute grin before toddling over to her father. He lifted her onto his lap, kissing her cheek and winking at me.

"Nice playing." Leo grinned over her head.

I laughed.

"Ting!" Angel raised her chubby little arms in the air, nearly smacking Leo in the nose. He ducked out the way just in time. "Ting!" she yelled again.

Leo grabbed her hands and gently lowered them before smiling at my confused frown. "She wants you to sing."

"Oh! Okay." I wriggled my butt on the armrest, trying to think of something good. Glancing at Angel's cheerful face, I couldn't think of any other song but "Happy Girl."

I tapped my heel in the air and started strumming. A smile stretched my mouth wide when I started singing. Angel clapped her hands and squealed. I let my voice take over and went for it, closing my eyes and loving the feel of singing my thing, my way.

Halfway through the song, Angel wiggled out of Leo's arms and jumped off the stool, dancing in a little circle as only a toddler can. I started to laugh, chuckling my way through the second chorus. I managed to pull myself together and ended the song with a flourish. Leo joined in Angel's clapping and then pulled her back onto his knee. He rested his chin on the top of her head and smiled at me. "You were just shining."

My cheeks grew hot with a blush, and I dipped my head.

"That's a decent set of pipes you've got there, little lady. You write your own stuff?"

I pursed my lips while my nose wrinkled. I wasn't sure whether to admit the truth or not. I didn't want to have to play anything for him.

His penetrating gaze stayed on me. In fact, Angel started staring at me, too, so eventually I spat out, "I've tried a little, but I don't really want to share it."

"Why not?"

"Because! It's like...I'd be baring my soul. It's terrifying. What if people don't like it?"

"I get that." He tipped his head with a nod before gently running his hand over Angel's soft curls. "But what if they love it? What if it touches their hearts?"

I lost the ability to breathe, the air thickening to fog in my lungs as I listened to him.

"You never know the kind of power your song could have on another person. Songs can change your life, make you see things you've never noticed before. Music comes from here, remember?" He pointed at his heart. "That's why it moves us. If you can write from the heart, you'll have a masterpiece; one that you don't need to be afraid of sharing."

And with that, he stood and left me to my guitar. I waited for the click of the door before sliding onto the couch. Resting my feet on the ground, I leaned against my guitar and strummed again.

I liked Leo's theory of music impacting another person. I understood that. Songs had been affecting me my whole life. I thought of Josh and the look on his face when I'd sing for him. I think he loved me in those moments, even if he never did say it.

I missed him.

I missed the way he looked at me, spoke to me…made me feel safe.

Fingering the yellow bruises on my face, I could only imagine the thunderstorm he'd unleash on Aren if he could. I didn't want him to. I hated the idea of him getting in trouble for beating on Aren, but I loved the idea of hiding behind him or being wrapped up in his arms. I missed my head on his shoulder when we'd fall asleep at night.

I knew better now.

Nothing could beat that feeling.

It was home…and it broke my heart to think I might never get it back.

My fingers rested on the strings, and I strummed an A before dropping down to a D and finding my rhythm before changing up to an E. The riff quickly grew into a tune and words started flowing out of me…straight from my heart. Josh would probably never be willing to hear it, but that song was for him—my feeble attempt at an apology that would never be good enough.

THIRTY-SEVEN

JOSH

"I thought love was supposed to be something you ran to, not away from." I went to pour myself a beer but changed my mind and filled my glass with Coke as I waited for Ness to keep talking.

"Not when it burns you." She scoffed at me, shaking her head and blinking at tears.

"Who is he?"

"My best friend, Jimmy." She leaned forward, pulling a photo from her back pocket and dropping it on the counter.

She tapped on the face of a good-looking guy with sharp features and a pair of bright blue eyes.

His hair was covered with a floppy beanie and his cocky smirk made me dislike him immediately.

"I've been in love with him since freshman year." Ness picked up the photo and gazed at it with a wistful smile. "The first time I saw him, I was messing around playing drums in the music room. He followed the noise inside and asked me what I was doing. He was so gorgeous I could barely speak." She chuckled. "And then I opened my mouth and said, 'What does it look like I'm doing?' He just gave me this slow grin. Sexy as hell, that boy, and all kinds of wrong, but I wanted him just the same. The next day, he showed up at school with his guitar and found me at my locker. He told me he wanted to start up a band and needed a drummer, and I was going to be it."

The look on her face told me everything. In spite of her heartache, that girl was still in love.

"I couldn't have said no if I'd wanted to." She dropped the photo with a sniff.

"What was your band called?" I collected it up and looked at the photo again.

"Chaos."

"And how long did you last?"

"We're still together...apparently." She muttered a curse and thumped the counter. "We just won *Shock Wave*, this reality TV show, and our prize was a recording contract with Torrence Records. An album plus a tour."

"Wow, congratulations."

"Yeah, I don't know if I'd be saying that right now. I'm supposed to be in LA recording as we speak, but I just couldn't do it anymore."

Her face bunched with agony, and I had to lean toward her again. "What happened?"

"We got together." She gave me a trembling smile. "The night we won. We'd been working our asses off, and we were so stoked to win. Everybody was celebrating and after the party it just...it just kind of happened. One night of pure magic, that I'd been waiting years for. I thought he meant it, but it ended up driving a wedge between us. He kept on seeing other girls—his damn groupies—and he pushed me away. I'm not his best friend anymore. I'm now just another girl he's slept with." She sucked in a ragged breath. "I don't even know why I love him so much! He's the world's biggest jackass!"

Her final shout almost echoed in the empty bar, making the following silence heavy and suffocating.

I cleared my throat and ran my finger along the edge of the bar. "I understand why you left. I wouldn't have been able to stick around either."

She pressed her elbow onto the counter and pushed her fingers into her hair, gripping a small handful. "I couldn't face him anymore. I mean, I know I have to go back at some point. Torrence Records will be flipping a switch right now, but I can't work with Jimmy when I feel like this. I can't go on tour with him, watching him take all these other girls to his bed. I need to get over him and move on, and then I can go back with my head held high." Her shoulders slumped after her impassioned speech, her voice weak and pathetic. "I don't know how I'm supposed to do that. He's the only guy I've ever loved and he doesn't want me."

"I know that feeling." My voice was deep and husky. Her pain was so real to me. Rejection was a punch in the face from a mighty fist.

Her face bunched. "I have to be able to be around him without feeling like my heart is being torn in half. It burns." She whimpered, pressing her fingers between her breasts. "How do I do it? How do I let him go?"

"I don't know," I croaked, reaching under the counter and pulling out my framed picture of Rachel. It used to be on display by the piano, but I'd moved it a few nights ago. I'd wanted to throw it away but couldn't bring myself to do it. Instead, I threw it under the counter and just hoped I'd forget.

Ness sat straight, picking up the photo and running her thumb over Rachel's face. "Wow, she's beautiful."

I couldn't speak for a second, having to swallow a couple of times in order to find my voice. "She chose something else over me, too, and it hurts like no pain I've ever felt. It's like walking around with this heavy burden weighing me down, and I don't know how to get past it."

Ness reached for me, slapping her hand over mine, her expression empathetic. "We can't spend the rest of our lives like this. We cannot let them own us!"

Her fiery passion spurred me on and I bobbed my head. "I know."

"We have to let go, no matter how raw we are."

"Okay." My head was still bobbing. "How do we do that?"

"Hell if I know." She shrugged and then her eyes pinged wide, her fingers wrapping tightly around the picture frame. "Let's burn 'em."

"What?"

"They've burned us, it's only fair." Ness jumped down from the stool and headed over to the jukebox, her long curls smacking against her back as she walked. "We're gonna need music."

I still didn't know what the heck she was talking about, so I just stood there like a confused idiot.

She glanced over her shoulder. "Well, go on. Take the picture out of the frame, find some matches."

Realization finally dawned, and with a wry grin I headed back into the kitchen. I snatched a metal can from the recycling pile, plus a box of matches off the shelf, then walked back into the bar as "Picture to Burn" by Country Matters started playing.

"Nice choice." I grinned, slapping the tin onto the counter.

"I thought so." She jumped back onto the stool and grabbed Jimmy's photo. Running her finger over his face, she gave him a sad smile before dropping his picture into the can. I took Rachel's picture out of the frame, my stomach jerking as I folded it in half and slid it next to Jimmy's face.

"All right." Ness sighed. "Light the match."

I did as I was told before I could go changing my mind. The match striking against the box sounded loud and ominous. I watched the flame dance at the end of the stick, uncertainty tearing through me.

"Do it. We have to." Ness nodded. "They don't want us and we've got to move on."

With a soft sigh, I dropped the match. We leaned in together, lightly knocking heads as we watched the flames take hold. The pictures curled and bubbled, going black and finally turning to ash.

We didn't say anything...just watched our loved ones burn in a feeble attempt to let them go.

THIRTY-EIGHT

RACHEL

I played for a half-hour, fiddling with chords and words until I was happy. I doubted I'd ever have the courage to sing it to Josh. I doubted he'd ever have the courage to hear it. I knew what he was like. I'd burned him, and he would take a long time to get over that. As much as I wanted to see him, I was scared he wouldn't accept my apology. If I went back to Payton and he didn't take me in, I'd have nowhere else to go.

A knock sounded on the door and I laid the guitar down, turning in time to see Jody waltz in.

The smile on her face was so wide, her blue eyes

so sparkly, my insides jumped.

She had good news for me.

"You're free." She giggled.

"What?"

She yanked on my wrist, pulling me off the couch and wrapping her arms around me. "We just got a call from Bobby. Aren's terminated your contract."

My insides jumped and skittered. "But what about the money I owe him?"

"Oh, please!" Jody let me go, flicking her hand in the air. "That contract had so many holes in it, he had nothing to stand on. When Bobby's lawyer laid out the cost of legal fees he'd have to shell out, he dropped your debt on the spot, not to mention the fact he freaked out when it was suggested you might lay assault charges." Jody shook her head. "Feeble little asshole. He, of course, doesn't want you going anywhere near Club Liberation again, but as if you would, right?"

I shook my head, still too shocked to speak.

I was free?

I was free!

"So anyway, I thought you'd want to know right away."

"Thank you." I wrapped my arms around Jody again and relished her tight squeeze. It hurt my back a little, but I didn't complain. At that moment, all I could think about was my mama. She was smiling down from heaven, I could tell.

Jody and I hugged until it started getting awkward and I had to pull away. Jody didn't turn to leave so I rocked back on my heels, waiting.

"Leo told me you've got an amazing voice, and I heard some of it when you were singing to Angel."

I blushed again. Those two and their compliments!

"I don't know what your future plans are, but you're welcome to audition for our production, or if you're interested, Bobby has a lot of connections in the music industry. He could get you an audition somewhere decent, and we wouldn't let you sign anything before running it past his lawyer first." She winked and then squeezed my hand with a chuckle.

I couldn't speak. I was too blown away by the fact that I was once again being offered an opportunity on a silver platter.

"I...I'm..." I swallowed.

Jody giggled again. She had such a melodic, merry laugh. "There's no pressure, I just wanted you to know that you can stay in LA if you want to. We could set you up, and you could really make something of this dream."

She shook my arm and I squeezed her hand back, managing a shaky smile. She grinned at me and planted a swift kiss on my cheek before turning to the door. "Dinner's in about an hour."

I nodded, held in my spot until she'd closed the door.

Audition for them. Work with nice people under a legit contract that would keep me safe. It was mighty appealing.

I spun on my sock-covered heel and headed for

my room, still a little dazed. My mind was working like a Ping-Pong ball, bouncing from one side to the other.

Part of me yearned for the chance to redeem myself...to make it all right again and show Mama that I could make her proud.

But another part of me was consumed by thoughts of Josh. I was pretty sure he wouldn't take me back, but what if he did? What if I spent the rest of my life regretting not at least taking the chance to find out?

I didn't know what to do.

Either way, I was walking away from something.

One could potentially lead to bright lights and the life I always thought I wanted.

The other could lead to certain disaster...or home.

That word scared the heck out of me. I never wanted to be tied down like that, but I couldn't deny the slight flutter in my chest when I thought of Payton and my blond grizzly bear.

THIRTY-NINE

RACHEL

I made a pros and cons list for staying in LA. It was the only thing I could think to do. Snatching a pencil and blank sheet of paper from inside Leo's piano bench, I got to work jotting down everything I could think of. It was a painful exercise and I didn't do too well.

Scratching my curls, I tapped the pencil on the wooden table and scanned my points. One list was way longer than the other, but...

A hint of music caught my ear. I stopped tapping and looked over my shoulder. It was coming from next door. I thought I recognized the song, and it was the perfect excuse to walk away from that dang list and have a breather. Maybe a little dinner conversation would help me make a more definite decision about what I wanted to do.

The pros list for staying and letting Jody and Leo help me chase after my dreams was pretty long, but I couldn't quite buy into it, because there was one word on the cons side that I couldn't move past.

"I Love You" by Martina McBride was blaring when I tapped on their front door, so they didn't hear me.

I tried one more time before giving up and reaching for the handle. The door was unlocked as always and I eased it open. The sight in front of me disintegrated my pros list and had me making a decision right there on the spot.

Jody was singing along with the words, dancing around the kitchen and flirting up a storm with her new husband. Angel was in her highchair, clapping and grinning at the lovesick couple. Leo chuckled, grabbing Jody into a hug and kissing her soundly on the neck. She giggled but kept singing, draping her arms over his shoulders and running her fingers through his fine hair. They gazed into each other's eyes, and she sang about being totally in love with him.

I could only see his profile, but there was a wide grin on his lips, and you could feel the love pulsing between them.

JOSH.

It was the only word I'd written on the cons side

of my page, and it was now the only word that mattered.

Jody held the final high note, and Leo spun her around. That's when she saw me standing there.

"Hey." She grinned, her face flushing pink as Leo pulled her against him and kissed her shoulder before letting her go.

"G'day, Rach. How's it going?" Leo winked at me.

I nodded, smiling at Angel as I approached the kitchen counter.

"Hi, day-dee." Angel waved, her chubby arm pumping up and down wildly.

"Hey, sweetheart." I tinkled my fingers at her, making her giggle.

"You ready for dinner?" Jody placed some cutlery on the counter before turning for the stovetop. "We're having nachos tonight."

"Actually, um, I'm not sure I have time for dinner. I need to get going."

"Excuse me?" Jody's head snapped back to face me, her expression crinkled in confusion.

I scratched my shoulder and flicked my curls away. "I've been thinking a lot about your offer and I really do appreciate it, but the thing is, I got someone I have to see first." I swallowed, tears making my voice thick. "He may not want to see me, and there's a real strong chance he ain't gonna take me back, but I'll regret it for the rest of my life if I don't try."

Jody glanced at Leo, a soft smile cresting over her disappointment.

"It's time for me to go home." My voice wavered on the last word. I'd never called Payton home before—not out loud anyway. But it suddenly felt like the only home I'd ever really known, and I wanted to get back there as fast as I could. "Don't suppose one of you could drop me at the bus station."

"Of course we can." I relished Jody's warm smile, nodding my thanks as I turned away to go pack up my stuff.

*****

Less than an hour later, Jody was dropping me at the station. I bought my ticket and was scheduled to leave forty minutes later.

"You don't have to stick around." I pointed at the parking lot. "I know you got things to do and family to take care of. Thank you so much for everything you did for me."

I lurched into her arms, wrapping her into a breath-stealing hug.

She squeezed me back, her fingers digging into my shoulders as she whispered, "Of course. I'm just so glad we were there to help."

"I'm sorry for smashing that window."

She giggled. "Don't you worry about that." Pulling away from me, she held me at arm's length for a minute, her blue eyes going misty as she gazed at me. "He'd be a fool not to take you back."

My forehead wrinkled with a sharp frown. "I've given him every reason not to."

"Well, when you get back, you'll just have to give him every reason to fall in love with you again. Either way, I think you're really brave, and I wish you all the happiness in the world."

I couldn't talk. My throat was too swollen with tears and the gushy words just couldn't break free.

Jody seemed to understand my dilemma and smiled at my silence. "Before you go, Leo asked me to give you this."

"Another gift? You've already bought me a guitar!" I pointed to the shiny new case at my feet.

With a sweet chuckle, she pulled a small iPod from her pocket and handed it to me.

"What's this?"

"It's a playlist." She rolled her eyes but was grinning like a monkey. "He always has a song for every moment, and the bus ride is like twenty hours or something, right?"

I nodded.

"He wanted you to have some tunes."

I rubbed my thumb over the screen. "He's a good man."

"He most definitely is." She beamed. "You take care of yourself, Rachel. No matter what happens in Payton, you're always welcome back here."

"Thank you." I pressed my lips together and gave her one more tight squeeze before swiftly turning for the door.

I stopped and waved one last time before finding a quiet spot in the waiting area. I tucked the guitar between my legs and balanced my bag on my lap before putting my earphones on.

"Coming Home" was the first song on Leo's list. I didn't know it, but the girl's haunting voice captured me, and the words seemed perfect. Closing my eyes, I let the tune sink in, even enjoying the rap part, which wasn't usually my style.

I grinned and checked the rest of the playlist while Diddy rapped for me. A huge chunk of the songs included the word 'home' in their title. I shook my head with an impish grin. Talk about driving the point *home*.

By the time I hopped on the bus, I was listening to "Home" by Johnny Swim. I slumped into my seat and gazed out the window as we drove from the station. I did need me some home, and the thought that I'd finally found it made me feel so warm on the inside that it outweighed the frosty reception I'd no doubt receive.

FORTY

JOSH

The beeping alarm jolted me awake. I hadn't slept well. I kept on dreaming of Rachel's face bubbling and warping as the flames turned it to ash. My soul hurt with a heavy ache that I was hoping to be rid of after my previous night.

I rubbed my face and sat up with a groan. It was only six, but I wanted to get to Little Rock and grab some supplies. That could sometimes turn into a half-day affair, and I wanted to be back in time for lunch.

Scratching Duke's back, I briefly lamented the fact he was a poor bed companion. At least I had someone, I guess. That girl, Ness, who'd been wallowing in my bar the night before, had no one. When she left, she mumbled something about having a place to stay already, but I couldn't help worrying that maybe it'd been a lie and I should have offered her the spare room.

It was too late to do anything about it, though. Swinging my legs over the bed, I shuffled through my morning ritual of showering and shaving before pulling on my jeans, boots, and a checkered shirt. I tied my hair in a ponytail and pulled my cap on before thumping down the stairs.

I skipped breakfast, wanting to hit the road quickly. Duke would usually be at my heels begging to come, but he'd no doubt been kept awake by my restless dreaming and was still upstairs and out for the count. With a soft chuckle, I closed the door behind me and phoned Brock, asking him to swing by and let Duke out on his way to work.

With that done, I headed out of town, stepping on the gas in a bid to make the trip a quick one.

Ten minutes later, I was slowing at the main crossroads out of Payton. Left would have taken me back to LA. I scowled down the road and shook my head, turning right and fiddling with my radio as I started my journey east. I took another right about a mile down, preferring to take the quiet road that only locals knew about. It was narrow and bendy in parts with a steep bank along the left side, but with hardly any traffic it was easy to speed. I pressed a harder on the gas, easing up a little as I took the first corner.

That's when I saw it.

A cloud of steam rose in the near distance. I couldn't figure out what it was until I crested the rise and my stomach jackknifed.

I slammed on my brakes to avoid the upturned pick-up blocking the road and pulled my truck to the side. Flicking on my hazard lights, I snatched my phone off the dashboard, threw my cap in the passenger seat, and raced toward the black vehicle.

"Hello! You okay?" I crouched down beside the shattered window.

A male passenger who looked to be in his late-fifties hung upside-down, a large gash ripping his forehead open. The blood that had gushed from the initial wound was now dried and caked to his face. I grimaced, reaching into the cab to feel for a pulse. I struggled to find one, my heart rate tripling as my fingers scrambled for a feeble beat. After a fair minute of trying, I closed my eyes and pressed my head against the hard metal of the truck.

Nothing. I couldn't find a pulse or feel any kind of breath coming out of his mouth.

My hands were shaking as I stood. Brushing the glass off my pants, I stumbled away from the truck, about to call the police when something caught my eye.

With a sharp intake of breath, I lurched around the back of the vehicle, jumping over the motorcycle and dropping to my knees beside a small body. It was a girl. She was sprawled on her back, her left arm trapped beneath the heavy bike.

"Are you okay?" I gently shook her shoulder.

I got no immediate response, which scared the hell out of me.

Yanking the zipper on her leather jacket, I pushed my fingers into her neck and breathed for what felt like the first time. Her pulse was faint and erratic, but it was there.

"Help me," she whispered in a small voice.

I jerked, wanting to cry that she was alive and speaking, although I could barely hear her with the helmet in the way. I swallowed, wiping my hands on my jeans before gently lifting the visor.

The first thing I saw was a small stud in the girl's button nose.

"No," I whispered, bile surging up my throat. "Please, no." I gripped my forehead, my eyes burning as I recognized her. She'd been sitting in my bar less than twelve hours earlier, burning a picture of some guy called Jimmy.

"Please, help me." Her face was squished within the helmet, but it didn't hide her anguish. Her pale brown eyes were dark with fear. "Help me," she whimpered.

"It's okay. I'll help you, Ness."

Her eyes flicked to mine, cloudy with confusion at first and then suddenly clearing. "Josh?" she whispered.

I smiled at her, tears burning my eyes. "Hey, Ness. Don't you worry now. I'm right here to help you."

I didn't want to take the helmet off or move her in case she had some kind of spinal injury, but I thought taking that bike off her arm was the right thing to do, so before dialing the ambulance, I jumped up and wrapped my fingers beneath the weighty machine.

With a grunt, I hefted the bike off her arm, nearly dropping it when she started screaming. Her hand was caught within it somehow, and I had to quickly lower the bike back down.

"I'm sorry." I puffed. "I don't think I should be moving that without help." I fell to my knees and tried to peer under the bike, but all I could see was blood and black leather. I couldn't tell how her hand was caught.

It was time to call 911.

Gripping the phone in my quivering hands, I dialed, nearly fumbling it when I lifted it to my ear.

"Nine-one-one, what is your emergency?"

"C-car accident and motorcycle. I think the man driving is dead, but the girl on the road is alive and breathing, although she's trapped."

"Can you please give me your location, sir."

I blinked, struggling to orientate myself for a moment, but then rattled off the back road details, describing a few key landmarks that would help the ambulance find us.

"Thank you, sir, an ambulance is on its way. Can you please give me some details of the female victim." The woman's voice was so damn soft and calm. I guessed that was a good thing. It was forcing me to keep my cool and think straight.

I swallowed, wiping my sweaty forehead. "Ah, her name's Ness, she's nineteen, a skinny little thing. She's pretty beat up. Her arm is trapped beneath her motorcycle."

"Is she conscious?"

"Yes."

"Could you please ask her if she has any allergies or special conditions we need to be aware of?"

"Allergies?" I mumbled at the girl.

Her eyes looked distant and confused for a second, but then she blinked and mumbled, "No. Nothing. I'm healthy."

She didn't sound healthy, but I knew what she was saying.

"No, ma'am."

"Is she on any medication at the moment?"

I scowled, hating that I had to bother Ness with another question. "You on anything? Meds or anything?"

"Just the pill," she croaked, her eyes fluttering closed.

"Ness?" I gripped her shoulder, shaking it until her eyes popped back open. With a relieved sigh, I relayed the information to the operator.

The lady asked me a few more questions before assuring me the ambulance would be there soon. My job was to keep her talking and as comfortable as I could.

Upon the operator's suggestion, I raced to my car after the call and snatched Duke's blanket out of the bed of the truck. It smelled like dog and was covered in fur, but I shook it out as best I could. It'd have to do. Ness wasn't allowed to go into shock.

Kneeling back down beside her, I wrapped the blanket around her body, tucking it beneath her tattered legs. Her jeans were shredded near her hip, and there was some nasty road burn beneath the fabric. I could tell it stung, because she hissed when the blanket brushed it. I readjusted the fabric with a mumbled apology.

"It's okay," she managed.

She wasn't crying and sniveling like I expected her to. The glimpse of her hand that I'd seen was pretty mangled; surely that must hurt something fierce.

Her skinny limbs trembled beneath me as I laid my hand on her arm.

"Ambulance is on its way, Ness. You just hang on now."

"My hand," she whimpered.

"It's going to be okay." My voice wobbled over the lie. She saw it on my face anyway.

Her lips quivered as she pressed them together, her eyes welling with tears. It was only then that it dawned on me.

She was a drummer…and drummers needed their hands to play.

Not only was she lying on that deserted road with a broken heart, but her body was a mangled wreck, and potentially she had to face the fact that her career soon would be, too.

FORTY-ONE

JOSH

The ambulance took forever to arrive. I kept talking to Ness while we waited, telling her to be strong and hang on. She cried and whimpered a little but never fully broke down. She grew real drowsy near the end and about gave me heart failure when she wouldn't respond. I struggled to find her pulse again and was about to start pounding her chest and doing CPR when I felt a faint beat. I kept my fingers against her neck and held my breath until I recognized a steady rhythm.

She woke shortly after that, just in time to hear the distant sound of sirens. I jumped up and waved my arms, warning the oncoming traffic of the crash. A police cruiser appeared first, pulling to the side of the road. A competent officer greeted me and quickly took charge. I was more than happy for him to do so. He spoke to me while he worked, asking me questions. I mumbled my replies, still feeling dazed as I hovered near Ness's broken body.

Paramedics arrived about two minutes later, and I was shoved aside as they got to work. Although, they soon called me back, asking me to steady the bike while they freed her hand. She screamed when they finally yanked her fingers free. They were crushed beyond recognition, a mess of broken bone and skin.

My gag reflex kicked in and I fought the threatening nausea, turning away from the mangled appendage and squeezing my eyes tight.

"It's okay, sweetheart. I know it hurts. We're going to give you some medicine to take the pain away." The paramedic had a calm voice that was soothing.

Ness's breathing was still short and rapid as the other guy assessed her injuries. Together they gently removed her helmet, making sure her neck remained stable, and brushed the matted hair away from her face.

"Neck brace," one of them murmured.

Snatching it off the stretcher, they wrapped it around her neck. As soon as it was secure, the male paramedic turned away to prep an IV line. Holding Ness's arm steady, he slid the needle into her vein, patting her good arm gently before laying it down beside her trembling body.

Ness looked so tiny sandwiched between them. I stood in awe of their efficient, emotionless manner. I was a quaking wreck, running my hands through my hair and pinching the back of my neck. I got to pacing pretty quickly, avoiding the other ambulance crew as they worked to free the dead man from his vehicle. My eyes scanned the bank, following the chatting officers as they tried to figure out what happened. Judging from the skid marks, I was guessing the truck hit the bank and rolled. Ness must have busted around the corner and not been able to stop in time, glancing off the side of the truck and flipping over it. I couldn't figure out how her bike landed on her, but it didn't even matter, did it? The truth was, it *had* landed on her, catching her hand and completely mangling it.

I stepped back from the bank, nearly crashing into one of the new officers that had arrived a few minutes earlier. He was setting up barriers around the accident. Thankfully, we were on one of the quietest roads in the area. Hardly anyone took these back roads to get from town to town. I only used them because I'd been living around there my whole life and I hated traffic.

"Okay, sweetie," the female paramedic said. "We're gonna lift you onto the stretcher and take you to the hospital now."

I spun back to the paramedics and held my breath as they moved Ness, then wheeled the stretcher toward the open ambulance. I followed in their wake. "It's okay, Ness. They're gonna take good care of you."

She lifted her good hand, reaching out for me. "Josh?"

"Sir, will you be traveling with her?" The paramedic caught my attention. She was waiting at the ambulance door while her cohort stepped up into the vehicle.

"I'll follow in my truck," I choked out the words. "Ness, I'm gonna follow in my truck. I'll be right behind you!"

The paramedic nodded and slammed the doors closed before moving to the front of the ambulance.

I yanked out my keys and stumbled to my truck. The officer waved me through so I could follow the ambulance. They were moving at a fast clip, but I managed to keep up okay. I'd been to the hospital a few times before. Aunt Lindy had died there, and we'd visited daily leading up to her final breath. Memories taunted me, eating at my brain and making me weak.

Ness couldn't die. She wasn't allowed to go out like that, not with a burned heart and all.

She deserved to find her happiness before leaving this earth.

It wasn't fair.

It should have been that jackass Jimmy lying on the road, not sweet Ness. Not the girl who was trying to move on.

We'd made a pact the night before to mend our burned hearts and move forward. She still had things to do on this planet.

I wasn't much of a praying man. I usually left that up to my aunt and uncle, but in that truck, rushing after that ambulance, it was all I could do.

I was fair begging God to save her by the time we pulled into the hospital parking lot.

That girl had to live.

I don't know why I was feeling it so bad. I ran toward that emergency room like it was my own flesh and blood being taken in there. Most likely, it was the idea that I'd just lost Rachel, and I couldn't handle losing anyone else...not even a girl I barely knew.

FORTY-TWO

JOSH

My knee bobbed like a jackhammer as I sat in that hospital waiting area. It took an eternity for anyone to come out and give me an update. I'd already argued with the nurse at reception twice, but I wasn't family, and she stayed tight-lipped over anything to do with Ness.

Glancing at my watch, I figured I wouldn't make it back in time for opening, so I pulled out my phone with a sigh and called Melody.

"Hey, Josh." Her answer was bright and sparkly as usual.

"Hi, Mel. Listen, I'm caught up with something.

Could you open up for me today? I'll hopefully be back in time for the evening rush."

"No problem. Everything okay?"

"Sure. Just fine." I nodded. I couldn't let on. Mel's heart was softer than pillow fluff. She'd hate the idea of some young girl in a bad accident...even if she didn't know her.

"Okay, well, if you need me."

I was nodding and about to say thanks when I saw a tired-looking doctor walking into the waiting area.

"I gotta go." I hung up and stood, towering over the lady in her green scrubs.

She gave me a curious look before indicating I sit again.

I reluctantly slumped back into my chair. She perched on the edge of the one next to me and introduced herself. "I'm Doctor Kennedy. Are you the guy who's here for Vanessa Sloan?"

"Ness. The bike accident victim."

"Ness." The doctor nodded. "How well do you know her?"

"She was in my bar last night. Not drinking or anything." I had to clarify that one. There was no way I wanted her getting any kind of blame for the accident. "That's the first time I met her, and then I found her on the road. Is she okay?"

The doctor made a face that told me she wasn't.

"She's still alive though, right?"

"Yes." The woman pressed her lips together. "We did everything we could in surgery. She's in post-op, and I'm confident she'll make a full recovery."

"Her hand?" I croaked, remembering the mangled digits on her left hand.

Dr. Kennedy's sad expression made me close my eyes and whisper, "No."

"I tried my best, but it was crushed beyond saving. I had to amputate just above the wrist. She didn't take the news very well, but thankfully for her, the pain meds are making her pretty drowsy. It's helping her remain calm."

"She was a drummer." My voice quaked, my airwaves thick with emotion.

The surgeon closed her eyes, obviously upset by my news. "She'll learn to adapt."

I shook my head, my jaw working to the side as I tried to hold back my anger and grief. A nurse bustled past us, her shoes squeaking on the shiny floor. I watched her wide hips swishing from side to side as she barreled down the hallway.

"What's your name, sir?"

"Josh." I sat up a little straighter. "Joshua Clark."

Her head tipped to the side. "You don't own Clark's Bar in Payton, do you?"

I nodded, trying not to get distracted by the call for a "Doctor Matthews to ER" over the PA system.

The doctor next to me smiled. "My daddy drinks there all the time. Daniel Kennedy."

"Ol' Dan." I grinned. "We love him."

The connection obviously softened her toward me, because she nestled back in the seat and turned to face me more openly.

"The girl, Ness, we're struggling to find an emergency contact. Her driver's license says Vanessa Sloan, but the only next of kin information we can find is a dead grandmother in Chicago. Her phone was crushed in the accident and isn't working. She's not saying a word either."

"Well, maybe she doesn't want to be found."

"She needs someone who cares about her. This is an extremely traumatic time, and her stubbornness is doing her no favors. Whether she wants the support or not, she *needs* it. Please, can you help us out?"

I leaned back in my chair, battling to decide where my loyalties lay. If I was in a hospital bed facing a grim future, would I want someone to call Rachel?

The answer was a whisper in my brain, but definitely loud enough to hear.

"Jimmy," I muttered. "She's in love with a guy called Jimmy. They play in a band together." My knee bobbed again, my mind racing to remember the rest. "They just won a competition in LA. Shock something. I can't remember." I winced, hating that I hadn't retained more of the information.

"Shock and band. We can try Googling that."

"Chaos." I clicked my fingers. "Her band's name is Chaos."

"Thank you." Dr. Kennedy smiled. "That's really helpful."

She lightly squeezed my shoulder and stood to leave me.

"Can I see her?"

The doctor paused, her thin lips pursing as she gazed down at me. "I'm not really supposed to let you in. You're not family."

"But she doesn't have anyone right now."

"Which is why I'm going to say yes, but don't be telling anybody." She pointed at me.

I rose and quietly followed her into the post-op unit. I hoped I could handle it. My stomach was in knots, and it plummeted down to my shoes when the doctor pulled back a curtain and I got my first look at Ness.

Her skin was pale, her lips barely pink. Greasy hair covered the pillow beneath her, although it had been arranged to one side. A tube was attached to her hand and connected to a machine beside her. I assumed that was the morphine, keeping the excruciating pain at bay.

My gaze roved her body, which looked small in the cumbersome hospital bed, and I had to bite my lips together when I noticed the white-bandaged stump on her left arm. Tears burned my eyes but I didn't let them fall, putting on a brave face as her eyes fluttered open.

"Hey." I smiled, lifting my hand in a feeble greeting.

"Hi." Her voice was dead and doused with sorrow.

I sat down on the seat beside her bed and gently collected up the fingers of her right hand.

She didn't say anything, just looked at our hands linked together and blinked real slowly.

I didn't know what to say to make it better.

There wasn't anything I could do but sit there and hold her hand. After a space of silence that was long and painful, her eyelids fluttered closed and sweet oblivion captured her. It was a small mercy.

I remained where I was, gently rubbing the back of her hand with my thumb and praying she'd make it through.

I sat there until my backside was numb, but didn't budge until a nurse came through well after dark.

"Josh, right?"

I turned and nodded at the tall redhead. She had a kind smile and freckles splattered across her nose.

"You really need to get home. Get yourself some rest. We'll look after her for you."

Glancing at my watch, I saw that it was well past the busy rush and felt bad I hadn't showed up like I said I would. I'd probably make it for the last hour if I drove fast enough. With a sigh, I stood from my spot. I'd make it up to Mel by letting her leave early and dealing with close-up myself.

I gazed down at Ness, so slight in the big bed, and whispered, "I'll be back in a couple of hours."

The nurse smiled at me. "You don't—"

"I'll be back." I looked at the nurse.

Pressing her lips together, she stepped aside to let me pass. "We managed to reach Jimmy a few minutes ago. He's on his way."

I stopped at the curtain, relieved by the news...and also not. I hoped she wasn't mad at me for giving away that information, but the doc was right. No one should have to suffer an accident like

301

that alone. At the end of the day, she still loved Jimmy, and maybe having to take care of her would make him fall in love with her, too.

"That's good," I murmured, "but I'm still coming back."

"I know." Her soft smile relieved me some. I didn't want to have to fight my way back in.

But there was no way in Hades I was letting Ness endure the night alone.

FORTY-THREE

RACHEL

It was past eleven when the bus finally pulled into Payton. Sheryl Crow was singing "Long Road Home" in my ear, and I left her in there as I walked to Clark's Bar. Although it'd only been a couple of months, it felt like a really long road home for me. Mama had been the only home I'd ever known. When she died, I'd been lost. The only anchor I could cling to was Mama's dream for me. But it was different now.

Josh had become my new anchor, and I'd been too blind to see it.

My eyes were wide open now, and I was willing

to do whatever it took to get him back.

I paused across the street from Clark's. The road was empty and quiet. Mid-week traffic was always nonexistent in Payton at that time of night. The air was cool, kissing my skin as I clipped across the road. My boots sounded loud in the quiet air.

Breathing was a challenge as I stopped outside the main door. It'd no doubt be locked already, but I tried the handle anyway. To my relief, it turned and let me in.

"We're closed," Josh called over his shoulder.

He was wiping down the bar area. I couldn't move as I stared at his broad back. That sexy little ponytail stub just above his shoulders made tingles skitter down my spine. I swallowed, unable to respond, frozen by a mixture of fear, longing, and regret.

Josh let out a sharp huff and turned. "Look, I said we were—"

His eyes bulged wide, his blue gaze trying to knock me off my feet.

"Hi, Josh," I finally managed, my words swallowed up by the clicking of Duke's claws on the wood. He barked and shot toward me, rising on his back legs and thumping his paws onto my chest.

It was an effort to stay upright, and I was forced to drop my bags and greet him properly. I couldn't help chuckling as I scratched his ears. "Hey, Dukey." He dropped down and scampered around my feet, sniffing and snuffling at my boots and luggage, his tail going a mile a minute.

I petted his back with a grin and glanced up at Josh, my smile disintegrating as I took in his hard gaze.

"What are you doing here?" His voice was icy, his eyes narrowing as he stared at my banged-up cheek. Duke sensed the tension right away. His head snapped toward his owner, and he let out a little whimper before trotting away from me and nestling at Josh's feet.

It wasn't the dog's fault, but it hurt like one of Aren's blows to the face. I clenched my jaw, glancing away from them both and fighting the burn of tears in my eyes.

I wanted to tell Josh I'd come home, but I couldn't say that word. The way he was glaring at me said I wasn't welcome...and if he didn't accept me, then Payton couldn't be my home after all.

Pressing my lips together, I stared at the floor as if my courage was somehow hiding between the cracks in the wood. It wasn't. I had to take a breath and force myself to look back up. "I just wanted to explain why I didn't come back right away...when everything fell to shit."

His forehead wrinkled with a deep frown. He tucked a stray lock of sandy hair behind his ear and looked away from me. His sigh was heavy. "Listen, I've had a really long day and I've still got some place I need to be, so can we do this another time?"

"Oh...you're going out now?" I couldn't hide my surprise. Josh was such a homebody. He didn't go out on late-night prowls, which could only mean one thing.

My throat restricted into a tight knot that nearly suffocated me. He'd moved on already. He'd found another woman to warm his bed.

"Yeah, I've got..." He shook his head, his pursed lips confirming my assumptions.

My eyes started smarting real bad, and it took all my willpower to throw him a shaky smile. I crossed my arms, all set to tell him that he deserved someone who could make him happy, but I couldn't manage those words. Instead, I tipped onto the sides of my boots and nodded. "Okay. Well, I can come back."

I snatched my stuff and turned for the door, frantic to get away as fast as I could, but Josh's deep voice stopped me.

"Do you have someplace to stay?"

I brushed my hand through the air. "I can find—"

"Sleep upstairs if you want." My lips parted, and I looked over my shoulder. Then he drove a spear straight through me when he muttered, "I'm gonna be out all night."

I wanted to get out of there so bad, but I didn't have any place to sleep. I'd barely caught a wink on that uncomfy bus, and the idea of a real bed brought a small sense of comfort. As much as I wanted to disappear out the door, the logic of spending the next few hours roaming Payton in the dark for a place to sleep versus clomping up the stairs to a familiar bed was an easy battle.

Turning back to face the bar, I gripped my guitar case and forced a tight smile.

"Okay," I whispered. "Thanks, Josh."

He didn't say anything, just nodded and flicked his head toward the stairs. I did as I was told and walked across to them without one glance at Josh. My heart was breaking with every step, but as much as I wanted to ditch Payton and head back to Jody, I couldn't leave without telling Josh the truth. Even if he had moved on, he deserved to know why I'd let him down so badly.

FORTY-FOUR

JOSH

Rachel was the last person I'd expected to walk through my door that night, and it totally threw me. I didn't know what to say to her. I couldn't even think straight. The pale, yellow bruise on her cheek didn't help with that.

The idea of someone hurting her made me want to kill something. It took all my willpower not to vault the bar and wrap her in my arms, find out every detail before heading to LA to damage whichever weasel laid a finger on her.

I gripped the wheel as I steered my truck into the hospital parking lot. The day had been more than harrowing. First Ness, now Rachel. I didn't know what to do about either.

The low-lying anger brewing within me was beginning to burn. I wanted to hate Rachel. She had no right waltzing back into my life, not when I was trying to let her go. And Ness, the injustice of the whole situation had me seeing red. She didn't deserve to be in that hospital bed, broken and shattered. It should be that numbskull Jimmy! She wouldn't even be in this situation if he had just opened his eyes. I'd spent one evening with her and I could see she was gold. The guy was an idiot!

Thumping the wheel, I shouldered my door open and headed for the post-op unit. I'd said I'd be back, and I had no intention of leaving her again that night.

The nurse who sent me home to freshen up was walking out the door as I stepped in.

"I thought I told you to get some sleep." Her reprimand was hampered by a grin.

"I can sleep in a chair. How's she doing?"

Her soft sigh made my heart sink. "We've moved her to her own room now. She's on the second floor, down the end of the corridor. She's not sleeping well...keeps getting woken by nightmares."

I closed my eyes, feeling wretched.

The nurse squeezed my arm. "She'll get through."

"I hope so."

"People who love and care about her are on their way, and in the meantime, she's got you...a stranger with a heart of gold."

I flicked my hand at the compliment and walked away before my ears started turning red. I didn't have a gold heart. If anything, it felt black. With a heavy sigh, I slipped into the elevator. I found her room easily. A nurse at the station knew I was coming and led me down there. Ness was sleeping, albeit with a frown on her face, but I didn't care to wake her.

Slumping quietly into the chair, I rested my head back and closed my eyes. Rachel's face swam into view immediately. I squeezed my eyes tighter, trying to get rid of it, but I couldn't. Her battered face didn't do anything to mar her beauty. Those big eyes of hers still undid my insides, making my stomach rumble with butterflies. She'd always had a power over me, and she probably always would.

All I could hope was that she'd be gone when I got back in the morning, because I didn't know if I had the strength to kick her out my door. But I didn't have it in me to forgive her either. So there I was, stuck in an impossible place that I couldn't run away from.

*****

"Tell me where the fuck she is! I have to see her right now!"

The harsh shouting jerked me from my sleep. I winced at the kink in my neck and rubbed the sore spot as I sat tall and straightened my clothing.

"Jimmy, calm down, man." Another voice, lower and definitely more in control, wafted down the hallway. "We're Troy and Jimmy Baker. We're here to see Vanessa Sloan."

I rubbed my eyes and brushed the hair off my face.

"I'm sorry, but visiting hours don't start until eight." The nurse was obviously annoyed. Her voice was pulled tight and coming out firm and terse.

"I don't give a shit when they are! I have to see her *now*!"

The nurse on duty mumbled something I couldn't hear.

I stood and moved to the bed. Ness's pale face was bunched tight. She was either dreaming or in pain, I couldn't quite tell, but it was enough for me to want to wake her. Unsure what to do, I cleared my throat and hoped the noise might stir her out of whatever nightmare she was having.

She winced, a small whimper coming from her throat.

It broke my heart and I leaned over her, whispering softly, "Hey, Ness, it's okay. I can get the nurse for you."

"Jimmy." The word slipped out of her cracked lips. Her eyes squeezed tight as she came to.

I gripped the edge of the bed, but forced my voice to come out gentle and even. "You don't have to see him if you don't want to."

"Jimmy," she repeated the word, her eyes

cracking open to look at me. "He's here?"

"Yeah, he came as soon as he heard. He's currently fighting with the nurse to get down here." I pointed behind me as his voice wafted through the door.

"You think I give a rat's ass about policy!"

"Jimmy, seriously." The calm one, who I assumed was Troy, had a deep, mellow voice that I guessed was normally quite effective. At that particular moment, it wasn't doing anything to calm his irate brother.

Ness's lips rose into a soft, fleeting smile.

I brushed a strand of hair off her cheek. "Do you want to see him?"

"No," she croaked, "and yes." Her eyes filled with tears, the brown orbs looking lost and broken. "I don't know," she whispered. "I don't want him to be the only person I need right now, but he is."

I knew that feeling.

Part of me wanted to tell her to be strong. She could make it on her own, but I couldn't.

Leaning over the bed, I pressed a soft kiss onto her forehead. "I'll go get him."

Stepping out of the room, I forced a calm breath as I strode to the nurses' station. I stopped beside the short, round nurse, who was doing her damn best not to let that cussing rock star through. I eyed him carefully, unable to hide my frown as I scanned him from head to toe. He was wearing skinny jeans and a Ramones T-shirt. His young face was puckered in anger, his locks of hair hidden beneath a gray beanie. The only thing that stopped me from hating him on the spot was the desperate look in his bright blue eyes. He was scared, which could only mean one thing...Ness meant more to him than he'd let on.

I cleared my throat, bringing the argument to an abrupt end. "She wants to see him."

"Who the fuck are you?" Jimmy glared at me.

I glared right back, annoyed by his punk attitude.

His brother, a towering guy with large arms and an apologetic smile, reached out his hand to me. "Troy Baker."

"Josh Clark. I'm the guy that found her."

Jimmy's lips pinched into a tight line and he looked ready to throw up. Breaths spurted out of his nose, and I swear he was fighting tears.

"For some reason, she wants to see you," I muttered.

He nodded, ignoring my snarky tone and brushing past me.

"Remember how lucky you are," I called over my shoulder.

He swiveled back to me, his forehead wrinkled with a frown.

"You don't deserve her," I muttered.

Anger flashed across his expression, but nothing came out. Instead, his face folded with a look of agony before he whispered, "I know, but that's going to change."

He spun away and near ran for the room. I turned back to his brother, my frown skeptical.

Troy nodded. "Yeah, he's got his work cut out

for him."

"She's pretty damaged. Make sure he doesn't do any more."

"I'll do my best." He reached for my hand again. "Thank you for everything you did for her."

I gave it another shake. "I wish I could have done more."

Troy shrugged. "You can't stop life from happening. People make mistakes. Accidents happen. People get hurt. All we can do is forgive and move forward, right?"

My gaze was sharp as my face bunched into a tight scowl. "She's lost her hand, not to mention the fact he completely broke her heart. She's going to have to do some pretty big forgiving."

"Yeah." A sad smile swept over Troy's face. "My brother's an idiot, and he might never win her over, but I can tell you one thing: he sure as hell is gonna try. All I can hope is that she'll find it in herself to let him."

"Why should she?"

Troy let out a long sigh. "Because they're meant to be together." His pale eyes hit me, penetrating my very core without even meaning to. "Sometimes it takes losing someone to realize how much you need them."

My throat felt hot and dry. I couldn't even squeak out a response.

"No one ever said love was easy, right?" With a firm slap to my shoulder, Troy moved past me and down the hallway. I remained stock-still in my place, the war within me raging into a full-blown storm.

FORTY-FIVE

RACHEL

The bar was quiet when I woke. Josh still wasn't back from his night, and why should he be? It was still early. He was probably waking up beside some gorgeous girl who appreciated him and hung on his every word. That's what he deserved. Not some wandering hussy who left him at the first chance she got.

My mind played games with me, trying to figure out who it was, jealousy ripping through me like hot knives.

"Just stop!" I eventually had to yell at myself. "Knowing won't change anything."

I rolled out of bed and patted Duke's back before making my way downstairs. The bloodhound followed me, loyal in spite of my absence. His tail wouldn't stop wagging. I gave him a sad smile as I crouched down and popped open my new guitar case. I still couldn't believe Leo had given it to me. It would never replace Mama's gift, but it came in a pretty close second. Those people changed my life, and I was grateful for the small reminder of their overwhelming generosity.

Angel's chubby little face flittered through my mind.

"Ting!" That's what she'd be yellin' if she was with me.

I sat on the old wooden stool, center stage, and nestled the guitar on my lap. Looking out across the empty bar, I felt it then, stronger than I ever had before. I was home. I was safe.

I strummed the first chord of "Safe" and settled into the rhythm. The words oozed out of my mouth, and all I could think of was Josh. A smile crested my lips and I closed my eyes, picturing him standing before me.

I was just hitting the second verse when Duke barked and trotted toward the kitchen. I pressed my hand against the strings and waited, holding my breath as jittery nerves shredded my insides.

Josh appeared, his towering body filling up the doorframe.

I smiled at him, my lips taking on a mind of their own.

He didn't return the gesture.

Poor guy looked dead on his feet, gray bags under his eyes, messy whiskers dotting his face.

"Big night, huh?" I swallowed, desperate to hide my heartache.

He deserved happiness. I had no right to make him feel bad for moving on.

Leaning against the frame, he gave me a long, assessing stare before finally answering, "Just...long."

My eyes filled with tears. I couldn't help it! I wasn't made of stone!

Clearing my throat, I dropped my gaze to the floor and nodded. "I'm happy for you, Josh. You deserve it."

"What?"

I glanced up at his confused growl, my eyes rounding as he strode toward me.

"I deserve this?" he barked.

"Well, yeah. I mean, if she makes you happy then you do." I tapped my finger on the guitar, fighting the lump in my throat.

"You thought—?" His scoffing laugh made me cringe.

What was I missing?

"I wasn't with..." He closed his eyes and sighed. "I mean, I was, but it's not what you think."

His pale face washed with a sick look of agony before he finally gazed at me.

"I came across an accident yesterday morning. The girl was injured pretty bad, and she didn't have anybody nearby, so I was sitting with her until friends arrived."

Damn if he didn't make it impossible not to love him!

Why the hell did I leave?

How could I have messed it up so badly?

The stingy tears sprung forward again, threatening to really fall this time.

"You're a good man, Joshua Clark." I sniffed and pressed my knuckles into my eyes. I didn't want to cry!

He didn't say anything.

In fact, the only noise in the bar was my sniffing and Duke's thumping tail.

Josh licked his bottom lip and shoved his hands in his pockets.

I couldn't tell if he wanted to say anything or not. He'd always been a tough one to read, and getting feelings out of him was damn near impossible.

The awkward silence stretching across the bar was suffocating, so I filled it before he could.

"You should go sleep. I won't make any noise. I'll stop playin'."

"No, don't stop. I don't mind." He waved his hand in the air and slumped to the stairs. I waited until he'd reached the top before continuing with my song.

My voice shook pretty bad knowing he could hear me. I wasn't usually nervous playing for anybody, but the rift between us was like a chasm. I had to cross it. I just didn't know how.

*****

It was past noon. Brock had been by, given me some muttering speech that made me feel like shit. I knew I'd done wrong, I didn't need reminding!

I hated that the rumor wheel would already be spinning. Gossip spread too damn fast in this town. They were going to burn me on a stake if I didn't make it right…and fast.

There was only one thing left to do. I had to tell Josh the truth, and if he didn't want me back after that, my only choice was to walk away.

The idea killed me. It'd taken me way too long to figure out this place was home, and to have to leave it so soon stung like poison ivy.

Climbing the stairs like an old woman, I stopped outside the bedroom door and lightly knocked. A low grumble came from behind the wood, so I creaked the door open and stepped inside.

He hadn't bothered closing the curtains to sleep, so I could see him clear as day. He was still in his clothes and boots, like he'd just fallen onto the mattress and slept.

"Josh?" I nudged his shoulder with my hand and stepped back when he rolled over to face me.

As soon as his bleary eyes cleared, I wished to God I had stayed downstairs. Sleep had done nothing to revive his mood. If anything, it'd only made it blacker. Curse dreams and nightmares. What's the bet his nap had stirred up all kind of emotions I wasn't ready for.

He sat up with that angry dog look on his face and made me feel as big as a snail. "What the hell are you doing here, Rachel?"

I lifted my chin against his tone, crossing my arms to hide my shaking. "I needed to come back and see you. To make it right."

"You can't make it right!"

"I can sure as hell try!"

His face pinched with a tight frown and he looked away from me.

"Just let me tell you what happened."

"What happened?" His head snapped back in my direction. "I can tell you exactly what happened. The love of my life walked out that door and went to the big city to whore herself to some no-name agent who treated her like a worthless piece of trash. Was it him? Did he give you them bruises?"

I brushed my face, acting like it was nothing. I could never tell Josh the details of that beating. Whether he loved me still or not, he couldn't tolerate violence against women, and I didn't want him committing murder.

"Look, I know I made a mistake, Josh. Please, just let me explain. I didn't whore myself to anybody."

He shot me an incredulous look.

"I didn't! I may have danced half-naked and posed for photos, but no one touched this body. It's yours. Only yours. I—"

His pointed look didn't help my nerves none. I was hoping my *only yours* statement would soften him, but it didn't.

I swallowed a couple of times and pulled my shoulders back.

"I shouldn't have signed that contract. I was a fool who rushed in without thinking it through and understanding all the details. I got caught up in what I thought would be something amazing and it wasn't. It turned out to be a total con. I never read the small print. I should have listened to you."

His right eyebrow rose in a silent *I told you so*.

My forehead wrinkled in desperation. "I can't *change* that now."

"How could you stay and let them do that to you?"

"Because I was under contract!" I threw my arms wide. "They threatened to sue me. I couldn't afford that and they knew it. They knew I'd have to come to you for help, and they *knew* you were the kind of man that would sell everything to save me. I couldn't let that happen."

His eyes swirled with a dark anger. "What makes you think I'd want to keep this bar over you? I loved you!"

He'd never said that to me before. I mean, I'd always been pretty sure he did, but I'd never heard him say it, and there he was, finally shouting the words, but in the wrong tense.

"You don't love me anymore?" I swallowed, biting my lips together and pinching my arms until it hurt.

He looked away from me, his jaw clenching tight.

It took everything in me not to cry. I could barely speak and ended up croaking out, "Well, I love you still, and I didn't want you to be ruined. I know how much this place means to you."

"You meant everything to me." He shot off the bed, turning away from me and leaning against the window. "Seeing you like that..." His voice was a broken whisper. "What you did to yourself...*that* ruined me."

I swallowed, bile surging up my throat. "You said you'd always forgive me."

"I can't forgive you for this," he muttered.

A sob shook my belly, a soft whimper coming out my throat. Pinching my nose, I covered my mouth and fled from the room before he could see me fall apart. I busted into the single room we used to share and slammed the door behind me. Dropping to my knees, I curled over on myself and cried like I never had before.

I cried for my shame...for a past I couldn't undo.

I cried for my mother.

And I bled for Josh.

FORTY-SIX

RACHEL

Josh didn't come to comfort me. I knew he wouldn't. He'd been hurt too many times in his life to let me do any more damage. He'd lost his mother at birth, his father to war, his aunt to cancer, and I'd simply walked away. I was the only love he'd known that had rejected him, and he wasn't about to give me a second chance. Why should he?

I cried until I was weak with exhaustion and fell asleep right on the floor.

When I woke, I could hear the bar in full swing downstairs. The chatter was loud, that familiar buzz reaching me from the stairs. I couldn't stay another night. My time was up, so I dragged my sorry ass off that floor and threw my belongings into the small bag I had with me. The only thing left to get was my guitar, which I'd left down on the stage.

I didn't want to face everybody, but like hell I was leaving Leo's gift behind, so I clomped down those stairs in my favorite pair of boots and held my head high.

I'd done all I could do, and I just had to leave with as much dignity as I could muster. It wasn't much, but I clung to it anyway.

No one noticed me at first. I kept my gaze on the wooden floor and moved to the stage, but the second I stepped up to get the guitar, a hush raced across the room. I glanced over my shoulder and took in the crowd of familiar faces. A few low murmurs and whispered words fluttered into the air, but nothing could cancel out the oppressive silence and range of stares. Most people were glaring at me.

I worked my jaw to the side, wanting the earth to open up and take me right there, but it didn't, and I was stuck as the center of attention. I glanced at Josh. He was staring at me with a sad hollowness that hurt. It was easier to bear than his anger, maybe because there was an openness to it.

With a soft sigh, I turned back to my guitar, and I don't know what compelled me to do it, but I lifted the strap over my shoulder and settled it against my stomach.

Switching on the mic, I adjusted it and spoke before I could get booed off the stage.

"I know y'all probably hate me right now, and I guess you have good reason. Y'all won't ever know the full story, but this much is true...I screwed up." My lips twitched, begging me to shut my mouth, but I ignored my instinct and kept talking. "I don't expect you to forgive me, but I'd really appreciate it if you'd allow me to sing one last song."

I waited for the jeers and shouts, but none came. If anything, they seemed to settle into their seats.

I couldn't look at Josh as I tuned my guitar. I could barely breathe. I was about to do something I'd never done before.

"This is a song I wrote for Josh and, ah..." I shrugged, tongue-tied and emotional. "It's called 'Home.'"

Don't know why I thought my dreams lay far from you
Existed miles from your door
Had to chase them, get away and find the truth
But all I got was lost

City lights, the hum, the fame is what I craved
But it just left me feeling low
Tried to fight it, to deny all my despair
But had to finally face the truth

That you're my home, you're my home
You're the place where I belong
I rest my head upon your shoulder and I'm home

Your kiss is life, your love divine
It's the only place I shine
So I'm back to the only love I know
You're my home
My only home

FORTY-SEVEN

JOSH

She wrote a song for me—one she performed in front of everybody. Not only that, it was called "Home." She sang the word *home*, and she was talking about me.

My gaze was glued to her for the entire song. Her voice had never sounded so sweet and pure. It was raw with honesty and so incredibly beautiful, I forgot to breathe. I couldn't talk when she was done. No one could. Her song finished and the place fell silent.

I felt bad for her at first, until I noticed the tears in Millie Rae's eyes and a lopsided smile from

Brock.

Ol' Dan grinned up at the stage and shouted out, "Keep on singing, sweetheart, but don't you be thinking about making me cry again. Give me some country goodness!"

Cheers went up around the bar and Rachel chuckled, glancing at me for approval. I nodded my wooden head but couldn't crack a smile. Her song had stripped me naked and I was damn scared, still fighting my instinct with logic. What if she hurt me again? What if she meant it now but changed her mind later?

"Josh, get me another beer, will ya?" Brock's request pulled me out of my daze, and I grabbed out a fresh glass as Rachel started singing "Chicken Fried." Ol' Dan whooped and a few cheers went up. It was the perfect choice.

I ignored Brock's knowing smile as I plonked the fresh brew in front of him.

"Shut your face," I muttered, turning my back on him and fighting a smile of my own.

*****

Rachel stayed 'til closing, stacking all the chairs and sweeping the floor for me. She'd insisted Harriet get on home and won the argument pretty damn easily. I hadn't said anything to her. I hated that I was so useless with words, but emotions always tied my tongue in a big ol' knot and these particular words were the overpowering kind that had my throat restricting, as well.

Her boots sounded loud on the wooden floor, but not enough to drown out the jukebox. "I Hope You Dance" was playing—one of Rachel's favorite songs. It seemed to be the night for soulful tunes, and I almost dreaded what was coming next.

Rachel stopped at the bar, and I was glad for the barricade between us. If she came within a breath of me, I'd fall apart on the spot. Her sweet smell and delicate curls had always been my undoing.

"Do you want me to do anything else?"

I shook my head, focusing on the dishtowel in my hands.

She gripped the guitar case handle and nodded. "I know there's nothing I can say to erase what I did, and I know one song ain't gonna fix it either, but if you ever change your mind..." She reached into her pocket and pulled out a scrap of paper. "Here's my new number." She held it out to me.

"What happened to your old one?"

"It was..." She shook her head and muttered, "Broken."

I took the paper from her, wondering what she wasn't saying, and tucked it into my back pocket. Her gaze was sad as she drank me in.

"Thanks for letting me stay."

"Where you going tonight?"

"Millie said I could stay with her and Brock until I've got myself figured out." She pressed her lips together as if she didn't want to tell me more, but then blurted, "There was a couple in LA who helped me out. Saved my life, really. They offered to have me if you wouldn't…"

I looked away from her sad expression. I swear my chest was being pounded with a battering ram.

"I'm really sorry for ruining everything. I didn't—" Her soft sigh made me cringe. "For what it's worth, I love you and I can't see that changing…ever. You'll always be my home, Grizz."

As if fate was working for us, the jukebox started playing, "Feels Like Home."

I had to look at her then, drink in that beautiful face.

She glanced at the jukebox with a wistful smile and turned for the door. "Goodbye, Josh."

What the hell was I doing?

Snatching out my phone, I pulled her scrap of paper free and scrambled to dial the number before she got through the door. It was stupid, I know, but I couldn't seem to call out to her, and maybe if I did this over the phone, I'd do a better job.

Her phone rang just before she closed the door behind her. I could only just make out her profile in the dim light outside, but a grin twitched my lips at her confused expression.

She looked back into the bar at me and lifted the phone to her ear. "You know I'm still here, right?"

"I do need something from you." My voice was tight and small as I spoke into the phone. I swallowed, hoping to cure my parched throat.

She stepped back into the bar, placing her guitar case on the floor and gazing across at me. "And what is that?"

I clenched my jaw, the words fighting to get out of my stubborn, fearful mouth. Finally, I parted my lips and whispered, "I need you to stay."

It took her a second to register my words. Her eyes locked on to mine as if she didn't quite believe me, but then a relieved sigh, mixed with a smiling sob, burst out of her lips, and she dropped the phone to the floor. It landed with a clunk, but she didn't even notice as she raced across the room. I vaulted over the bar and met her halfway, catching her against me and lifting her into my arms. Her legs wrapped around me, squeezing my waist as her hot breath caressed my skin. Her lips were trembling as they met mine, and I swallowed her sob, cradling the back of her head with my hand.

"I missed you," she cried, kissing my lips between words. "I missed you so much."

I stopped her trembling voice with my mouth and walked toward the wall, slapping her body against the hard wood and squeezing her thighs. Her scorching kisses were trying to drown me. I'd forgotten how good she tasted.

Sucking her bottom lip, I forced myself to pull away so I could look at her. "I mean it, Rachel. I need you to stay forever."

"I love you." She held my face, her fingers digging into my hair. "And I'm not going anywhere. I'm never leaving home again." The look in her eyes told me she meant it, and I thought my heart was going to fly right out of my chest.

With a growl, I pulled her back against me, her

hot mouth consuming mine in a kiss that said everything we needed it to. My body responded with an intensity I'd never felt before. The low-lying home fire I'd kept burning for her flared with passion, heating my inner core. I had to have her. I had to be inside her and know without a doubt that she was once again mine.

Sliding my arm around her waist, I pulled her tight against me and carried her up the stairs. She clung to me, kissing my neck and sucking the sweet spot below my ear. I dropped her onto the bed and she giggled, kicking off her boots. Her big eyes gazed up at me, her teeth running over her lower lip and fueling the inferno raging within me. With a shy smile, she undressed herself, slipping off her jeans and shirt until she sat on my bed looking mouth-watering in nothing but a skimpy pair of hot pink panties.

I didn't miss the bruises on her body—the gash on her shin and the finger marks on her arm. I couldn't move for a beat, locked in place by the idea someone had hurt her.

She caught my anguished gaze and shook her head. "It's over. He can't touch me again."

"Why'd he beat you in the first place?" I ground out the words.

"Because I wanted to come home to you." Her eyes glistened. "I was too scared to leave when you came for me. I didn't know what he might do to you. I was trying to protect you, but when you walked away…" She dipped her head, disappearing behind her curls.

I stood in agony, listening to her sniff and clear her throat.

"It took me way too long to figure this out, but when you came for me, I realized that all this time, you were all I'd ever wanted. I couldn't stand one more second in that place, so I refused to do as I was told and I paid for it."

Her words turned me to stone for a second. Rage flared inside me with a mighty roar, but it was overshadowed by the resounding knowledge of what she'd done for me. She'd taken a beatin'. She'd suffered so she could get back...to me.

Rachel glanced up, dragging her curls over one shoulder and smiling at me again. "I don't want to talk about that night. I just want you to help me forget that I ever hurt you. Please," she whispered. "Please, let me be yours again."

I nodded, my head bobbing quickly as I tried to swallow the boulder in my throat. Her relieved smile grew and she let out a breathy laugh. Relief washed over her, drying up her tears, and then a glimmer danced into her eyes. They sparked with a sassy wildness I hadn't seen in a long time.

She dropped on all fours and crawled across the bed, looking like a lioness, her untamed curls glinting in the soft light. Her eyes danced as her fingers inched up my body and slowly unbuttoned my shirt. She slipped it off my shoulders and started trailing kisses down my body. Fireworks exploded beneath my skin, her soft touch being the first I'd had since she'd left.

I'd missed her. I'd ached for her and here it was,

a precious gift I'd nearly denied myself.

I cupped the back of her head as she licked my belly button and worked her way down to my belt. It was an excruciating, intoxicating dance she made me endure. A belt had never been taken off so slowly, I can assure you. I was harder than granite when she finally pulled my pants down, anticipation making me quiver. When she took me into her mouth, I nearly blacked out, my fingers digging into her hair while a slow moan clawed up my throat.

That mouth of hers teased me until I could barely see straight, and I had to push her away from me before I exploded everywhere. She leaned back with a flirtatious laugh and lay down on the bed. I drank her in from the tip of her bare toes to that mass of curls on the top of her head. I skimmed her injuries, not wanting them to ruin the moment. Yet in spite of them, she stole my breath away.

"You are so beautiful," I whispered, trailing my fingers over her beat-up shin as I crawled between her legs and gently kissed her.

She sighed as I slipped her underwear off and flung it over my shoulder. It was a sweet sound that lit the air and then changed in pitch as I caressed her body, sucking her breasts and making her writhe with my fingers. They remembered where to touch her and how to make her gasp and clutch my shoulders like I was the only thing anchoring her to the bed.

Her limbs began to tremble and quake as an

orgasm rocketed through her. She arched her back, clutching the mussed-up bed sheets and crying out like we were the only two people on earth.

A smile played with my lips when I kissed her chin, her husky voice begging, "Don't make me wait, Josh, please."

I nestled myself between her legs, her hips rising to take me. She'd always been so small compared to me, and I used to worry about hurting her, but her hungry desire had taught me how far to go, and I thrust into her just the way she liked it.

Her head tipped back, a lusty groan firing into the air. Her delicate center was tight, wrapping me in a heady embrace that consumed my entire body. I drove into her again, closing my eyes and getting lost. Her fingers scraped down my spine as she lifted her legs and wrapped them around me, allowing me to go even deeper. I obliged, much to my pleasure.

She cried out again, brushing her teeth across my shoulder and murmuring that she loved me.

I wanted to say it back, but not when I could barely see straight, let alone form a coherent sentence. Instead, I showed her by increasing the tempo, burying myself inside her until I came with an explosion of light and color that outclassed anything I'd seen before.

My body was fair shaking as I puffed against her skin. I put the pressure on my elbows, not wanting to squash her. She giggled beneath me—a soft, breathy sound.

"Oh my Lord, you are good at that." She

grinned, tucking a lock of hair behind my ear with a loving smile that told me she wasn't going anywhere.

I kissed her nose, then brushed my lips across the yellow bruising on her cheek. I still wanted to kill her boss, but it wasn't the time to think about it.

Right then, the only thing I was meant to do was pull her into my arms and let her fall asleep on my shoulder...at home...where she belonged.

FORTY-EIGHT

JOSH

The birds woke me before the sun. I hadn't really slept anyway. Rachel's body pressed against mine was enough to keep any man awake. I'd trailed my fingers up and down her naked back until they'd gone numb. She hadn't stirred once. It was like she hadn't slept the whole time she'd been away. There was a peacefulness about her that seemed to permeate the entire room.

The pale curtains didn't do much to hide the light as the sun rose. I ran my fingers through Rachel's golden curls and kissed her forehead. She stirred in my arms, her hand gliding over my waist as she woke.

"Morning," she finally croaked, her eyes peeking open.

"Hey, baby," I whispered with a grin.

Her smile was sweet and relieved, like somehow she thought I might have changed my mind after a good night's sleep. It wasn't until I saw that look cresting over her face that I realized what an ass I'd been. Sure, she'd left me, but she'd stayed to protect me and what she thought I'd wanted. She'd assumed the bar was more important to me than she was, and maybe I'd never given her reason to believe otherwise.

Shifting my arm from beneath her neck, I perched up on my elbow and gazed down at her, gently running my finger along her hairline.

A smile brushed my lips when I finally said, "I love you."

Her gaze shot to mine, her eyes rounding slightly.

"I should have told you before, every damn day, but I'm not that great with words. It wasn't just your fault, you leaving me. I should never have let you walk away so easy. I should have gone with you and protected you." I ran the back of my finger across her cheek, cringing at what had no doubt been an ugly, painful bruise.

"It's done now." Rachel smiled at me, her eyes glistening. "Let's just forgive each other and move on."

"That's what I want, and I'm sorry for saying I couldn't forgive you. That was a lie." I brushed my lips against her. "When you love someone as much as I love you, you have to forgive them. It's impossible not to."

Her smile was sweet. "Well, I ain't gonna be giving any more reasons to. At least I hope I ain't."

I chuckled at her cute expression. "Me too. All I want is to be with you, and build a life here. Is that what you want? To build a life with me, here in Payton?"

Her gaze warmed, her eyes fair glowing as she looked at me. "Yes, that's exactly what I want. I told you, I'm never leaving home again, so that means…" A cheeky smile lit her face as she pushed me onto my back and straddled me. "That means that wherever you go, I'm going, too. You can't get rid of me now, Joshua Clark."

"That suits me just fine." I ran my hands up her waist and gave her perfect breasts a squeeze.

"And why is that?" She leaned into me, her pink tongue poking out the side of her mouth.

"Because I love you."

Her smile was pure sunlight.

"Say it again, Grizz." She rocked against me, lighting a quick fire in my belly.

"I love you."

"And again," she sing-songed, bursting into giggles as I flipped her onto her back with a growl and nipped her chin.

"I love you, Rachel Myers, and I will keep on loving you until the day I die."

EPILOGUE

RACHEL

A fall chill was starting to touch the air and I wrapped my arms around myself, crunching over leaves as I walked through the backyard.

"Come on, Dukey. Let's get inside." I clicked my fingers and ushered him in the back door. He trotted up behind me, bashing my legs with his tail when he scampered through the door and headed for his water bowl.

I grinned, scratching him behind the ears and kissing his head.

"Love you, you crazy bloodhound."

I stepped behind him and flounced through the

kitchen, checking my watch and figuring I had at least an hour before I had to start setting up the bar.

Josh was out running a few errands, so I skipped over to the stage and picked up my beloved guitar. My fingers nestled onto the strings and I started strumming. I didn't know what to play, but fell into a chord structure that led me to singing, "I Just Call You Mine."

A smile brushed my lips as I thought of Josh...my grizzly bear.

Since finally letting go and having the courage to admit that he was all I really wanted, and I didn't need to follow Mama's dreams to be happy, I'd found a new level of contentment.

Success, as Leo would say.

I never thought I could be happy in Payton, but I was. I loved it. I mean, sure, there were still the old gossip biddies and the odd glare from stuck-up grandpas. I still had to flick off wandering hands on busy nights, but none of it mattered, because each night I went to bed and I lay my head down on Josh's shoulder. His big arms wrapped around me, and I fell asleep with a blissful sigh on my lips.

I was a country girl, in love with a country boy, and I didn't need anything else.

Duke, who had wandered in and flopped at my feet, jumped up, his tail going crazy. He let out a gruff bark and trotted for the kitchen, meeting Josh halfway.

I grinned like I did every time I saw my man. Yes, it was safe to say we were in the *honeymoon* period, but I was hoping it'd last a good long while. I loved those butterfly tickles and heady rushes. They were so much more potent now that I knew how precious they were. Living without someone you crave is a damn good way to get your priorities straight.

"Hey, honey." I propped my guitar against the piano and jumped down from my stool.

"You got some mail here." He dumped his bag on the bar and unzipped it.

"Really? Mail? When does that ever happen?"

"I know it." He chuckled, catching me against his side and pecking my lips before handing me a white envelope.

A delighted laugh punched out of me as I read the return address.

"It's from Leo and Jody. You know, the couple in LA who helped me out."

Josh nodded, his hand tightening on my back the way it did every time LA was mentioned. I'd told him everything, early morning pillow talk bringing out more honesty than I'd expected. Josh was livid when I got down to the nitty-gritty of what Aren had been forcing me to do, but I'd convinced him that Leo and Bobby had done enough. I didn't need Aren and Parker to pay for their lies. Besides, Bobby seemed pretty set on making sure no other girls could fall into the same trap I did, and last we'd heard, Club Liberation was being closed down due to building-code violations. Yes, that tickled my fancy some. I'd laughed pretty hard over that one.

Ripping open the envelope, I pulled out the letter and a card dropped onto the floor.

Josh bent down to collect it while I read the letter aloud.

Hey Rachel,

I was cleaning out the studio apartment and stumbled across a postcard that was addressed to Josh. I don't know why I felt compelled to send it to you—maybe it was your four-word message that touched me, I'm not sure—but here it is anyway.

I often think of you and wonder how you're doing. I'm glad everything worked out and you were able to stay.

Angel still points to the studio every now and again saying, 'Day-dee ting.' It makes me laugh every time. You'll always be a very sweet memory in our lives, and I hope we get to see you again one day.

You won't believe how small this world is, but I was talking to my best friend, Ella, yesterday and she told me that Nessa Sloan had stopped for a drink at Clark's Bar. She met Josh. Apparently, he saved her life."

I looked at my boyfriend. A pained smile crested over his face as he tapped the postcard against his thumb.

He'd always wished he could have done more.

Ness had flown back to LA a few days after her accident. Josh had gone to see her one last time before she left, but he figured he never would again. She'd still not been in a great place, and Josh worried about her all the time.

"Does it say how she's doing?"

I blinked, glancing back at the letter.

Can you tell Josh that she's hanging in there? Ella didn't say much, but Chaos fans are hopeful and Torrence Records announced recently that the album and tour are still going ahead, although they have been delayed. There's still a very big question mark over whether Ness will be part of it, but we're all crossing our fingers.

Anyway, I hope this letter finds you well and that you've found that dream you were searching for.

Lots of love,
Jody

I folded the letter with a wistful smile and gazed up at Josh. He was looking at the postcard, his expression like melted chocolate.

"With love forever more," he finally whispered.

"Of course I was going to sign it that way. You told me to."

Flipping the postcard over, he studied the picture of the California sunset, his expression pensive.

Nudging his leg with my hip, I started singing the song he'd given me...well, just the line about how something always made her stay.

"You're my reason, Josh. I may not have stayed, but you pulled me back, so thank you."

Flicking the postcard over his shoulder, Josh

tugged me against him, lifting me up like I weighed nothing. I wrapped my legs around his hips with a grin as he hummed the rest of the tune, dancing around the empty bar. I giggled and kissed him, pushing my tongue into his mouth to cut the song short. His hum turned into a moan, and I pulled away with a laugh.

"I think it's time we find ourselves a new song."

He tipped his head to the side, his eyes sparkling as his deep voice started singing, "You're my home, you're my home, you're the place where I belong."

My smile was so damn wide it hurt my face. Hearing my own song sung back to me was the coolest thing ever. Sliding my arms around his neck, I pressed my forehead against his cheek and closed my eyes, letting his deep voice wash over me and remind me of everything I was staying for...and everything I'd never leave again.

THE END

Thank you so much for reading *Home*. If you've enjoyed it and would like to show me some support, please consider leaving a review on the site you purchased this book from.

The next Songbird Novel is due for release in November 2015

TRUE LOVE

One night can change everything...

Nessa Sloan has been in love with Jimmy Baker since the ninth grade when they started up a rock band together. Five years later they're about to hit the big time—*Chaos* wins a recording contract and nation-wide tour with Torrence Records. After their celebration party, the two best friends have a one-night stand that will tear their relationship apart.

On the run from Jimmy's rejection, Nessa takes off on her motorbike, but an accident brings her escape to a tragic end. Now trapped in a broken body, Nessa has to face a future stripped of the one thing that's gotten her through every past challenge—playing the drums.

Jimmy never meant to break his best friend's heart, and he will forever regret taking her to bed then treating her like one of his groupies. But once he'd crossed that line, he couldn't go back. Now Jimmy's on a mission to do something he's never done before—win a girl over.

Angry and confused by her new disability, Nessa doesn't want Jimmy's help. But she has nobody else to rely on...and his pigheaded ass won't leave her alone. Can these two stubborn hearts get past their own insecurities to figure out what true love really looks like? Or will they drive each other crazy before they finally see the truth?

It's infuriating, irresistable, and all-consuming...it's true love.

*****

If you'd like to stay up-to-date with the SONGBIRD SERIES, please sign up for the newsletter, which will include cover reveals, teasers and new release info for all the Songbird Novels.

http://eepurl.com/1cqdj

You can find the other Songbird Novels on
Amazon.

FEVER

Ella & Cole's story

BULLETPROOF

Morgan & Sean's story

EVERYTHING

Jody & Leo's story

.

<u>ACKNOWLEDGEMENTS</u>

It's so cool to get to work with all these amazing people to pull together a project like this.

Thank you so much to:

My advisors: Lisa and Pete. Thank you SO much for your medical and technical advice for this book. I couldn't have written those accident scenes without you.

My country music girl: Ashley. Thanks for your suggestions and opening me up to a bunch of songs I'd never heard before. I've seriously fallen in love with country music, so thank you!

My critique readers: Cassie, Theresa, Ashley and Rae. As always, your thoughts and opinions are invaluable. Thank you so much for your time.

My editor: Laurie. I'm in love with your eagle eyes and brilliant brain.

My proofreaders: Kristin, Marcia, Lindsey, Suzy and Karen. Love what you guys do for me. You're amazing.

My cover designer and photographer: Regina. What can I say other than *you rock*, lady!!

My publicity team: Mark My Words Publicity. Thanks for all your time and effort. You guys are the best.

My fellow writers: Inklings and Indie Inked. Thanks for your constant support and encouragement.

My Fan Club and readers: THANK YOU! Those words never seem enough, but I am so grateful for your support.

My family: You guys make life worth living. Thanks for your belief and your love.

My savior: Thanks for helping me find my home, and for never leaving my side no matter where I travel to.

OTHER BOOKS BY MELISSA PEARL

THE SONGBIRD NOVELS

Fever—Bulletproof—Everything—Home

Coming in 2015: True Love

THE FUGITIVE SERIES

I Know Lucy — Set Me Free

THE MASKS SERIES

True Colors — Two-Faced— Snake Eyes — Poker Face

THE TIME SPIRIT TRILOGY

Golden Blood — Black Blood — Pure Blood

THE ELEMENTS TRILOGY

Unknown — Unseen — Unleashed

THE MICA & LEXY SERIES

Forbidden Territory—Forbidden Waters

Find out more on Melissa Pearl's website:
http://www.melissapearlauthor.com

ABOUT MELISSA PEARL

Melissa Pearl is a kiwi at heart, but currently lives in Suzhou, China with her husband and two sons. She trained as an elementary school teacher, but has always had a passion for writing and finally completed her first manuscript in 2003. She has been writing ever since and the more she learns, the more she loves it.

She writes young adult and new adult fiction in a variety of romance genres - paranormal, fantasy, suspense, and contemporary. Her goal as a writer is to give readers the pleasure of escaping their everyday lives for a while and losing themselves in a journey…one that will make them laugh, cry and swoon.

MELISSA PEARL ONLINE

WEBSITE:

melissapearlauthor.com

YOUTUBE CHANNEL:

youtube.com/user/melissapearlauthor

FACEBOOK:

facebook.com/melissapearlauthor

TWITTER:

twitter.com/MelissaPearlG

PINTEREST:

pinterest.com/melissapearlg/

You can also subscribe to Melissa Pearl's Book Updates Newsletter. You will be the first to know about any book news, new releases and giveaways.

http://eepurl.com/p3g8v

CPSIA information can be obtained at www.ICGtesting.com
Printed in the USA
LVOW08s0418131016

508538LV00003BA/195/P